RATTLESNAKE AND
OTHER TALES

This collection of stories is dedicated to the memory of my beloved parents Peter and Betty.

RATTLESNAKE AND OTHER TALES

ROBERT DODDS

Polygon
An imprint of Edinburgh University Press Ltd
22 George Square, Edinburgh

Typeset in 11 on 13 pt Linotype Sabon
by Hewer Text Ltd, Edinburgh, and
printed and bound in Great Britain by
Creative Print & Design, Ebbw Vale, Wales

A CIP record for this book is
available from the British Library

ISBN 0 7486 6294 4 (paperback)

The Publisher acknowledges subsidy from

THE SCOTTISH ARTS COUNCIL

towards the publication of this volume.

CONTENTS

Acknowledgements

Thanks to Katy Gardiner and David Jackson Young for encouraging me in my folly. Thanks also to Elpy Sawdon, Kim Auston, Jane Cooper, Donald Holwill, Sue and John Loudon, Chris Miscampbell, Elizabeth Shove and Roddy Simpson, for various reasons.

Two of these stories have been published before: 'Running Away' was published in the anthology *The Devil and Dr Tuberose* (HarperCollins, 1991) and 'The Seventh Egg' was published in the anthology *The Laughing Playmate* (HarperCollins, 1992). Both stories were also broadcast on BBC Radio Four.

Also by Robert Dodds: *The Midnight Clowns*, a supernatural thriller for children, published by Andersen Press, 2000.

RATTLESNAKE

The country and western on the car radio had started out as something that marshmallowed Miranda's mind, calming her down. It went with the flat uneventful desert landscape that slipped by outside the windows. Then somehow it had started to become irritating, without her really noticing, until finally, as 'Stand by your Man' started up, she punched the off button like she was poking out the singer's eye. In the sudden absence of music she heard the phlegm-throated burr of the engine and the long kiss of the tyres on tarmac. The road stretched ahead in an impossibly straight line to a horizon that someone had made with the same ruler. The sun sat symmetrically on the end of the road, like a big swollen half orange. Maybe this desert highway followed some old migrant trail to California, and the settlers had guided themselves westwards by the sun. Anyway, it was lousy for the eyes. To save them, Miranda concentrated on the desert off to one side, where the cacti slipped by like phantoms. The thought came to her that they could be the spirits of migrants who had failed to make it across this desert. They'd have rattled out their last breath in the dessicated air, pleading for God to send them water. Then a cactus had grown for each corpse, thrusting up through a huddle of bones picked clean by squabbling vultures. 'Give us a ride', the cacti would have said, if they'd had voices, 'give us a ride if you're going to California!'

How long was it since she had seen another car? This road was endless. She pressed her foot down a little harder, sending the needle well past the statutory fifty-five. Then she saw it. Shit! The gas-tank needle was flat on empty, and the warning light was on.

She forced her mind backwards over the last hour. How long ago had she driven through that place – Wackenburg, Wickenbird, whatever? There'd been gas stations there for sure, although she couldn't bring them into focus. They'd slipped by, as irrelevant as the cacti, the other cars, the big signs for motels. If only she'd paid attention. Now what?

Miranda slowed the big Dodge right down so she could think. She checked the rear-view mirror, and her attention was held by the eyes that looked back at her. They were like voids. The low sun straight ahead threw the minute landscape of her face into sharp relief. For a change she looked every minute of her forty-three years. The car wandered into the middle of the highway, and she shifted her gaze quickly from those stranger's eyes to steer it back to the right.

It must be too far now to go back to Wackenburg. There had to be another gas station ahead somewhere, and besides, the idea of turning back gave her a horrible sensation. She had to keep going now, like some space probe, sent out into the depths of the cosmos. She didn't know what she'd find there, but, please God, just let there be a gas station. He could surely just do her one favour – he owed it.

As each mile clicked on to the clock like a gasp for petrol Miranda found she had to fight off a tension which made her grip the steering wheel with knuckles like blanched bones. She tried to breathe deeply, using the old tension-ridding exercises they'd taught her in drama school. She stretched her cramped muscles, tightening then relaxing them, bunching up and releasing. But the tension crept back, until she felt she would scream. Fighting the urge to go as fast as possible, she let her speed drop to around forty, to eke out the petrol. She felt as if she was wading on foot through deep sand and sagebrush, getting nowhere. It was a slow-motion sequence, a nightmare.

Then, against the setting sun, a miracle. A dark blob of buildings, and a sign. A lit-up sign. A lit-up sign that said 'Mr Happy's Gas Station'. Miranda swung the Dodge off the tarmac in a graceful lazy curve and on to the dusty forecourt. God had turned up trumps after all.

There were two pumps, and a little kiosk with a light on but no-one inside. There was a house behind the kiosk. Kind of an apologetic-looking house, wooden, with flaking white paint. Off to one side were a couple of sheds that looked like they couldn't be bothered falling down completely. Behind them, there was the desert again.

Miranda waited a few seconds, then hit the horn once, briefly. Nothing happened. Maybe it was self-serve. She turned off the engine, and opened the door. The heat was starting to diminish now that the sun was low. The sky was faceless blue, deepening to black already out in the east, where she'd come from. Miranda stood stretching for a moment, and smoothed out the crumples in her white linen skirt and jacket. Where was Mr Happy? She called out, in the direction of the house.

'Is there anybody there? Hello? Is there anybody around?'

There was no reply, but an old metal sign for some kind of engine oil creaked slightly in the merest hint of an evening breeze. Oh well, must be self-serve anyway. She unlocked the petrol cap and reached for the holster of the nearest pump. But it was padlocked. The light on the pump was on, but the pistol grip of the hose was padlocked to the holster. She checked out the other pump. Same story.

Miranda reached into the car and pulled her handbag off the passenger seat. She found her cigarettes and lighter. Agitation was making her fingers clumsy. Where the fuck was the attendant, and why the fuck were the pumps padlocked? She needed nicotine like those migrants needed water, and the first lungful of smoke sluiced relief through her. The thin backwash of the smoke streamed out of her nose, but before she could pull again a voice came from the house. It was disembodied, as if the house itself were speaking.

'Excuse me, you can't smoke there!'

It was a young man's voice. Now at last maybe she'd get somewhere. She pulled more calmness and strength out of the cigarette, then dropped it into the dust and ground it out with her heel.

'I'm sorry!' she called out towards the house. 'Could I have some gas, please?'

The screen door of the house opened slowly, and the owner of the voice emerged onto the little porch. The low sun picked him out like a warm golden spotlight. He was of medium height, slightly built, maybe nineteen or twenty years old. He had on jeans and a checked shirt, and a

4

baseball cap with a name on it in big red letters. 'Harold', the hat said.

Harold stood for a moment on the porch. Miranda saw an Edward Hopper painting, the solitary figure transfixed in a momentary beauty by the sun's late glow. Then the boy came down the three wooden steps. There he stopped again.

'Station's closed, ma'am.' It was said neutrally, just a statement.

Miranda held the last of the smoke in her lungs a moment longer, then let it out slowly.

'But your sign's all lit up.'

'Sure – I was just going to turn it off. We shut at six, and now it's five after six.' Harold's voice was a little squeaky, as if he'd used it too much when it was breaking. Miranda turned a moment, and looked up and down the empty highway. Then she swung back. She had a big friendly smile now. She'd constructed it while her back was turned to him, and now it was as good as she could make it.

'Just five minutes late? I wonder . . . Harold . . . if you'd do me a big favour and just let me have some gas? You see, I'm right out.'

Harold also looked out at the empty road. 'Gee . . . that's a problem. You see, I just don't have the authority to open up the pumps after we've closed for the night. Mr Ozark wouldn't like that.'

'Who is Mr Ozark?'

'It's Mr Ozark who owns the gas station.'

'It says it's Mr Happy's gas station on that sign.'

Harold came forward a little. He stood just beside the kiosk, where it cast a deep shadow.

'Oh, that's just a name Mr Ozark thought up.'

'So there is no Mr Happy?'

'No.'

Miranda's smile had not withstood this exchange. She felt it curling at the edges like an old sandwich. She abandoned it before it walked and looked business-like instead. She reached for her handbag again.

'Listen, Harold. What if I were to offer you . . . five dollars, say, just to open up the pumps for me and let me have some gas?'

Harold lifted up his cap and pushed some sandy hair back away from his forehead. He was just a boy, Miranda thought.

'Gee, I'm real sorry, but I just can't . . .'

'Ten dollars?'

'I'm sorry, I truly am, but Mr Ozark's rules are pretty definite. I just can't serve anyone after six.'

Miranda put the handbag back on the car seat. Harold moved some stones around with his toe, then shot her a look she couldn't work out.

'You got enough gas to get to the next station?'

'I don't know. Where's the next station?'

'West?'

'Yes.'

'That'd be at the junction with Interstate Forty. That's forty-one point four miles from here. You got enough gas for that?'

'Fuck knows. I don't know how long the warning light was on before I noticed it. What is there between here and Interstate Forty?'

'Nothing. Just desert, ma'am.'

'I see. And the other way?'

'Wickenburg's the first town, ma'am. That's forty-five point six miles.'

Miranda considered the figures. What if she set off and got about twenty miles? It would be pitch dark. She'd have to sleep in the car. Walk in the morning. Get gas in a can. Get a lift back to the car. She didn't like it. The feeling of wading through sand and sagebrush came back. She must persuade this boy somehow.

'Listen, Harold. Is Mr Ozark in the house?'

'No, ma'am. He's got a house out the other side of Wickenburg. Forty-eight miles away exactly.'

What was all this distance shit? Miranda looked at Harold, trying to appraise if he were being funny. Or was he a bit simple? She thought a minute. A bright idea came.

'Listen, Harold. What if you were to telephone Mr Ozark? Or let me speak to him. I'm sure he'd let you bend the rules a little in the circumstances. Only five minutes late. A woman travelling on her own, right out of petrol.'

'You from Boston or someplace?'

'What?'

'Petrol's a kind of a fancy word for gas, ain't it? Are you English?'

This was getting ridiculous. The boy wanted to make small talk for God's sake.

'Yes, I'm English. Now, what about that telephone?'

'Telephone's gone down.'

'What? You mean it's broken?'

'Sure. Mr Ozark got mad at it. Broke it right up against the wall. Slam! Just like that. He's got some temper, Mr Ozark.' Harold looked uneasy as soon as he'd said these words. He looked along the road towards the east. 'Oh, I ain't saying nothing against Mr Ozark. But he sure as hell has a temper!'

Miranda looked at the boy. In spite of her situation, she felt a twinge of sympathetic interest in his nervous glances along the road, and his obvious fear of this Mr Ozark. But behind her facade of calm there was a seething rout of demons screaming and stamping their feet with impatience and frustration. She needed to get back on that road, back into her drift into deep space. Urgent drift. What could she do? Without much hope, she tried bribery again.

'Listen Harold . . .' she opened her handbag, '. . . I've got about fifty dollars in cash on me right now. You can have it all, every cent, if you just give me five gallons of gas.'

Harold was already shaking his head. One foot insinuated itself backwards a few inches in the dust, as if reluctant to remain out there at the end of Harold's leg. 'No way, ma'am. I'm really sorry, but no way. Mr Ozark – well, he'd be so mad at me if I did that . . .'

'For fuck's sake, Harold! Mr Ozark's probably in his house right now, isn't he? Do his ears twitch when he hears a gas pump working forty miles away?'

'Forty-eight miles away.'

'Well – do they?'

'I just can't do it ma'am. I'm sorry.'

'Well, what do you suggest I do?'

Harold looked into infinity over her shoulder. 'Me, ma'am? Gee, that's a tough one. I guess you might hitch a ride, but there's some strange characters around you know, at night. On the roads, at night.'

'I can take care of myself, don't you worry!'

' Oh, sure ma'am, I'm sure you can. It's just, well, there's some strange people on the roads. At night.'

'Well anyway, hitching a ride is no good to me. I need my car. Hey – are you going back to Wickenburg tonight?'

'No, ma'am. I stay out here.'

'Do you have a car? Is there a car parked out the back of the house?'

'No, ma'am. I don't drive. Mr Ozark brings me out here.'

'And he's not coming to get you tonight?'

'Nope.'

The sun had reached that stage in its sinking when the shadows seemed to lengthen even as you watched them. Miranda stood looking at the dark shapes creeping across the dusty ground. The shadows of the gas pumps, the kiosk, her car. The earth was turning, but she was still. Stranded. Beached. She took a deep breath.

'OK. Thanks to your Mr Ozark's rules, I'm stuck here, aren't I? I'll spend the night in my car then. Will that satisfy you? I'll sleep in my car and fill up in the morning when you unlock these sodding pumps. What time do you open in the morning?'

Harold's voice squeaked between octaves. 'Well, there's a problem right there, ma'am . . .'

'What's that? Mr Ozark doesn't like people sleeping in their cars at his station?'

'No – it's that tomorrow's the Lord's Day. We don't open Sundays.'

'Jesus Christ!'

'Amen!'

For a second, Miranda wanted to hit this little punk. She wanted to grind his nose in the dust. But there wasn't a trace of irony in his face, or triumph. He really must be simple. Leading his life according to a simple set of rules. Besides, he was scared. Definitely scared of this Ozark character. But what the fuck was she going to do?

Harold cleared his throat. 'There is one thing. Mr Ozark is coming out here tomorrow morning. I don't know what he'll say, but he might open up the pumps specially. I don't know.'

That seemed to close the conversation as far as Harold was concerned. He went into the kiosk and flicked a switch. The lights on the gas pumps went off. Then he flicked another switch, and the big sign saying 'Mr Happy's Gas Station' went out. Instantly the desert seemed to press closer, and Miranda shivered a little. As the sun went down, the warmth was draining out of the air fast. A big truck thundered by, heading east. She realised it was the only vehicle that had passed since she'd been there.

Harold had finished in the kiosk. He turned out the lights

in there, and came out. He paused as he locked the door. Then gave Miranda a longer, more direct look than he had done so far. She met his gaze angrily. She wasn't just going to go away and cry in her car. Let him feel guilty. His eyes were pale, like his skin. He was so fair as to be almost albino.

He put a hand to his chin. 'You know, I have this funny feeling I know you!'

Instantly, Miranda saw it coming. This was all she needed.

Harold was looking at her hard. A sort of half smile started to appear on his face. 'Yeah! I've seen you on TV, haven't I?'

What could he have seen? It must have been old, whatever it was. 'It's possible . . . you might have.'

'Yeah . . . I got it. *The Carltons*. You were in *The Carltons*!'

'That was a long time ago . . .'

'Our local station was running a repeat of the whole darned thing last year in the afternoons. I never missed an episode. Gee – I got it! You were the English governess . . . Miss, Miss . . .'

'Miss Seymour.' Might as well get it over with.

'Miss Seymour! Wow! Those kids sure gave you a hard time Miss Seymour, huh? I don't know how you stood those brats!'

He was transformed. His shuffling nervousness was gone. He looked as if he might explode with excitement. He took a couple of steps towards her. 'So, what are you doing out this way, Miss Seymour? They send you out here to get a break from those kids?'

Miranda took an involuntary step back towards her car. 'Now hold on, Harold. It's only television. It's not real. I'm not Miss Seymour – I am . . . myself.'

Harold stared into some inner place for a moment, then

he blushed and looked at the sky. 'Gee! That was real stupid of me, huh? I'm sorry – er . . .' he wiped his hands on his jeans, '. . . could I shake your hand, Miss . . . er . . .'

Reluctantly Miranda held out a hand. 'Solheim. Mrs Miranda Solheim.'

He took her hand and shook it reverently. Then he backed off a couple of feet and started a kind of breathless tuneless noise.

'A da da dee, a da da dee, a dat dat da da da dee! That's some catchy theme tune that show had, huh? I bet you catch yourself whistling that in the tub don't you, Mrs Solheim?'

'No.'

'So what brings you out this way, Mrs Solheim? You on vacation?'

'Yes – sort of.'

There was a pause. Harold couldn't take his eyes off her. It was as if she might fly up into the air over the forecourt and hover above him, a celestial being. She broke the moment crudely. Maybe she could milk this sudden fan worship to get out of this hell hole.

'So, as a *Carltons* fan, are you going to give poor Miss Seymour some gas, Harold?'

He looked genuinely distressed. 'Gee, I'm real sorry about this. This is the most awful thing that ever happened here. I just can't break the rules, even though I want to help out.'

'So I've got to spend the night in my car, and hope that your Mr Ozark will open up the pumps for me in the morning?'

'Well . . . I guess that's about it, Mrs Solheim.' Then, incredibly, he was turning round, heading back to the house. She couldn't believe it. Was that it? She watched him go slowly up the steps, pause on the porch, pull open the screen door, and disappear inside. Seething, Miranda grabbed her handbag, scrabbled for her cigarettes, and lit up. She called out:

'I'm going to smoke all I sodding well like! I don't care what the rules say!' There was no response. She got back into the car and locked the door. The sun was just a thin segment of orange on the horizon now. The landscape was nearly dark. No lights showed up on the long straight highway. The temperature was dropping down the scale. She looked in vain for a rug or something on the back seat to cover up with. Nothing. It was going to be a fucking uncomfortable night. She thought about drastic actions, but they all seemed unreal. The only solution was patience. She hoped to God this Mr Ozark was able to bend his own rules.

Off to the other side of the road, far off, there was a line of low hills which marked the edge of the flat desert. The moon was coming up over the top of the hills. As she watched the sun vanish, and the moon rise, Miranda felt the cold start to penetrate her limbs. She started the engine, to run the heater, and after five minutes the engine coughed and died. That really was it then. Completely out of gas. She wondered if Harold had heard the engine and thought she might drive off. No light showed in the house. Had he gone to bed? She watched the red and orange afterglow fading in the western sky. In spite of the cold, she started to feel drowsy. After all, she hadn't slept since the night before last. Her thoughts started to wander away from the present into the past.

The knock on the window made her leap forwards in a panic, banging her arm on the steering wheel. She looked out to see Harold with a flashlight. She wound the window down a fraction.

Harold looked sheepish. 'I was thinking, Mrs Solheim, you could come in the house if you want. It must be real cold out here.'

Miranda weighed it up. She decided she could handle anything he threw at her. It was better than freezing to death out here. She got out of the car, and followed Harold's frail silhouette as he led the way with the flashlight towards the house.

Inside, the first thing Harold did was to lock the door. 'Mr Ozark's rules,' he explained. They were in a bare hallway with four or five doors opening off it. Harold opened the first door on the right and led her into what was presumably the sitting room. A single light bulb dangled from the ceiling, illuminating a comfortless room with cheap shoddy furnishings. It wasn't much warmer than outside. Miranda glanced towards an electric bar heater standing on a threadbare rug in the middle of the room. It wasn't on. Harold saw her looking.

'You cold? Thing is, the heater works on a kind of a slot meter thing, and I'm clean out of quarters.'

Miranda found a couple of quarters in her purse and gave them to Harold. He pushed them into the meter, and the fire buzzed and crackled into life.

'Mind if I sit down?'

'No, make yourself feel right at home, Miss Seymour!'

'Solheim. Mrs Miranda Solheim.' Was he doing this deliberately? Harold looked away, towards the window. 'Your husband know where you are?'

'What?'

'I just . . . I was just wondering . . . your husband's maybe expecting you someplace? Tonight? Where are you headed?'

Miranda resisted the impulse to tell him to fuck off and mind his own business.

'I was on my way to see someone else . . .' She thought quickly, '. . . my sister. My sister lives in Los Angeles.'

'LA? Gee, that's four hundred and seven point five miles from here. You'd have been driving all night, Mrs Solheim!'

'Is it as far as that? Well, I . . . I might have stopped over at a motel somewhere.'

Miranda sat down on the black pvc couch in front of the fire to close the subject. She took in the rest of the room. An armchair in the same hideous black material. A reproduction of Salvador Dali's *Christ of St John of the Cross* on the wall. A bookcase with a few cheap paperbacks and some car magazines scattered on its shelves.

'Does this house belong to Mr Ozark?'

'Sure.'

'Doesn't provide much in the way of home comforts, does he? Haven't you even got a television?'

'Used to have a television, but Mr Ozark took it away. Said the station didn't make enough money to support a television. I got a radio though, in the kitchen.'

'Are you going to make me a coffee or something?'

'Sure – do you like milk?'

'Yes, please.'

'We're out of milk – sorry.'

'I'll take it black then.'

'OK. Do you take sugar?'

'No.'

'That's lucky. We're out of sugar too. I like sugar myself. Mr Ozark said he'd bring some out this week.'

'How long does Mr Ozark leave you out here for at a time, Harold?'

'Oh . . . maybe a month, maybe six weeks.'

Miranda was horrified. 'Six weeks! Stuck out here on your own! I'd go up the wall!'

'Pardon me?'

'Up the wall – crazy – stuck out here all that time.'

'Well, Mrs Solheim, the thing is . . .' Harold hesitated, then seemed to decide something. He perched on the edge of the sofa next to Miranda, and lowered his voice, as if he might be overheard. 'The thing is, Mrs Solheim, that Mr

Ozark thinks this is the best place for me to be. He says I'm like Christ, sent out for forty days and forty nights into the wilderness. Only I got it easier than Christ, 'cause Christ was tempted all that time by the Devil. And out here I ain't got no Devil to tempt me.' He lowered his voice almost to a whisper now. 'And the thing is . . . you won't say nothing will you, Mrs Solheim?'

'I won't say anything to anyone Harold.'

'Well . . . I have given way to temptation in the past, and Mr Ozark thinks this is the safest way for me to be – you know – out of the way of temptation and all. You see . . . I know you won't say nothing to anyone Mrs Solheim?'

'No, of course not.'

'Well, I could have got sent away, Mrs Solheim, if Mr Ozark hadn't stepped in and vouched for me. And there was things he knew that the law hadn't found out about yet. He sure saved me from a heap of trouble. Mr Ozark's my preacher you see, Mrs Solheim, and he's my protector.'

'I thought he owned this gas station?'

'Sure he does. And another one the other side of Wickenburg. But the money they make is all for his ministry.'

'I see. But what about your family – haven't you got a family that you'd like to see more of? A mother and father?'

Harold stood up. 'I guess. Well, I'll make that coffee.'

While Harold was out of the room, Miranda turned over these fragments of information. It was pretty clear this boy was being exploited. Stuck out here in this miserable half-furnished house for weeks on end, terrified to break Mr Ozark's rules. Ozark. Strange name. From nowhere another thought came – maybe there was no Mr Ozark! Maybe Harold made it all up. Maybe he just wanted to exercise a little power, a devious tyrant in his lonely little kingdom. The thought was a disturbing one, and she pushed it away. Harold wasn't dangerous; he was just a simple boy. She decided she needed to take a leak. She went out into the hallway.

Harold came out of the kitchen to point out the door of the bathroom to her. There was a light cord dangling outside it.

When she came out of the bathroom, Miranda thought she'd glance into one or two of the other rooms. She could hear Harold making coffee in the kitchen. One door was ajar, and she pushed it open gently, so that it wouldn't creak. There was no window, but the moon shone into the room through a small skylight. But there was nothing illuminated by its pale light that she could recognise. There seemed to be some kind of glass cases along the walls. She flicked on the light switch.

A gust of hissing and rattling greeted the light. In the glass tanks that lined the room, what seemed like hundreds of rattlesnakes slithered and reared and arched about each other. Miranda recoiled, trying to fight down the scream rising in her throat. But it wouldn't stay down, and she stumbled out of the room into the hallway with a gasping shriek of fear and disgust. She hunkered down in the hallway, her stomach heaving. If there had been any food in there she'd have thrown up, but instead her stomach twisted up into a hard knot that hurt. Harold came rushing out of the kitchen. When he saw what had happened, he closed the door of the snake room. He seemed more puzzled than angry.

'Mrs Solheim! You didn't ought to have gone in there! I showed you where the bathroom was. Why did you go in there?'

Miranda pulled herself together. She stood up slowly, putting a hand on the wall to steady herself. Why *had* she gone in there?

'I . . . I'm sorry Harold. I was just being nosy. But . . . I mean . . . is that a hobby of yours?'

16

'Sure'. A fatuous smug expression came on to his face. The expression of every boy proud of his collection of whatever it is he collects. 'Caught them all myself too, in the brush and the rocks around the station.'

'But . . . aren't they . . .'

'Poisonous? Sure as hell they are. You gotta be real careful how you pick them up. I got a kind of a stick with a fork at the end – keep it right there in the room with them. You wanna see how I pick them up?'

'Christ! No!'

'Well, it ain't so difficult. You just pin 'em down with the stick and then reach down real easy and grab them just behind the head. Then you can do what you want see, 'cause they can't bite you as long as you hold on. Got names for 'em all too!'

'I . . . I see. Don't tell me any more.'

But Harold was on a roll. His eyes shone with enthusiasm. He became confidential. 'You won't let on if I tell you a little secret, Mrs Solheim?'

'No.'

He was grinning now, at some private joke. 'There's one big diamond-back in there. Nearly six feet long. Caught him last summer. Well, I call him "Mr Ozark". Hee! Hee! I like to get him mad, then he puffs himself up and rattles his tail like crazy and he's just the spitting image of the real Mr Ozark!' Harold suddenly looked doubtfully at Miranda. 'Don't get me wrong, Mrs Solheim – I ain't saying nothing against Mr Ozark – but he sure as hell has a temper. You wouldn't say anything about this to Mr Ozark tomorrow, would you?'

'Of course not. Can we go and drink that coffee now?'

Harold fetched the cups from the kitchen, and Miranda went to sit down again on the sofa in the sitting room. She realised how incredibly tired she was now. Her eyes were aching from the long day's drive, and she closed them for a moment. In the darkness, a thought formed. A thought about Harold, and Mr Ozark protecting him. About Harold tormenting the snake. Why would he want to get back at Mr Ozark? She opened her eyes. Harold came in with the coffee. He put hers down on the low table at the end of the sofa, and sat down opposite her in the armchair. He had got hold of one of those Rubik's cube things, and was rotating it absently in his hands. He was just a young boy. What was going on here?

'Harold . . . this is none of my business . . . but is Mr Ozark blackmailing you?'

Harold looked blank, as if he didn't know the word. 'Pardon me?'

'Are you working out here for Mr Ozark because you're afraid that he'll tell the police about . . . whatever it was you did?'

Harold's hands gripped the cube. 'No way. No, ma'am. Mr Ozark wouldn't let me down.'

Miranda let it drop. There was something wrong, but she couldn't put her finger on what it was. The idea that Mr Ozark only existed in Harold's head was the most worrying possibility. Mr Ozark. Weren't there some Ozark mountains somewhere? And what about his confusion over whether she was a real person or a character in a soap?

Harold's thoughts had returned to her television career too. He cleared his throat. 'I . . . I guess you must be in a lot of television stuff huh?'

Well, to be fair, he didn't have a television. 'I've . . . given that up now, more or less.'

'Oh, why's that?'

Bless his naive little socks. 'Well . . . when I was Miss Seymour in *The Carltons* I was young and quite good looking . . .'

'Very good looking I'd say.'

Oh my God. 'Well, I'm a good deal older now, and there

aren't so many parts for . . . middle-aged women on television.'

'You ain't middle-aged are you?'

The boy was on the level. He was absolutely on the level. It was flattering, in a crazy way. 'Well, tell that to the casting directors. I could get parts when I was young by looking good and being a reasonable actress. But when you've got to my age you can only get parts by being a damned good actress. And I'm not.'

'Well – you're sure a star in my book.'

The boy was blushing even. This was unbelievable. He wasn't going to come on was he, for Christ's sake? No, luckily he was too shy to take it any further. That would have been all she needed.

But Harold did have something up his sleeve. He cleared his throat again. 'You know, Mrs Solheim. I been wonderin' . . . about your husband.'

Her husband? What the fuck did he know about her husband?

'You see, I listen to the radio a lot in the day, and I specially like listening to the police reports. Now, yesterday, there were four homicides in Arizona. There was a Mrs Edna Schneider hacked to death with an axe in her own back yard in Lake Havasu City. They picked up a suspect for that one – guy who'd bought the axe in a hardware store earlier in the day – but they ain't got a motive. Then there was a Mr Alexander Cabeza who was crushed under the wheels of a blue station wagon by an unidentified man following an apparent dispute over a parking space. The other two were shot in the head – one in Phoenix and one in Tucson – but I got distracted by a car coming in for gas, and I only remember the names. There was a Gerry Snyder, and a Frank T. Solheim. Now that surely couldn't be your husband, could it, Mrs Solheim?'

He doesn't know anything. Breathe easily. Like a drama exercise. Improvise. Now: 'Of course not! My husband's name is Andrew, and he's away on a skiing trip in Oregon. Do you think I'm a murderess? On the run from justice?' Perfect.

'No, no, I surely don't. It's just one of these coincidences that happen. But I did think maybe if it was your husband that had been shot in the head – twice I think it was – then it'd be best you heard about it now, you know. So it wouldn't be a shock later on, you know.'

'Well, that's thoroughly thoughtful and decent of you, Harold. And if I'd said "My God! That's my husband! I must get back to Tucson!" you'd have filled up my car with gas and let me go, wouldn't you?'

Harold hadn't considered this one. The Rubik's cube tumbled round and round in his hands like he was spin-drying it. 'Well, that's a hard one. I'm expressly forbidden by Mr Ozark . . .'

Miranda interrupted him. She could change the subject here. 'You're enjoying this, aren't you?'

Harold stopped tumbling.

'You're stuck out here in the middle of nowhere, and now you've got a chance to wield a little power haven't you? That's why you collect the snakes, isn't it? So you can have something to bully? And now you've got me where you want me, haven't you?'

'It's just the rules . . .'

'It's nothing to do with rules. You know what? I don't even believe in your Mr Ozark! I think you made him up as an excuse.'

Harold put the cube down. His thin face was agitated. His finger wagged at her. 'Don't say that now! That's wrong. You'll find out tomorrow.'

'Are you telling the truth, Harold? Mr Ozark is coming out here tomorrow?'

'Sure. He comes out every Sunday to take the money out of the safe.'

'That's a fine Christian mission! I thought he was a preacher? Why isn't he in his church on Sunday?'

Harold was on the march now, up and down the room. His agitation couldn't be contained any other way. Miranda was afraid she might have stirred him up too much. But hell, why shouldn't she stir him up? It was thanks to him that she was here at all. Well, let him start to regret it. He needed a shake anyway. This Ozark was a bastard, and she would get Harold to acknowledge that fact properly.

'How long have you been working out here, Harold?'

'Two years, one month and sixteen days.'

'And how many holidays have you had?'

'I've had seventeen full days, and one half day on account of the pumps needed maintenance work.'

'Seventeen days off in two years! And what does Mr Ozark pay you?'

'That's private information that Mr Ozark said I wasn't to let out.'

'Can't you see that he's just taking advantage?'

'You mustn't talk like that, Mrs Solheim! That's the voice of the Tempter speaking through you!'

This shit was starting to get to her. Couldn't the boy understand anything? This Ozark had filled his head so full with the Bible and rules that he couldn't see he was being screwed. The desire to shake him up was overwhelming. If there really was a Mr Ozark, then it was thanks to his bloody rules that she was trapped here, and she was as much a victim as Harold was. Ozark was one of these fucking vampires that lived on other people, sucking them dry.

'Mr Ozark is an exploiting bully as far as I can make out.'

'He looks after my family! He's a good man!'

She had him on the run now. He was pacing up and down the room like crazy. She had him squirming.

'Who's your family?'

'Ma and three sisters?'

'What happened to your Pa?'

'Listen, I ain't supposed to talk to strangers . . .'

Miranda threw back her head and laughed. Theatrically. But it was funny too. Mr Ozark didn't want Harold talking to strangers. But he'd invented a rule that meant Harold had a whole night with a stranger to get through. She'd get to the bottom of this.

'Does Mr Ozark stay with your mother and sisters?'

'No – he don't stay. He just visits.'

'Just visits, huh? But you're never there, are you? How does he treat your mother and sisters? Does he have a bad temper there too?'

Harold was going up and down, up and down the room. She had a shrewd idea.

'Had you ever thought that Mr Ozark was the Tempter, Harold? Had you ever thought that he might be the Devil himself?'

The effect on Harold of these words was startling. He stared at her with a look of intense horror, but with something pleading in his eyes, as if he was in need of help. Then he drew out a tiny crucifix that hung on a chain around his neck and which had been hidden beneath his tee-shirt. He held it towards her, B-movie style, warding off a vampire.

'Get thee behind me, Satan!' he exclaimed. Then he moved towards her, his eyes shining with that strange mixture of horror and pleading. Miranda was terrified. She'd gone too far. What was he going to do? In a panic, she grabbed her handbag and ran out into the hall, thrusting her hand into it as she went. Yes. Her hand closed around the grip of the small handgun. Harold was coming after her, and she whirled and pointed the pistol straight at his face as he came out of the sitting room door. He stood stock still. Lowered the crucifix. And his jaw.

'I put two bullets through my husband's head in Tucson

yesterday. I've not got a lot to lose if I put the rest through yours!' She didn't know why she had told him that. Why hadn't she just pointed the gun at him?

Harold was goggling at her in just the same way as when he'd realised she was in *The Carltons*. 'You killed Frank T. Solheim in Tucson yesterday?'

'Yes.'

As they continued to stand in their frozen positions it dawned on Miranda why she had said it. It was the relief of being able to share it, even with this strange boy. She looked at him, his eyes now lowered to the gun barrel. Even now, she felt as if some of the weight of that heavy secret had been shifted. It had been an unendurable burden to carry alone, even for a night and a day. She was glad that someone else knew what she'd done.

While her body continued to stay stock still, her thoughts raced on further, and she realised why she was glad that Harold knew. There was an affinity between them. He might not see it yet, but she was going to force him to see it. She felt renewed strength and control. She weighed the gun in her hand, its handle snug against her palm.

'You know why you made me want to say that to you about Mr Ozark, Harold? It's because you're just like I was for years and years and years. Terrified of some bullying bastard who's sucking the life out of you like a vampire. God! The world needs sweeping clean of these people!'

'If you mean Mr Ozark . . .'

'Shut up! I understand your Mr Ozark even if you think the sun shines out of his ass! That's the way with these vampires. They can fool you for years and years.'

Harold's stare was disconcerting. He was frightened, obviously. But there was also that look of admiration that she'd seen before. He pointed at the gun.

'Would you mind pointing it at my legs or something. I ain't going to do nothing.'

Miranda lowered the gun. Tiredness swept into her as if it had only been waiting for this action. The moment was past. It was her fault anyway, winding him up like that.

'Let's go in the kitchen, Harold. I want another coffee.'

The kitchen was as bare as the living room. There was a jumble of dishes and pans in the sink. The table had coffee rings on its formica top, and crumbs. Miranda put the gun back into her handbag and sat down on one of the two wooden chairs by the table. Harold put the kettle on the stove behind her. She sensed that he was hesitating, looking at her back.

'So . . . what are you going to do now, Mrs Solheim? I mean . . . you were going someplace when you stopped here, weren't you? You were going to LA?'

'Sure – I was going to LA To see someone.'

'Your sister?'

'No. Someone who loved me, once. Before I married. A long time ago.'

'Will he help you?'

'No, I don't think anyone can help me. I just wanted to talk. But now I feel so tired, and it's four hundred miles to go. And I forgot to fill up with gas.'

Harold busied himself with the coffee pot. But he was itching to know more. 'I guess you and your husband didn't get along too good?' he said eventually.

In the circumstances it was a pretty funny comment, or at least it struck Miranda that way. She found herself hooting with laughter, howling like a maniac, as if Harold had made the world's best joke. Through the hysteria she was vaguely aware of him coming forward and looking at her, his jaw slackened off again. She must seem a pretty strange fish to him, a husband-shooting English television actress who drove around in deserts without filling up her gas tank. The thought of it sent her off again in a gust of laughter. She felt the spring that had been wound up for two days in her guts was unwinding in a crazy unleashing of tension. Then her head was on the kitchen table, and she was sobbing like a child. But it felt good. She needed it.

'I'm sorry Mrs Solheim, but you said you wanted to talk.'

Miranda reined in the horses of her laughter and tears. She did want to talk. She found a handkerchief and mopped up. Harold put a cup of coffee in front of her. Where should she begin? How could she tell this story for the first time? Her mind went back through the years to that initial, shocking revelation. When she discovered the truth about the man she'd married. That was the proper point to begin. She took a sip of coffee and blew her nose. Harold sat down on the other chair. It was as if he were settling down for an episode of *The Carltons*. But she didn't care. She was telling this story for herself as well as for him. Maybe it was for him too, if he could understand its relevance to his own sad exploitation.

'I worshipped my husband at first. I worshipped him from the first day I met him until the first time he beat the shit out of me. That was the night of our wedding day.'

'Gee, that's awful! On your wedding night?'

'Yes. My wedding night.' She shut her eyes, the better to watch the movie of her past. The words came easily in the darkness. She felt it was absolutely necessary to share this story with this strange boy. This asteroid she had encountered on her space drift.

'I was all dressed up in white silk underwear. He turned up the radio in the hotel room so no-one would hear. It was a programme of that old Dixieland music. I remember all the songs: 'You're Some Pretty Doll', 'Nobody Knows You', 'That's a Plenty'. He beat me in time to the music you see. That was his sense of humour there. He had a wonderful sense of humour did Frank.'

'But you stayed with him even after that? You stayed with him for years?'

'Sure I did. You know why he was beating me? Because I'd been talking all the time at the wedding reception with some guy. It was a friend of Frank's – he was from out of state, and he didn't know anyone there. I was just being friendly. So then I knew not to be friendly with other men – at least not when Frank was around. But I was still in love. So – he had a violent streak – but, hell, I thought his being jealous like that showed how much he loved me. But I was wrong. Jealousy is to do with power, not love. And Frank was very interested in power. I loved him for years before I really understood that properly.'

'So how long were you married?'

'Oh, sixteen years exactly. It was our wedding anniversary yesterday. It seemed an appropriate day for . . . for what I did.' Was it really only yesterday? Was Frank alive yesterday?

'Gee – had you planned it like that, Mrs Solheim? Had you planned it that you'd kill him specially on your wedding anniversary?' This was *True Detective* stuff for Harold. He was on his collector's kick now. Not snakes, but murder details. First hand. Miranda recalled his recitation of the details of those other Arizona homicides. But she didn't care. He was only a boy. And he would understand more, later.

'No. If he'd have acted differently it might not have happened. I hadn't made up my mind to do it. It's a funny thing Harold. If you come to hate someone you've once loved, there's still some of that love lingers on somehow, mixed up in the hate.'

Harold seemed struck by this bit of wisdom. He nodded agreement. 'I guess. You know, I feel a little like that about my snakes. I sorta love 'em and hate 'em a little at the same time.'

'And Mr Ozark?'

But that was forbidden territory. Harold's eyes went cold

for a moment. Then he urged her on. 'Go on and tell me what happened, Mrs Solheim. If you don't mind, I mean. How did you work up to pulling that trigger?'

Miranda shut her eyes for a moment. Some of that old pain bit into her again, just like the pain of an old operation that the nerves never forget. 'Over the years, Frank got into some strange ways of treating me. I'm not going to go into details. He liked . . . he liked to degrade me. Always in private, never so anyone else could ever guess what was going on.'

'What kind of things . . .?'

'I'm not going into all that. I was just an animal to him, once the doors were locked for the night.'

'Did you have children?'

'No – we never had children.'

'So why'd you stay? Why didn't you get a divorce? Or just leave? You coulda gone back to England, couldn't you?'

'I left him dozens of times. But he always came after me. And always with promises and roses. Always swearing that it would all be different. Always full of regret and broken hearted that I could go away and leave him. I was such a fool. Over and over again I took it for love, all this pleading and swearing and promising. And for a few months it'd be better. Then, one night, it would start all over again. And you know, Harold, there's something else about being bullied and treated like a dog. You admire Mr Ozark don't you?'

'I don't know why you keep on bringing in Mr Ozark . . .'

'Ah, but it's you who keep bringing him in. I don't even know him. I only know him through you Harold. Anyway, what happens – what happened to me – was I sort of came to see myself in Frank's terms. When you've been beaten and treated worse than a slave, worse than a dog that's crawled in out of the gutter – you start to feel that's something to do with you. That it's something to do with the way you are. Maybe you *are* worthless and weak and fit only to be used and abused. Maybe anyone would treat you that way, once they got to know you. Maybe you're even lucky that, even though you get beaten and used worse than a whore, at least someone wants to be married to you, and live with you.'

Miranda paused for a moment. She felt different now to that woman she was describing. Vaguely she tried to reach out for a description of that difference, even to describe it to herself. It was self-esteem, or something like that, because ever since she had shot Frank, she had felt a new strength in herself. She was frightened, and tired, and on the run from her fate, but she felt that she had seized the steering wheel of her life again. That was why it was so crazy that she was here now, under the thumb of this obscure Ozark. Why didn't she just force Harold at gunpoint to give her the gas? Why hadn't she pulled a gun when he first refused her? It was too late now. Maybe even at first something inside her had recognised a fellow victim. She couldn't shoot him. And anyway, she knew the police would find her soon. She was only trying to keep her freedom a little longer. Los Angeles. She thought of John, her old lover. The startled look that would come over his face when he saw her standing at his doorway. Would he even recognise her? And what did she want from him anyway? Maybe just this, just what she was getting now. A listener for her story. Harold broke into her reverie.

'So why'd you shoot him last night? What happened?'

'What happened? Well – Frank took me out to lunch. An anniversary lunch. Really expensive place. We drank champagne. He treated me like a queen in public, always. I think it must have given him an extra thrill to do that, to treat me like two separate women in public and in private. He got a little drunk anyway, a little excited. He was reminding me of our wedding night, started kidding on about that white silk underwear. Said he wanted me to wear white silk underwear that night. Said we'd listen to a little Dixieland music. Right there in this expensive restaurant I started sweating you know, with fear. And he kept right on talking about what he was going to do. He ordered more champagne. He was getting pretty drunk. Then he said 'I've got a surprise for you Miranda', and he took out this brown envelope. He must have planned this all out, to have it with him like that. When the waiters were done with our plates he showed me these pictures – photographs. They went back a few years. They were all of women – some had him in them as well. These women were tied up, or gagged, or . . . whatever. He used to photograph me sometimes. Well, all these years I'd thought it was just me, you know? All these years he'd been beating up other women – prostitutes a lot of them, I guess. There were dates on the back of the photographs. They went back almost sixteen years you know. All that time, I was just one of them you know – just one of his victims. He put the pictures away and started on again about the night. And I looked at his eyes . . . his skin . . . his teeth . . . his neck swallowing champagne, and I saw a dead man, Harold. I saw the place on his forehead where the bullet was going to go in, as if I had it marked with a cross. You see, Harold? Even though I hated him, I loved it that I was special to him. I'd always thought that, all along, that I was special to him.' The stupidity of it! She would have shot him again, a thousand times. Furious that he was now beyond her reach, she grabbed the empty coffee cup in front of her and hurled it at the wall as hard as she could.

'You bastard, Frank! You vicious, vicious bastard!' Then she was sobbing again, in a confusion of anger and relief that he was gone, and horror and pity that he was gone. He was like a cancer in her soul that had been cut out, but now she felt scoured out inside, incomplete. She remembered how her eyes had been voids when she saw them in the car mirror. Was there more to her than what Frank had made her? Was she just an empty husk? Incapable of anything but running away? But when Harold's hand rested shyly on her shoulder, she felt that she could do something. Something good. Something redemptive. She could help him to help himself.

Harold was trying to calm her down. 'There, there, Mrs Solheim. Take it easy! It's all over now!' He waited a moment, then took his hand away from her shoulder. 'Was he asleep?'

The collector again. Gruesome facts. 'You really want to know it all, don't you, Harold? Why is that?'

'Oh, well . . . I never got to talk to a . . . to anyone who killed someone before. And I just love those police reports you know.'

'And do you think it's a help to me to have someone to talk about it to?'

'Well . . . I guess I didn't really think of that. But if you say so . . .'

'You're pretty honest I think, Harold. You don't bullshit do you? You're just plain burned up with curiosity about what it's like to shoot someone, huh? But I wonder . . . didn't you ever think there was someone you'd like to shoot?'

'Me! No sir, ma'am! No sir. I maybe done some bad things, but no sir! Who would I want to shoot? Tell me how you shot, Mr Solheim.'

She shut her eyes, and watched the movie. 'That night, I put on silk underwear. I let him do whatever he wanted. He was too drunk to be as vicious as he'd talked about. And all the time I was thinking about my little Smith and Wesson, tucked under the mattress on my side of the bed. All the time he was hurting me I was picturing how he'd look later on, with half his head blown away. It's pretty funny being beaten up by a corpse you know. When he'd done I took a bath while he just fell into the bed. I took a really long hot bath, just relaxing into my hatred, letting it grow. Nursing it, Harold – do you know what I mean?'

'I . . . I don't. That ain't the Christian way, Mrs Solheim. I can't imagine it. No sir.'

'Well, when I came out of the bathroom he was snoring like a pig in the sty. I eased the gun out from under the mattress, really gently. Then I released the safety catch, and pointed the barrel at Frank's head. I'd had that gun for ten years or more, and I'd never fired it. It felt like I was acting some part.'

'How far away were you? Were you kneeling on the bed?'

Miranda was in that bedroom again. She stood up. 'No – I was standing. Like this, legs apart, both arms out, the gun pointing, pointing at his forehead. The barrel about three feet from his forehead.' She stopped. Sat down again. This wasn't a play. It was what she'd really done. It felt so much like a scene in a play.

'And then – then you shot him?'

'No. I stood there, like I said, and I willed myself to pull the trigger. But I couldn't. I just couldn't.'

'So what'd you do?'

'I . . . I called out. 'Frank!' I called. 'Frank, wake up!' I shouted it over and over. He was in a deep sleep, but then he moved his head a little. Then he opened his eyes. I watched his eyes. They stared back at me, blank, like a dead man's eyes. I called again, gently, because I sort of felt sorry for him now, now that I knew I was really going to do it. His eyes opened wider. He saw the way I was standing, the gun. He started to lean forward. "Miranda! No!" he said. And then I pulled the trigger. Twice.'

She stopped and looked at Harold. So now he knew everything. He returned her gaze. His eyes were shining.

'You know, I admire you for what you did, Mrs Solheim! Yeah, I really do. That took guts, what you did right there!'

Miranda stood up and went to the window. The moon was riding high now, and the desert was blue and silver, a landscape of dreams. Somewhere a coyote howled, a long, long way off. It was empty out there. Clean. She wanted Harold to enjoy that big world out there. It wasn't there for her any more. She'd forfeited all that. But Harold might have that freedom, if she could help him. She must help him. She turned away from the window.

'Well that's all my secrets out in the open, Harold. What about yours?'

'Secrets?'

'Sure. I won't tell. What did you do that Mr Ozark knows about?'

'Mr Ozark told me that I was never to tell anyone about that in any circumstances whatsoever.'

'Or else?'

'Mrs Solheim . . . I . . . my whole family . . . owe an awful lot to Mr Ozark. My mother and sisters have only got a roof over their heads on account of Mr Ozark takes care of all the bills.'

'And why does he take such a kind interest in you and your family?'

'I told you, Mrs Solheim. Mr Ozark's our preacher. It's his duty on this earth to look after the poor and the unfortunate. Excuse me now, I gotta go and get some mice for my snakes.'

He was out of the room before she could speak again. Agitated. But Miranda was surprised by how quickly he came back.

'That didn't take long!'

'Well, I just kinda throw them in quick. I don't like to stay and watch. Those mice are pretty scared.'

'The mice are alive?'

'Oh sure. Rattlesnakes have to have their food fresh.'

'Oh my God!'

'I stay and watch once in a while. The mice all kinda huddle together in a corner you know. And the rattlers just kinda watch them for a while.'

'Don't tell me any more. It's disgusting.'

'It's only nature though, Mrs Solheim.'

'Yes . . . it's only nature. And you believe in a god that set this all up do you Harold?'

' 'Course I do. Don't you believe in God, Mrs Solheim?'

She thought of that Blake painting, *The Ancient of Days*, the bearded patriarch leaning down from his clouds. But the face was not a benevolent one. 'Oh, maybe. Maybe he's up there watching us. His own private snake pit. The biggest bullying sadist of them all!'

Harold was shocked. 'Mrs Solheim! That's the worst talk I've ever heard! That there's blasphemy! Blasphemy is something Mr Ozark comes down real heavy on. You're sure lucky he ain't here tonight!'

Miranda seized the opening. 'What does Mr Ozark do when he "comes down real heavy"?'

'He's got some temper! But it's all in the cause of the Lord's work.'

'Has Mr Ozark ever beaten you, Harold?'

Harold looked away, out of the window at the moonlit desert. He spoke mechanically. ' "The rod and reproof give wisdom" Proverbs twenty-nine, verse fifteen.'

Miranda moved up behind Harold. 'Is that what he does when he beats you, Harold? Does he quote the Bible while he beats you?'

Harold kept looking out of the window. 'I didn't say nothing about him beating me. You're twisting things around . . .'

Miranda leaned in close. 'Do you like Mr Ozark?'

'I don't have to like him.'

'What does he look like? I bet he's fat, is he?'

'Sure, he's a little fat.'

'Big man? Tall? Strong?'

'Sure, he's pretty much on a big scale.'

'Drive a big expensive car?'

'He's got a Cadillac.'

'What does he pay you, Harold?'

'I told you I can't say that.'

'So he visits your mother and your sisters, does he?'

'Sure – he looks after us.'

'Your mother live in a big house?'

'No, it's real small. I have to sleep in the living room when I go home.'

'But Mr Ozark – I bet he's got a big house, hm?'

'Sure – but he's a big man, Mr Ozark, an important man.'

'Everyone looks up to him, hm?'

'Yeah.'

'So, how often does he beat you, Harold?'

'That's . . . that's none of your business.'

'I told you everything.'

'That's . . . that's different. You wanted to talk.'

Miranda couldn't see his face. But his voice sounded close to tears. She was getting somewhere. She put her hand on his shoulder. He was no taller than her. She felt the muscle in his shoulder tighten up at the contact. She moved her fingers against the muscle, relaxing him. 'Listen – I'm trying to help you, Harold. How can I help you if you won't tell me? Hm?'

'Mr Ozark would kill me if he found out I'd been talking . . .'

'He'd kill you, would he? I don't think so, Harold. You're more useful to him alive. But he might just beat you within an inch of your life, mightn't he, Harold?'

Harold turned. Now there really were tears coming. He was angry, but she could see that he was relieved too, just as she had been relieved to tell her secrets. 'He does that pretty much every time he comes out here. There! I've told you now. Are you satisfied?'

'And what about your mother? Your sisters? Did you see some bruises last time you went home, Harold?'

Now Harold tore himself away, walked into the middle of the room. He banged his fist on the table. 'Stop it! He pays the rent! Who else is going to pay the rent?'

She had to make him see. 'You're paying it! You and your family! You're paying it with your pain, your separation, your loneliness, your victimisation, your degradation! That's the price of Mr Ozark's filthy dollar bills!'

Harold slumped into a chair by the table. Then he was sobbing, his head in his hands. 'Stop! Please stop!'

Miranda desisted, letting his tears finish flowing in their own time. She remembered all the times she'd cried, in the long years of her marriage to Frank. These bastards! At least there was one less in the world now, although she knew there were thousands and thousands of Mr Ozarks and Frank T. Solheims still out there. They were to be found everywhere, in positions of power, humiliating their subordinates, abusing their families, riding roughshod over the weak and the humble. But at least this mouse had struck back, sinking its tiny lethal teeth into the rattlesnake's head. As Harold's tears started to turn to sniffs, Miranda felt another wave of tiredness. This time it was as if a cloak of lead had landed on top of her, and she felt weight in all her limbs. She had to sleep. This business with Harold and Mr Ozark was unresolved, but she couldn't pursue it any further now.

'Harold . . . Harold?'

He looked up, finding a handkerchief in his pocket, and blew his nose.

'Does your bedroom door have a lock on it, Harold?'

'Yes.'

'Any snakes in there?'

'No.'

'Then that's where I'll sleep. I need to sleep now.'

Harold showed her his bedroom door, and shuffled off with a blanket to the sitting room to sleep on the sofa. He, too, seemed suddenly exhausted.

Miranda locked the door and surveyed the room quickly. It was austere, and spotlessly neat and clean. The only furniture was the bed itself, a little table beside it and a chest of drawers with brush, comb and mirror symmetrically laid out on top of it. On the little table was a bible. There were no pictures on the walls, but there was a big plain crucifix on the wall opposite the bed. There were curtains of a plain green material, which she drew across the window, shutting out that moonlit emptiness that pressed so close to the house. The bed itself was made, and the sheets seemed clean enough. Miranda took off her skirt and top and climbed in under the blanket. Then she reached over to switch off the bedside lamp on the little table, and welcomed the darkness.

In her dream, Miranda was small, and white, and furry, and running as fast as she could go along a dark tunnel which echoed to the sound of her flight. She was conscious of being a mouse, but she was wearing a bridal veil and stiletto shoes. At the end of the tunnel was a corner, and from around the corner she could hear the blows of a leather belt on flesh. She rounded the corner, and there was Harold, also in the guise of a mouse. Frank was standing over him, with a bullet hole in his forehead. He was whipping Harold with what she at first took to be a belt, but then he saw her and paused, and she saw that the belt hanging limply from his fist was a rattlesnake. The rattlesnake slithered out of Frank's grasp, and at the same time it grew huge. It reared over Harold and herself as they huddled together in a corner. Frank disappeared, but now the rattlesnake had

Frank's face. It was leering down triumphantly at its victims, its tail rattling behind it as it prepared to strike. Then she found her gun in her hand, and fired twice, bringing the huge snake toppling down on top of them, lashing and rearing in its death throes.

She woke with a start. The lashing sound in her dream was coming from another room in the house. Had Mr Ozark come in the night, and was he belabouring Harold for allowing a stranger to stay at the station? Fearfully, she unlocked the bedroom door and opened it a crack. Yes, she could hear blows, and Harold whimpering. She went back for her handbag and found her gun. There were still four bullets in the chamber, she knew that.

She crept along the hall. The whipping was going on in the snake room. She hesitated a long time at the door. There were long intervals between the blows, and she could only hear Harold's voice. He moaned when he was struck, but then in the intervals he sounded as if he were chanting something repetitive, like a prayer. She listened for long enough to be absolutely certain that there was only Harold in there. She thought about returning silently to her room, but she knew she wouldn't sleep. So, with a sense that she was trespassing on something very private, she pushed open the door.

The snake room was lit only by a candle on the floor. It threw flickering monstrous shadows of the snakes in the tanks against the white walls. It was like a vision of hell. In the middle of the floor, Harold was kneeling. He was naked, and along his back were the weals of the blows he had been inflicting on himself with a heavy leather strap.

For all the hideous quasi-religious ritual of the scene, Miranda recognised what lay at its heart, what drove Harold to do this, because she had felt it herself. It was self-hatred and despair. She knew why Harold felt that he deserved to be beaten, why he hated the flesh he was made of, because it was the flesh that a vampire feasted upon. She knew then what had to be done, what she had nothing to lose by doing. What she could achieve for Harold. She knelt down beside him, and took the strap gently from his hand.

'Do you know what I'm going to do tomorrow, Harold? Tomorrow, I'm going to shoot your Mr Ozark dead!'

Harold closed his eyes, and clung to her like a baby in its mother's arms.

The sun was already high in the sky behind him at ten o'clock as Mr Ozark made his way along the familiar stretch of highway between Wickenburg and the gas station. To his eyes the almost featureless road had its landmarks. There was the slight rise about eight miles out from Wickenburg, where occasionally Officer Sherman would park with his radar speed gun to catch truckers in a hurry to get through the desert. He would catch them just as they crested the slope, his patrol car only then visible a hundred yards away in a dip. Officer Sherman wasn't there this morning of course, this being a Sunday. But Mr Ozark stuck to the limit anyway, not being in any particular hurry.

Then at twenty miles out from Wickenburg, there was the 'Giant with a baseball bat' cactus as he liked to call it. No-one else could see the similarity, and he had to admit he couldn't see it too well himself, but one night driving east the big cactus had caught the light in such a way that he thought it looked like a big man standing at the plate, waiting for the pitcher's delivery. He thought of it as the half-way point of the drive out to the station.

The third landmark was about four miles short of the station, where he'd erected a sign saying 'Mr Happy's Gas Station in four miles. Last gas before Interstate Forty'. The sign had blown over in the strong winds of last month, and he kept meaning to fix it. There was no big rush though. Most people had filled up in Wickenburg, and the light business that the station did was mostly coming along the highway from the other direction.

Mr Ozark was sweating a little. It was going to be another hot one, and the air-conditioning wasn't working too good. That was another thing he needed to get fixed. How was it that nothing worked for long without needing to be fixed? He hoped Harold had some beers left at the station.

Finally, after the usual one hour from his house on the other side of town, Mr Ozark swung the car into the forecourt. He saw the brown Dodge parked in front of the pumps, and wrinkled his brow. Who could that be? It was a Tucson plate. Maybe somebody broke down.

He pulled in his own car, an old Cadillac, between the house and the pumps and gave his customary toot on the horn to let Harold know he was here. He took out a handkerchief and mopped his brow, then stepped out into the mounting heat outside.

Inside the house it would be cool. He went up the steps, pushed the screen door open and stood in the hallway.

'Harold? Where are you, boy?' he called. Surely he wasn't still in bed? After a moment, Harold's voice came back. He was in that snake room of his.

'Hi! I'm just feeding the snakes.'

Mr Ozark went in. He didn't like the room too much. Jesus! There seemed to be more of these critters every time he came in. Harold had just put a mouse into one of the tanks. It was rigid with terror, huddled into a corner, its sides pulsing rapidly. One of the rattlers was lazily un-coiling, lidless eyes watching the prey, forked tongue slithering in and out as if it were licking its lips. The mouse's eyes were wide and dark. Mr Ozark repressed his distaste. After all, if it kept Harold happy . . . the boy needed a hobby.

'Sure don't like it in there, does he?' he said. He looked at

Harold for agreement. Harold nodded, then went over to another tank with a second mouse.

'You look tired, Harold. You get a good night's sleep?'

'Sure.'

There was something a little strained about Harold. 'You in one of your moods, Harold? Did you take your medication this morning?'

'Sure I did.'

'Whose is the Dodge parked out front?'

'Oh, that belongs to some guy from LA. It was running rough, so he left it out here. He's coming out from Wickenburg with a mechanic tomorrow.'

'How'd he get to Wickenburg without his car?'

'Oh, he just hitched a ride with the next car that came in for gas.'

'Wasn't there nothing you could do for him?'

'Well, no. It wasn't any of those simple things you taught me to look for. It needed a mechanic.'

'OK. So . . . you gonna smarten up a bit now, and then we'll ride back into town and pick up mom, huh? How do you feel about the seafood platter at Big Joe's Diner?'

'Sounds good to me!'

Mr Ozark clapped a friendly hand on Harold's shoulder. 'OK. Get going, boy!'

They moved out of the snake room and Harold turned into his bedroom. He paused in the doorway.

'Oh, by the way, I was forgetting. There's . . . uh . . . there's some problem with the ice box. Could you take a quick look in there?'

'Sure. What's the problem? Not cold enough?'

'Yeah. Seems like it.'

'You check the thermostat?'

'Well, I thought I did.'

Mr Ozark sighed inwardly. There was no getting around

it, Harold was just not the most practical of people. It was probably just the thermostat was set too low.

'I'll look at it. You get smartened up. Wear that white cotton shirt your mom gave you. Is it out here at the station?'

'Sure. I'll be right with you.'

Harold turned into the bedroom. Mr Ozark went on into the kitchen whistling to himself. He'd been whistling 'Tie a Yellow Ribbon Round the Old Oak Tree' for more years than he cared to count up. Sometimes he knew that's what he was whistling, and it got on his nerves. But usually, like now, it was just like breathing, just an unconscious noise he made when he was relaxed.

He opened the ice box door, and knelt down to get a better look in there. It felt cold enough to him. There was ice in the ice compartment. More important, there was a bottle of beer on the top shelf. He was just reaching in to get hold of it when a movement behind him made him turn.

His heart jumped like it was taking a surge of voltage at what he saw. There was some woman with wild uncombed hair and staring mad eyes standing at the kitchen door. And she was pointing a gun straight at his head. Jesus Christ!

'Don't move, Mr Ozark! Just stay right where you are, kneeling down! That's where a bastard like you belongs, on your knees.'

Now she had him. He looked just like she'd thought he would, a big powerful man, just like Frank was. His face was a mask of fear and bewilderment, but he knew the score, he knew the game was up.

'Who in Christ's name are you? What do you want?'

'Shut up! I just want you to know something important Mr Ozark. You're going to die because you don't deserve to live.'

For Christ's sake. She wasn't trying to rob the station as he had at first assumed. She was some sort of crazy. He yelled at the top of his voice. 'Harold! Help me!'

'Harold won't be your slave any more, Mr Ozark. Neither will his poor mother and sisters.'

'Sisters? Harold ain't got no sisters!'

Miranda was momentarily thrown. But then he was a devious, lying bastard, like Frank. He would try to throw her like that. 'Shut up! Don't think you can lie your way out of this!'

'Harold ain't got no sisters I tell you! Jesus!' Why should she think Harold had sisters? And what had that got to do with anything?

'Shut up! Don't try to talk, just listen. Men like you don't deserve to live on the same earth as innocent women and children.'

Where the hell was Harold anyway? Mr Ozark shouted desperately. 'Harold! Help!'

Miranda would have liked to have laughed. But all the muscles in her face were clamped rigid with tension. Did this sadistic victimiser expect help from his victim? She moved the barrel of the gun to point at his chest. It was a bigger target than his head. She wasn't going to miss.

He stopped calling for Harold. Tried desperately for calmness. For a cool, reasoning voice. But his voice was an unnatural croak: 'Listen to me . . .'

'No. You listen to me, you scum! You don't deserve to live, Mr Ozark!'

Mr Ozark started to stand up slowly. For Christ's sake! He had to take a chance if he was going to survive this. Miranda was shouting at him now.

'Stay down! Stay down, or I'll fire right now!' She looked like a tigress or a lynx snarling at its prey. He had to take a chance. He tried to talk again. He had to distract her, just for a moment.

'Listen! Who are you?'

As soon as she started to say something in reply he made his move. He lunged at her, grabbing desperately at the gun.

It went off as he charged her down, and he felt agonising pain in his left leg. He screamed. Then he was on top of her on the floor. The gun went off again and a bullet smashed into the cupboards. Then he managed to get his hand on it and force her fingers away from the handle. He was shouting, he didn't know what, a mixture of obscenities and inarticulate yells of pain. She sank her teeth into his shoulder like a wild animal, but now he had the gun. He slung it across the floor to the other side of the kitchen, and twisted her arm round behind her back. For a moment he didn't give a shit if he broke it. Christ! He ought to break her neck!

Miranda struggled with a fierce desperate strength, but the arm lock was excruciating. The bastard had beaten her. She screamed. 'Harold! Help me!' but he didn't appear. Was he going to abandon her now, after what she had tried to do for him?

Mr Ozark was puzzled. He squatted on her back, his left leg streaming blood on to her, his arms holding her own pinned behind her. 'You really know Harold? Or are you just bullshitting me? Who are you?'

'Let me go, you bastard!'

Mr Ozark felt vicious. His leg hurt like fuck. He could have been killed. He wrenched at her arm. 'Who . . . are . . . you?'

Miranda screamed in pain. 'Stop it!'

He eased off his grip slightly. 'Well?'

'My name is Miranda Solheim.'

He released her with a shove, and quickly slid himself across the kitchen floor to grab the gun again. His leg left a smear of blood along the floor. He pointed the gun at her. 'Stay real still now! I could shoot you cold and say it was self-defence. Jesus! I *should* shoot you!'

He raised his voice, and shouted for Harold again. But there was only silence in the rest of the house. Miranda was looking at him as if he were poisonous. 'Harold has told me all about you, Mr Ozark.'

Mr Ozark raised his eyebrows in an expression of disbelief, then his face distorted into a grimace of pain.

'I know all about your set-up, Mr Ozark. I know how you treat Harold and his family. Men like you don't deserve to live!'

Mr Ozark weighed this up. 'You been talking to Harold, huh?'

'Yes.'

'And what Harold told you got you all fired up to shoot me?'

Miranda nodded. Why hadn't she done what she'd set out to do? She didn't want to have to talk to this bastard.

'So – what exactly have I done, according to Harold?'

At least she'd wounded him. Maybe if she kept him talking he'd bleed to death. 'You've terrorised him into being a virtual prisoner out here, working for almost nothing because you blackmail him over something he did in the past. You beat him. You've abused your influence as a preacher, and you physically abuse his mother and sisters. You're like every other bullying bastard who's in love with power! The world would be better without you!'

'Lady . . .'

'You're poison. I know your kind.'

Mr Ozark interrupted angrily. 'Lady . . . just a minute. I don't know where you came from or why you're here, but did it ever occur to you that Harold might not be telling you the truth?'

'I believe Harold because he didn't want to tell me anything. I had to worm the whole story out of him, bit by bit. Don't think you can lie your way out of this.'

Mr Ozark waved the gun. 'Seems to me I don't need to lie my way out of nothing. Seems to me you're the one that's in the shit here. But let me tell you a thing or two anyway. Here's a few facts for you. First of all, Harold ain't a prisoner out here. He stays here alternate weeks. The other weeks it's another young guy called Ed. I got another gas station in town, and they take it in turns to look after that one too, see? I don't ask them to stay out here more than four nights at a time, maximum. Second of all, like I said, Harold ain't got no sisters. He's an only child. Third of all, I ain't a preacher. I run two gas stations, and I part own a motel, and that's it.'

Doubt hit Miranda like nausea, swiftly and overwhelmingly. Why would Ozark bother to lie when he had her at the end of a gun barrel? But he must be lying. She hadn't misjudged Harold's terror, his self-loathing. She looked into Mr Ozark's eyes for the first time, trying to read something there, something that would give her some clue. 'Why should I believe you and not Harold?'

Mr Ozark met her gaze. 'Let me tell you a little about Harold. I should know, 'cause I'm his stepfather – did he tell you that?'

Miranda felt another lurch in her guts. To quell it she folded her arms together, cradling herself, rubbing the red bruised flesh with her hands where Mr Ozark had hurt her. 'No, he didn't say that.'

'Well, I married Harold's mother – Barbara – five years ago, when Harold was sixteen. The year before, something bad had happened in their family. You see . . . what was your name?'

'Solheim.'

'You see Mrs Solheim, Harold is what they call a schizophrenic. He does not always act as one person from one day to the next. Sometimes he has delusions. And he's very suggestible – you know what I mean? He picks up on things, especially religious things. Or he might take something someone says and build a whole crazy fantasy around it. He tends to believe what other people want him to believe, you know?'

Miranda nodded. Certainty was draining away from her. The events of last night, her talks with Harold, were slipping into insubstantial vagueness. Mr Ozark's story made sense, but, surely, so had Harold's – or at least the story she'd pieced together from Harold's reluctant partial revelations. While she tried to reconcile the two versions of what might be going on here, Mr Ozark was going on inexorably, plausibly.

'I think something you said, Mrs Solheim, must have triggered him off into telling you all that stuff about me.'

'What, according to you, was the bad thing that happened? Was it something he did?'

'Well, I wasn't all that close to the family in those days, but the way Barbara tells it, when Harold was fifteen he got a sorta craze for religion, you know. He used to watch these television evangelists all the time. Took to learning big chunks out of the Bible and quoting them at you all the time. You might have noticed Harold's got some amazing memory?'

'Yes.'

'Anyways, to cut a long story short, when Harold was fifteen he got the idea into his head that his father was the Devil.'

'The Devil?'

'You got it. Barbara said he was always reading Revelations and trying to work out signs he saw in the sky and stuff. It was before they'd really realised that he was ill, and he wasn't on no medication or nothing. Anyway, one night at midnight Harold just up and went into his parents' bedroom and cut his father's throat with a carving knife. Afterwards he thought he'd killed the Devil. Thought he was gonna be made a saint!'

Nausea. Horrible dizzying sickness hit Miranda now, and the room flipped. She felt as if she were hanging onto the ceiling with straining fingernails in a world turned upside down. Was this the truth about Harold, poor Harold? She managed to speak.

'But then . . . how come Harold . . .'

'How come Harold is not locked up? Is that what you're wondering? Well, he was only a juvenile, and the medical evidence said he was not in his right mind anyway when he did it. He was kept for a year or so in a sort of secure hospital, where they worked out what drugs to give him. He started to get much better. That was the time when I got to know Barbara. By the time we decided to get married we were able to get Harold released on condition of us both being responsible for him at all times.'

'Do you think leaving him out here in the desert on his own was a good idea?'

Mr Ozark looked away. 'Well – he's been so well for the last coupla years . . . pretty much a normal boy you know. But maybe . . . maybe I shouldn't have . . . we can't check that he takes his medication out here.'

'Why is he terrified of you? The only reason I'm here is that he wouldn't fill my car with gas. He said you wouldn't allow it, if the station was shut.'

Mr Ozark shrugged, still looking away. 'Oh – I don't know why he seemed scared of me. I've always treated him kind. But the thing about the gas – well, I sorta understand that.'

He looked up again. 'You see, the thing is, you gotta give him firm rules to abide by, otherwise he can get confused. He doesn't like any of those little grey areas, 'cause he can't think too straight when it comes to making decisions. So I said to him, I admit this, I said to him: "Harold, on no account are you to serve gas outside the normal opening hours." That way, no-one can take advantage of him, see? There's a coupla truckers I know, use this road regular at all hours of the night. They'd be waking him up at three in the morning for gas just for the hell of it, if they didn't know what I'd told him. There's people like that, who'll take advantage.'

Mr Ozark paused. For a moment they both listened to the silence. Then Mr Ozark moved his leg a little and let out an involuntary gasp of pain. Miranda spoke:

'Where do you think Harold is now?'

'Well, he'll be about here someplace. Maybe the gun going off frightened him and he's hiding. Or maybe he just took off into the desert a little ways.'

Miranda was staring into a horrible pit. She'd been right on the edge of it, close to falling in. She'd nearly killed an innocent man. How could she have misread Harold so completely? It must have been her state of mind last night, sharing with him all her story, finding him beating himself in the snake room. She'd been so wrong. She had to be strong now, try to set things right as much as she could.

'Mr Ozark . . . please . . . if you can, please forgive me. I think . . . Mr Ozark . . . all I can say is I've gone a long time without any sleep, and I'm . . . I'm in the middle of some troubles of my own. I think I was a little out of my mind myself when I tried to shoot you.'

She looked at the blood still oozing steadily from his leg. She should get him to a hospital.

'Can I put something around that wound?'

Mr Ozark nodded. He was aware again of the dreadful pain that he'd managed to ignore while he convinced this woman of what was going on. He knew he couldn't drive back into town on his own. He needed her help, if Harold was no use. What was Harold doing anyhow? Had Harold actually wanted this woman to kill him?

Miranda found a clean kitchen towel in a drawer, and wrapped it tightly around the wound to staunch the bleeding. The bullet was still in his leg.

'Go phone for an ambulance from Wickenburg.'

'But Harold said the phone was broken . . .'

'The phone ain't broken. I spoke to him on the phone yesterday morning.'

'I don't know where it is.'

'It's in the kiosk out front. The key to the kiosk'll be in the back of that drawer where you found the towel.'

Miranda found a bunch of keys. Now that she had discovered that Harold had lied to her, she was afraid of him. When he'd heard the shots, what had he done? Where had he gone?

Mr Ozark saw her hesitation. He couldn't walk. Could he trust her now? He made a decision. 'Here, take the gun. Don't worry about Harold. He'll be all confused – he's probably run off a little ways into the desert. He's more danger to himself than to us.'

Miranda took the gun. Would she be able to fire it if she encountered Harold? Would he threaten her? Would he know that Mr Ozark had revealed his lies for what they were? She moved cautiously out of the kitchen, glancing back at Mr Ozark. He nodded her on. She called out in the hallway: 'Harold? Are you around the house?'

There was only silence in reply. Slowly, her hand like a vice on the handle of the gun, she went to the front door and opened it, then pushed the screen door, and stood on the porch. The highway was deserted, as usual. Nor was there any sign of anything moving around the station. The cacti stood about at a little distance, the ghosts of the pioneers, watching in silence. She let go of the screen door and the springs swung it shut. Then she stepped out from the shelter of the porch into the blasting sunlight, her eyes squinting. She ran, her shadow moving in front of her, deep black and small, scurrying across the dust in fear. At the kiosk she had to hold the gun in her left hand, her right hand tremblingly trying the keys on the bunch until she got the right one and opened the sliding door into the kiosk.

Inside the kiosk it was stifling. The sun beat on the glass

sides as she scanned the walls, the little desk, everywhere for the telephone. Finally she saw a phone socket. But there was no phone. Harold! He must have removed it, either last night or this morning, to prevent any calls out.

Then Miranda saw a switch. It had a handwritten label stuck on the wall below it. The label said 'Pumps'. She looked again at the bunch of keys in her hand. For sure the keys for the padlocks on the pumps would be on this bunch. She had it in her power just to turn on the pumps, undo the padlock, fill her car, and drive out of this nightmare. She looked along the empty highway to the west. She could be a hundred miles from here in two hours. Her hand went towards the switch. The temptation to get away, just to resume that drift into featureless space, was overwhelming. She could imagine herself on the empty road, listening to country and western music, not thinking about the future. Her finger touched the switch. But she couldn't do it. Mr Ozark had trusted her. He was bleeding badly. An innocent man, and she'd shot him. If she couldn't ring for an ambulance, she'd have to help him into his car and drive him back to Wickenburg. With a huge effort of will, she left the kiosk, and headed back towards the house.

She almost put her foot on the rattlesnake. It was coiled like a fat mound of rope on the first step up to the porch, and it reared and hissed just as she was raising her leg to the step. She threw herself backwards with a scream, straight into Harold's arms. With the advantage of surprise, he wrested the gun from her grasp quite easily, and twisted her arm behind her back just like Mr Ozark had done earlier.

'Harold!' she managed to gasp out. 'Harold! Let me go! What are you doing?'

Harold hissed in her ear, like a serpent. 'You messed up, Mrs Solheim! You were supposed to kill Mr Ozark, but you messed up!'

Miranda struggled fiercely, but he had a wiry strength

that was too much for her. 'You bastard, Harold! You lied to me!'

He said nothing, and forced her up the steps, frighteningly close to the rattlesnake, which rattled its tail as they passed. When the screen door banged behind them, Mr Ozark shouted out from the kitchen. 'Mrs Solheim, is that you?'

Miranda was going to call out, but Harold put his hand over her mouth and shouted out instead. 'It's all right! I got her! I'm going to put her where she can't do any more damage!' Then he frog-marched her along the hallway and thrust her into the snake room, locking the door behind her.

Miranda sprawled on the floor where he had pushed her. The little skylight only admitted a shaft of light, which illuminated her at the centre of the room. All around her, the tanks of snakes reacted to the sudden noise. They rattled their tails, arched up to explore the lids of the tanks, and thrust their faces against the glass as if they would have swallowed her alive. Knowing it was useless and irrational, but without being able to stop herself, Miranda began to scream.

Harold went into the kitchen. Mr Ozark was lying in what was becoming a small pool of blood from his leg. It had soaked through the towel and dripped onto the floor. Harold shut the door behind him, deadening the sounds of Miranda's screams.

Mr Ozark was furious. 'You told that woman some damned lies about me, Harold!'

Harold squatted down beside Mr Ozark. He spoke urgently. 'Listen! I don't know what she said to you, but listen! Do you know who that woman is?'

'She said her name was Solheim.'

'OK. That ring any bells in your head?'

'Solheim? No – why should it?'

'You bring the Sunday papers out in the car?'

'Yeah.'

'Wait just one minute then . . .'

Harold went quickly out of the kitchen, ignoring Mr Ozark's protests. Jesus! What did the boy think he wanted the paper for, for Christ's sake? 'Harold! I need a doctor. I'm bleeding here! Harold!'

Harold came back in with the paper.

'Harold! My leg!'

'Your leg will be fine. Now . . . just let me find the crime summary. Here we are.'

'This is a fuck of a time to read the crime summary.'

'Now – you'll see. Just give me a minute . . . woman raped in park . . . small child abducted . . . man burns neighbour . . . axe murder . . . ah, here it is! Read that!'

Harold thrust the paper in front of Mr Ozark's face. Mr Ozark read the paragraph he was pointing at. It said 'After the shooting of Mr Frank T. Solheim in Tucson on Friday night, law officers have begun a nationwide search for his British-born wife Mrs Miranda Solheim. Neighbours say she left the house shortly after the shooting is believed to have occurred.'

'Are you telling me . . . are you saying . . .?'

'That woman in the snake room is Mrs Miranda Solheim! This gun is the gun she shot her husband in the head with!'

Mr Ozark pressed the kitchen towel against his wound. Whether it was from loss of blood or what he didn't know, but his head was spinning. He tried to readjust to this new information.

'I just can't believe this is happening. That woman . . .'

'That woman is a dangerous homicide on the run from the law.'

'She's sure dangerous. She tried to shoot me dead. Where in hell were you when she was trying to shoot me? Why didn't you warn me?'

'I was in the bathroom. Then I heard shooting. I was frightened.'

'In the bathroom! There's a crazy woman with a gun walking around the house and you're having a crap! And another thing – all that shit you gave me about someone breaking down in the Dodge and going back into town for a mechanic! And all the time you knew there was a crazy woman in the house . . .'

Harold put a hand on Mr Ozark's shoulder. 'Listen! Calm down! I'll tell you what it was. I'd sorta felt sorry for Mrs Solheim. She told me her story, you know? All about this Mr Solheim being a real bastard, you know? And how he used to beat up on her, and how it went on for years until she couldn't stand it any more.'

'She seemed to have a pretty strong notion that I beat up on you. Did you spin her some story, Harold? Did you start up on one of your fantasies?'

Harold stood up. He started to pace up and down the kitchen. The sound of screaming from the snake room had stopped. 'No! Of course I didn't. She's crazy right? Anything she says is crazy. Anyway, listen! After talking to her and all, I felt real sorry for her. So I said she could hole up here until we opened on Monday. I was going to tell you about her on the way back into town, then we coulda told the police and they coulda come and taken her in. I was just trying to help a little by letting her have a few hours of freedom. When you came out here I told her just to lie quiet underneath my bed until we'd gone.'

'Underneath your bed? Jesus!'

'Sure. I knew you wouldn't find her there.'

'Couldn't you have gotten her gun away?'

'No way. She didn't know she could trust me, did she?'

'What I don't get is why she was so fired up to kill me! You must have been laying some stuff on her, Harold! Don't bullshit me!'

'No way. Sure, we talked a lot last night, and she was pretty interested in me and all. I guess it was taking her mind off . . . you know, what she'd done. But now I know she was fixing to shoot you, it makes me realise that she might have got a hold of some wrong ideas.'

'Like what?'

Harold stopped pacing. He was facing away from Mr Ozark, looking out of the window at the desert. 'Oh, like . . . she seemed to think you must be taking advantage of me some way. Being my stepfather and all.'

'Did you tell her about . . . ?'

'About Pa? No. But I told her he died, and . . .'

'Hold on a minute there. She seemed surprised when I said I was your stepfather.'

'Oh, yeah . . . that's right . . . I didn't say that . . .'

'Seems to me you don't rightly know what you said to her.'

'No – I didn't say nothing that wasn't the truth. I just don't remember everything exactly. She was asking me a lot of weird questions.'

'Such as?'

'Oh . . . she wanted to know who owned the gas station – was it you, or was it . . .'

'Who?'

'Well . . . I don't know . . . she seemed to think it might be mine maybe. Or maybe that it should be mine. I don't know.'

'Yours? What in hell gave her that idea? Maybe it'll be yours when I'm dead and gone.'

'That right?'

'Sure that's right. Who the hell else do you think I'm gonna leave everything to? My cousin Florence?'

'Well, I didn't know that for sure.'

'Listen, Harold – it don't really matter so much anyway. I'm not an old man.' He looked down at the pool of blood, still spreading slowly on the kitchen floor. Faintness came over him again. 'Listen, Harold . . .'

Harold, turning from the window, cut in: 'And she was asking about the motel and the other gas station and stuff.'

'What about it?'

'Well – she seemed to have an idea that it all belonged to me, on account of it all belonging to my pa before . . .'

'What! And what about me? Did she think I was stealing it from you or something?'

'Sort of, I guess.'

'Well, that's crazy. Your pa's will left it all to your mother, and now she and me own it all jointly. Did Mrs Solheim think – after what you did – that it would all have come to you?'

'She didn't know what I did.'

'Oh, right. Of course. You didn't tell her about that, I did.'

'You told her about . . .'

'Sure – your pa – I had to. She . . . I . . . you know, I had to deal with what she said you'd told her about me. I had to . . .'

'You had to make out I was crazy?'

'Well . . . sure . . . I mean . . . I didn't know about her then! I thought she was some woman who'd got all worked up by some stuff you'd told her . . .'

'Oh, she's the crazy one, not me. You wanna know what she told me?'

'About what?'

'About this little gun here. About how she blew her husband's head off with it. Frank T. Solheim.'

Harold's eyes were fixed on Mr Ozark's. Mr Ozark thought they looked hard and cold, then Harold's face swam out of focus and back in. All this talk could wait for Christ's sake. 'I don't think we need to go into all that right now. Harold – I need to get to a hospital for fuck's sake!'

'She stood like this, with her feet apart . . .'

'Harold! For Christ's sake! What are you doing?'

'. . . and pointing it like this . . .'

Harold was going out of focus again. Only the stone cold eyes were sharp. Mr Ozark was seized with a terror he didn't want to acknowledge. 'Harold! That thing might still be loaded!'

'She did pretty well on Frank T. Solheim, but she made a bad job on you!'

'Harold!'

Harold squeezed the trigger and the last thought in Mr Ozark's head was obliterated in an explosion of pain. Then Harold fired again into the head, because he wanted a pattern to it. She was a dangerous woman, that Miranda Solheim, when she had that gun in her hand.

When Miranda, in the snake room, heard the two shots, she knew what had happened. She didn't know why Harold wanted Mr Ozark dead, but he'd done it now. And she had a feeling that he'd want her dead as well. She'd been thinking about this moment, with a clarity born from the desperate desire to survive. She had a plan – one hope. She had to be brave now. And quick. Controlling her fear and revulsion, she got hold of the corner of one of the big glass tanks and, grunting with the effort, edged it gradually forward towards the edge of the table it sat on. The rattlers seethed inside, disturbed by the movement. She looked away, concentrating on the weight of the tank, the balance of it, until she'd got it just how she wanted it.

Harold looked down at the body sprawled in a bloody pool in the kitchen. He had his story all worked out. He didn't need to lie about much. Mrs Solheim had pulled in after the station had closed. He'd let her stay the night. But when Mr Ozark had come out this morning he'd recognised her from the police reports, and he was going to turn her in. To stop him doing that, she'd shot him, then Harold had come into the kitchen and she'd run off into the snake room in a panic. He'd followed her in there, and in a struggle for the gun it had gone off, killing her. It was the most miraculously perfect opportunity to get rid of Mr Ozark. It must be God's will. Who could suspect him, when the shots were fired from the gun of a murderer on the run?

Harold walked to the door of the snake room. He called out through the door: 'You get away from the door now, Mrs Solheim! I'm coming in and I want you backed up against the far wall!' Then he turned the key.

Harold went in and shut the door behind him. The snakes were restless after Miranda's efforts, and they rattled and hissed at his entrance. He didn't notice that she'd moved one of the tanks. His eyes were fixed on her. He held the gun pointed towards her, at about waist height.

Miranda spoke, her voice straining to find a normal pitch. 'What happened? I heard shots?'

'That's right, Mrs Solheim. Two shots. Mr Ozark just got his head shot off. Like you were going to do, but you messed up.'

'Oh my God! He . . . he was a good man! He didn't do all those awful things you told me. Why did he have to die? You're a murderer!'

'Oh come on now, Mrs Solheim! You started it all. This little gun was already hot when you turned up here!'

'I trusted you. I thought you were like me, a victim. But you're not. You're a lying, devious snake!'

'Let he who is without sin cast the first stone!'

'Don't quote the Bible at me! You're evil! Your stepfather told me what you've done. He called it mental illness. I call it evil, pure and simple. I've met evil before! I know what it looks like!'

Harold seemed angered. 'And so do I, and I'm looking right at it! You know, Mrs Solheim, you're too evil to live on this earth. Like Mr Ozark. And your husband. In fact there are very few of the righteous who can face the day of the opening of the seventh seal. "These are they which came out of great tribulation, and have washed their robes, and made them white in the blood of the Lamb."'

Jesus Christ! What was he talking about? His eyes were shining with a kind of intoxication. He was working up to pulling that trigger, fuelling himself with these words. Miranda tried to take a deep breath. She knew she had a chance to save herself, but she'd have to get it right, she'd have to be perfect.

Harold raised the gun and pointed it straight at her head. 'Close your eyes now, Mrs Solheim!' He closed his own eyes as he squeezed the trigger. As the hammer clicked on an empty chamber, just as Miranda had known it would, she was already at the tank of snakes, wrenching it from the table. Harold was caught on the knee by the falling tank, and staggered. Miranda pushed past him to the door. He whirled around and grabbed at her. But he'd only got hold of her jacket, and as she hurled the door open she turned and delivered a fierce slap across his face with her free hand. His grip loosened, and at the same instant one of the rattlesnakes struck his leg. His face contorted in fear and pain, and he turned away from her to pull it away. Another of the snakes, the big diamondback he called "Mr Ozark" arched up almost waist high and struck at his groin. Miranda slammed the door shut behind her. The key was still in the lock, and she turned it just as Harold threw himself against the other side. He was screaming.

'Mrs Solheim! Help me!' Then he beat against the door with his fists, and the snakes that were hanging off his body smacked against it like pieces of rope. Miranda slumped against the opposite wall of the hallway, fighting down nausea. She put her hands over her ears, but she could still hear Harold hammering on the door and screaming. She started to sing to herself, to drown it out. 'Stand by your Man' she sang, and through the singing she was aware that the screaming turned into a sort of moaning noise that gradually trailed off to nothing. When she finally took her hands away from her ears it was silent on the other side of the door except for the faint dry stirring of slithering snakes.

Miranda made her way along the little hallway into the kitchen. She used her hand against the walls to steady herself. When she saw Mr Ozark's body with his face blown away, she had to rush out of that house immediately, out into the clean hot air of the desert, where at last she threw up violently. When the racking heaves of her stomach subsided, she looked about her. The ghosts of the immigrants stood impassively, offering no comment or judgement. The highway was empty as ever. The house cast no shadows in the high midday sun. It looked empty and innocuous, an unremarkable wooden house beside a road.

The kiosk was still unlocked, and the bunch of keys was where she'd left it, on the desk inside. She turned on the switch for the gas pumps, and unlocked one of the padlocks. She filled up her Dodge, then locked everything up again. She took the bunch of keys back to the house, but she couldn't go in, so she just opened the screen door a little and threw the keys into the hallway. Then she ran back to her car, climbed in, and pulled out on to the highway towards California. She didn't know what lay ahead of her, and she didn't want to think about what lay behind. After a couple of miles she turned on the radio, and listened to some country and western.

RUNNING AWAY

I'm sure I'm not the only man in the world whose wife has run away. But generally the lady actually absents herself by car, or train, or simply by omitting to return from the supermarket. Now my wife really did run away, moving off at a steady pace, while I poured myself coffee from a thermos jug. I watched her through the windscreen of our parked car, speckled with insect deaths, and from his car seat our three-year-old son watched too, his mouth stuffed with currant cake. We didn't grasp the situation at all, Thomas and I, as her figure dwindled into the distance.

We were on our way to Rosemary's parents. A longish

trek which we often punctuated with a picnic stop some-where on the uplands of Wiltshire. This was about our half-way mark. It can't have been Thomas that upset her. He had been no trouble. True, he had thrown up outside Stevenage. But then he had given us fair warning, and the bulk of the affair was conducted with decorum on the hard shoulder. Nor had Rosemary herself seemed troubled at all – no hint that such an extraordinary thing was going to happen.

It was a Thursday. In August. Warmish, a few fluffy clouds blowing across a mainly blue sky. The car was packed with the usual paraphernalia – all Thomas's junk and of course my golf clubs and fishing tackle. I didn't like to be kicking my heels too much around Rosemary's parents' place. Lovely place of course – big house, lawns, shrubberies and so on. But every time I urged our Skoda past the heraldic whatnots on the gateposts I began to feel intimations of inferiority. Drawn by the sound of tyres on gravel, the old biddy generally stations herself at the head of the steps to the front door. Daughter and grandson receive their welcoming simpers. I drag behind, snail-like, with the suitcases, and her look suggests that although the trail of slime I have left on the steps is invisible to others, she can see it well enough. And I've never felt very at ease with the colonel either – not since the day I made the mistake of talking politics. Hence the golf and fishing gear.

I suppose that in many respects I was very lucky to marry a girl like Rosemary. She was – is – a few years younger than me. Tall, lively, attractive. I'm pretty quiet myself and somewhere around the middle of the spectrum when it comes to looks and height. But inches aren't everything, and sometimes I remind Rosemary (and she agrees) that she's better off with me than hitched up to some horsey county type and bored to death in a swamp of gin and tonic.

As a schoolmaster's wife in a small town she's got a valuable social function. Or she had.

People have been very kind. But I made a mistake telling the truth. No-one believes a word of it, although they all pretend to. They think she's gone off with another man, or back to mother. The usual things. They won't accept that she just vanished. I don't suppose I would unless . . . well, I'm getting sidetracked. I was describing to you the events of that Thursday in August. The day it happened.

Bit of a tiff as we set off. This was normal. I had insisted that Thomas eat up every last bit of his muesli before we left. Rosemary was of the opinion that if he didn't feel like it, he should leave it. Events near Stevenage proved her right, on this occasion. But in general she overindulged him.

Once in the car, we listened to Radio Three most of the morning. Rosemary prefers pop music, but she can listen to that all day in the kitchen, so when we're in the car my taste prevails, by common assent. Thomas likes any sort of noise, so he's happy. I remember it was some rather 'difficult' twentieth-century stuff – Schoenberg I think – and Rosemary commented on how music in a car always made her feel like she was in a film. The Schoenberg apparently made her feel she was in a film about nuclear holocaust, looking out at the last moments of a dying world.

The spot where we left the main road for our picnic was an old favourite. A small lane rose between sparse hedges up and over a hill, away from the sound of the traffic. Then you were into another world. The round backs of the downs rolling away as if without end. Fields, mostly grass, but some with yellow wheat or barley, dotted with poppies. We turned off the lane on to the beginning of a widish straight path, a chalky line rising gently upwards across the down and disappearing against the sky. I switched off the engine and we wound down the windows. We didn't speak – even Thomas didn't speak. We just listened for a moment: the wind rustling in the barley stalks and hissing in the grass, insects humming, a skylark, the sounds of cooling metal and settling liquid from the car engine. The peace of it. The calm of it. I shut my eyes for a few moments.

Rosemary packs a good picnic lunch. We had some excellent sandwiches: avocado and cream cheese with a hint of Marmite in granary bread. We didn't talk much. I rack my brains to think of anything in particular we might have said. Thomas was feeling better. I told him the names of some of the things we could see – a barn in the flatter fields away below the downs, some cows grazing there, the difference between cumulus clouds and alto-cirrus. Rosemary thought just 'clouds' would do for a three-year-old. It was the word she'd used all her life. However, I didn't take up swords on that one. I felt very calm, contented almost – as you sometimes are in simple moments of peacefulness, looking at the world, thinking of nothing in particular.

We'd nearly finished eating when a little flurry of breeze took a paper napkin out of the car on Rosemary's side. Her window was open, and it whisked out as if with a mind of its own, and set off up the path, tumbling and flapping along.

I know Rosemary's inclination would have been to let it go. But I have a horror of litter, of which she was well aware. We watched it for a minute or so as the wind took it along the track. Although it wavered and wandered a little, it nevertheless had the air of a rambler, setting off on a favourite walk, and making good progress. It must have been fifty yards away when Rosemary said, 'I suppose I'd better go and grab it.' I hadn't said anything mind, and I just picked up the thermos and started to unscrew the cap, for a refill of coffee.

Rosemary got out of the car and set off after the napkin. Thomas wanted some cake, so I twisted around and gave him a piece, which he dropped. By the time I'd sorted him out and turned around again, things seemed to be taking a rather comical turn. The wind must have picked up a bit, and the napkin was further away than ever, a hundred yards maybe, and bowling along. Rosemary had started to run. She was wearing jeans, and a white blouse. Blue and white on a green, blue and white backdrop. As she got further away, the napkin well ahead of her, the scene seemed to have a humorous futility about it.

Thomas chuckled a little through his cake. 'Mummy's running away from us,' he said. I explained that Mummy was not running away from us, but after a piece of litter. Then he said 'Why's she running away from us?' so I left it and said, 'I don't know.'

The napkin was now a tiny white dot, still, amazingly, proceeding along the path. Equally amazing was Rosemary's persistence. She was fully two hundred yards away now, apparently running hard. The wind was gusting strongly, and the barley in the field beside the car rattled furiously in a wave-like riffling motion. It sounded like laughter.

It was when Rosemary had dwindled to a distant silhouette against the brow of the down that a horrible sort of feeling washed over me. A physical feeling in the pit of my stomach, and a prickling of the hairs on my neck and the backs of my hands. A flock of crows appeared from nowhere and flapped noisily overhead. They distracted my attention for a moment, and when I turned back to look for Rosemary, she had gone.

I spoke to Thomas, to reassure myself. 'Mummy must have gone bonkers, Thomas!' He laughed. 'Bonkers. What's bonkers, Daddy?'

'It's running off into the blue horizon after a scrap of paper,' I replied.

We waited. I sipped my coffee thoughtfully. It calmed me. Rosemary would reappear at any moment, at the brow of the hill. I tooted the horn a couple of times. She would come back down the long white path, clutching the napkin in triumph, glowing with exertion.

How long would you wait in such a situation? Five minutes passed. I was angry. Thomas kept asking where Mummy had gone. I turned on the radio but it was just crackle. I kept on looking at my watch, setting a limit after which, surely, she had to reappear. Thomas started to cry.

After ten minutes I'd had it. I was furious, but I was also worried. A mixture of odd thoughts came into my head: had Rosemary fallen and broken her ankle? Had some extraordinary brainstorm? Been attacked by some lurking rural maniac? Where had that flock of crows come from so suddenly? How was it that the napkin never stopped or blew off the path? I calmed Thomas down as best I could and thought over what I should do. Thomas couldn't be left in the car alone, especially as he was already in a bit of a state. The path was too narrow to drive the car up. The only thing was to get Thomas out and set off together after Rosemary, hand in hand up the path.

Thomas was unimpressed by the prospect of going to look for Mummy. In the end I had to carry him, and I was pretty fed up and hot by the time we'd struggled up to where Rosemary had vanished. I'd been expecting this to be one of those false horizons that anyone who has ever climbed a hill is familiar with. But, to my surprise, we really were at a high windy viewpoint, right on the spine of the down, and the path fell away below us into a long valley. Well over a mile away, the ground began to rise again in a new series of hills, until the prospect was lost in a bluish haze.

In spite of my anxiety, I felt a strange exhilaration, as if I were an eagle soaring high above the world. I scrutinised the landscape for any hint of Rosemary's figure, but nothing moved except the clouds and the grass. Putting Thomas down to give my arms a rest, my attention was caught by something close at hand. A few feet ahead on the path lay the napkin. It was absolutely still, the wind not moving it at all. I walked forward to pick it up, but when my hand was inches away – whoosh! – the wind caught it hard and it flew twenty yards down the path, where it settled once more. I raced down towards it. Again it set off, tumbling away down the hill. I had to get hold of it. Somehow, once I had got it in my hands, Rosemary would turn up again. Just then, a cry of 'Daddy!' brought me up short. I looked back. Thomas stood on the brow of the hill, looking down towards me, on the verge of tears. Already he seemed a long way off. With an effort of will I relinquished my chase, and climbed back up the slope to Thomas. I was shaking, my legs as unsteady as if I had run a marathon.

I sat down for a minute or two, and while I chattered about nothing to Thomas I continued to look intently at the landscape for any hint of Rosemary. I ignored the napkin, which didn't move. It had frightened me, the way it had seemed to pull me after it. In the end there seemed no point in going further on foot. I could see the path plainly for at least a mile ahead, and the surrounding fields were bare. It was as if she had flown up into the sky, transformed into a skylark.

I called out a few times, without much hope. Thomas was getting cold. I suppose we stayed up there for about a quarter of an hour, before turning back and descending towards our car, parked like a dinky toy down below. Nonsensically I expected to see Rosemary sitting inside when we got back, but she wasn't. Just her handbag and a half-eaten biscuit on the dashboard. I looked at the shape her teeth had bitten out. It was like a relic of a bygone age – a crusader's helmet or a fossil.

That, really, is the end of the story. I drove to the nearest village, where I found the local constable eating his lunch in the pub. He listened to what I had to say, and was very reassuring – he would get one or two people together and we'd all go out on to the downs that afternoon. If she was anywhere out there we'd find her all right. But of course we didn't. Nor did anything turn up in the following days, or weeks, or months. It has been nearly a year now. I go down to Wiltshire every other weekend, and I've come to know the hills in all their moods. White and silent under a sprinkling of snow; muffled and damp in shifting grey mists; dazzling green, blue and white, as they were on the day I lost her.

THE CHAIR

The plants, even the plants on her window ledge (begonias, geraniums, African violets), were going to survive her. She'd be scattered over the crematorium rose beds by the spring, while their roots would be clamouring for moist earth and bigger pots. Already she was like a twig that had fallen off the tree of life, and was lying on the ground waiting for the sap to harden into brittle decay. And to suffer it all in such discomfort! It was this chair, that's what it was. Sailing to eternity in this nursing-home chair with its cargo of cushions wedged around her. Why couldn't they find a chair that fitted her properly?

Freda squirmed as much as she could to ease the pain in her back and buttocks, and of course one of the cushions came tumbling out of position. And of course it was on the wrong side, so she had to reach across with her good arm. Clumsy as a crab out of its rock pool, her good hand clutched at the empty air. Another inch, and the cushion would be in its pincers. Another half an inch. Then she was gone, arse over tip, spectacles crushed between the side of her face and the carpet. The crab squashed beneath the weight of her useless old body.

Later on, Clifford eyed his wife's bruised face as he wound sellotape around the broken arm of her spectacles. She looked as if she'd been dropped randomly into place in the chair, from a great height. Her body was a twisted reproach to his own clumsy strength. Couldn't he share some of his rude health? He felt useless.

Freda had a use for him.

'I want a new chair Clifford. This one's no good.'

'Do they have any . . .'

Freda was not going to let a terminal illness interfere with the habits of a lifetime. She interrupted him.

'One of the nurses found something in a nursing magazine. Look – it's over there on the table.'

Clifford followed the shaking signpost of her good arm. Her good arm hadn't shaken before the fall. Almost every day brought some new evidence of decline. He went to the table and picked up the magazine, which was folded open at an advert. Clifford took in the glamorous sixty-year-old in the photograph, high-heeled legs elegantly aloft on a reclining chair proportioned like a battleship. *The High Plains Drifter,* he read, *the answer to all your seating needs. Its combination of hydraulic lifting and support mechanisms will lift you up or lie you down, and its unique vibratory massage pressure pads will take you to levels of comfort you've never imagined. And at a price you've never ima-*

gined too, Clifford guessed, scanning the small print for any clue. It wasn't as if there was much left in the kitty, with the fees for the nursing home whacking into their little fund of capital month after month.

Just then, Nurse Tallow came in to check the syringe driver. She was a huge Jamaican woman with a voice like a foghorn. The imminence of her arrival had been announced by a booming noise from the next-door room, where totally deaf Mrs Slocum had been in receipt of her attentions. Clifford looked intently at the fruit bowl while the syringe, which was pumping morphine into his wife's arm, was examined and adjusted. Freda, whose hearing had stayed bravely on deck while all her other faculties were taking to the lifeboats, winced as Nurse Tallow shouted nine bells and all was well and headed off again like a black typhoon into Mr Johnson's room, where she could be heard raging and rearranging furniture.

Freda returned to the subject of the chair. 'I get so uncomfortable Clifford. That one in the picture – it's got, what do you call them?'

'Vibrators?' suggested Clifford.

'Vibrators, yes. Massage your spine. I get so sore, Clifford. Try and find out about how to get one, will you?'

At Reception, on his way out, Clifford bumped into that Plymouth Brethren woman. She was putting her gloves on briskly, with the air of one who has seen a job well done.

'Ah – Mr Cook. And how is Mrs Cook today?'

After Clifford's stumbling answer had petered out, she leaned forward confidentially. 'I've been visiting my mother-in-law again. Do you know, since she lost her powers of speech last month, I've felt we're communicating better than *ever* we did before! We never used to see eye to eye about anything. Family – politics – religion – nothing! But now there's a look in her eyes that I never used to see. I feel I can sit for hours talking to her about everything under the sun, because I just sense this tremendous new *rapport* between us! If only she could still talk!' A severe black-brimmed hat not unlike a bowler was now on her head, and she turned towards the door.

'Well, goodbye, Mr Cook. My best wishes to your good lady!'

Clifford pretended to read the Shady Acres newsletter for a minute or so to let her get clear, then followed the woman out to the car park. As he drove away along the avenue of dripping lime trees, he felt that tickling sensation in his nose that meant a cold coming on.

The next day Clifford felt wretched, and stayed in bed. On the phone, Freda pointed out that he'd left the magazine with the advert for the chair behind, so how was he going to go about getting hold of one? The conversation was terminated, none too soon for Clifford, by one of those bouts of coal-shovelling coughing that hit her with increasing frequency. After she'd put the phone down, he felt a chill of remorse though. He went to look at the Yellow Pages, but there didn't seem to be an obvious source of special chairs. It would have to wait until he went back to the home.

Freda slept a lot that day. The sounds of the nursing home seemed to come from across a dark sea, distant sounds from a shore which was increasingly difficult to regain. But sometimes pain brought her back, reeling her in like a fish to land with a bump on the chair, where she'd been all along. Alerted again to her discomfort, she'd reach out for the magazine and eye the High Plains Drifter wistfully.

It was with the magazine in her hand that Clifford found her the following afternoon. Her hand was shaking hard, so that the pages rustled like the leaves of a tree in a high wind. He took the magazine from her gently and tried to still her hand by resting his own on top of it. Underneath his palm it twitched on, like a mouse or hamster that wanted to escape.

'I'll ring up today about that chair, Freda. We'll soon have you seated in style!'

There was a difficulty, the man on the phone said, about having one of their chairs for a short trial before deciding to purchase. Yes, even for a few hours. You see, the material was very special, soft, comfortable. And – he hesitated delicately – very *absorbent*. You see, you could get cheaper, inferior products made in various synthetic materials. But nothing could match the comfort of the High Plains Drifter with its soft airlock cushioning and strategically placed vibrator pads. It was no contest. But because of its absorbency – well, you couldn't risk a twelve-hundred pound chair being ruined in a test, could you?

Eventually Clifford was given to understand that in the circumstances Mr Beezley *would* let Mrs Cook try a High Plains Drifter for a few minutes as long as payment could be made there and then in the event of the chair being acceptable, which of course it would be. A date was fixed, for three mornings hence.

As the featureless days passed, Freda felt as if she was sitting on a throne of jagged coral. Clifford came and went, bobbing across the wine-dark sea towards her. She was a mermaid, uncomfortable in the light and air, anxious to return to deep waters where the sounds of the home would swirl about her in a deadened distant form, where even the raging storms of Nurse Tallow were subdued by the weight of the water. Clifford talked of the chair, how it was coming in two days, or one day. And occasionally she found a sentence or two to share with him before he went, about vibrator pads or cushions.

*   *   *

Mr Beezley was profusely apologetic the day after he'd been supposed to come, when Clifford finally got through to him on the phone. The van had been in for its MOT, and unexpectedly needed work done on it. He'd bought it only a month ago from a man in Ripon. You had to be so careful, buying second-hand vehicles. He'd come first thing the next day. There was something about Mr Beezley's reassuring tone which had the opposite effect.

However, he did come the next day. But without the chair. Jim, the man who usually drove the van and helped with the lifting, was away from work that day with a heavy cold. But Mr Beezley felt he should come anyway, to meet Mr and Mrs Cook and discuss the chair a little.

Freda was in no state to join the discussion. She started out of her sleep for a couple of minutes when Mr Beezley walked into the room, but she was soon off again. Mr Beezley was older than Clifford had expected from his telephone voice, but less smartly dressed. He had a very pale complexion, and a sad moustache, which had known better times.

They talked about the chair Freda was in. Clifford gave his impressions of its inadequacies, based on Freda's comments. Mr Beezley talked knowingly of the drawbacks of using cushions to pad out a chair that was essentially the wrong size and shape. Then they got to looking at pictures of the High Plains Drifter, and Mr Beezley demonstrated with the aid of pencil sketches in the margins how the hydraulics worked, and precisely where the vibrator pads were located. There was no chair like it in the world for comfort. It would transform Freda's quality of life. As soon as Jim was back in harness, they'd bring the chair in. Tomorrow, or the day after, at the latest. He'd see himself out.

Clifford stood and looked at Freda for a moment before slipping away himself to buy fish and chips for his supper.

The low wintry sun was about to call it a day, and its fading light made a relief map of her sleeping face – a landscape of hills and valleys, dry river beds and smooth glaciers, gentle slopes and forests of fine white hair. It was such a familiar country that Clifford couldn't imagine it as impermanent. He left the room quickly.

Three days later, the first snow of the year was falling gently outside as Mr Beezley and Jim bore the chair into the room. Freda was quite alert, her face slightly flushed, and she seemed to follow the progress of the chair to the corner by the window with eager eyes. It had a light dusting of whiteness on it, like fine ash, which quickly melted in the warmth of the room. Clifford, ignoring Mr Beezley's protestations, helped to shove the great heavy brute of a thing into position. He felt a twinge of pain in his lower back as he bent low to the work and pushed. Old fool, he thought, straightening up cautiously and pretending nothing had happened.

Nurse Tallow was on hand to assist Freda across the room with her Zimmer frame to try out the new chair. But just as Freda was about to try and stand, one of the coughing fits came on – a bad one. Mr Beezley and Jim went down to wait in Reception. When the coughing eventually subsided, Freda was shaking worse than Clifford had ever seen before. It was frightening, and he looked at Nurse Tallow to see if she was worried too.

'I don't think she's strong enough to try the chair just now, Mr Cook.'

Clifford spoke close to Freda's ear. 'They can leave the chair here, darling. Do you want them to leave it?'

Freda's eyes stayed shut, but she found her voice. 'Leave it.'

Downstairs in Reception, Clifford wrote out the cheque and handed it to Mr Beezley. Even fish and chips were going to be a luxury now. Mr Beezley was certain that Mrs Cook was on the threshold of a new level of comfort and relief. He bobbed his head and left, folding the cheque and slipping it into his jacket pocket. The snow was falling fast now, and Clifford watched the hunched figures of Mr Beezley and Jim vanish into the whiteness like ghosts.

A couple of days later, Clifford was beginning to get the hang of the chair. The vibrators were massaging his lower back, where he'd hurt it getting the chair into place. Freda was asleep as usual. She was in the bed, and they said she wouldn't be getting out of bed any more now. He pressed the control button and the motor hummed as the hydraulics sent his legs higher into the air. He wondered vaguely whether he could get Mr Beezley and Jim to bring their van and help him get it home afterwards.

Freda knew it must be day time because shoals of sound swirled past her carrying hints of the activity on shore. There was something that might be a television somewhere. Footsteps along a corridor. A sort of humming noise. Coming up somewhere towards the surface, she tried to work out if she was lying on her side or on her back, but no messages were coming back from the outposts of her limbs and torso. With a great effort of will she got her eyelids up, and saw Clifford. He seemed to be sitting astride a whale, which rose and sank in the waves. His head was silhouetted against the light. After a moment of bewilderment and wonder, she remembered – of course, it was the chair! He'd got her the chair after all. Had she thanked him? She tried to get her lips to work.

Clifford saw the little movement, and pressed the button to return him to earth. He went to the side of the bed and leaned close, to catch whatever she wanted to say. One side of her face had sort of fallen in, and her mouth was lop-sided. It was hard to catch words.

'What is it, dear? Do you want more water?'

Freda's eyes flickered towards the chair, then back to meet Clifford's gaze. She had a premonition that more water was indeed what she was going to get, that one of these times she would not return from the deep sea which was now her real home. While she still had a few words left, she wanted to call out to Clifford, standing solicitously on the shore. So she called out with all her strength, as the sound of the wind and the waves fought to carry her voice away.

Clifford strained to hear the tiny whisper. He couldn't entirely make it out, but it might have been 'chair.' He thought he knew what she meant however, and smiled at her. Then, since her eyes had closed again, he went back to sit down and seek the best position for his poor back. The humming noise of the chair's motor brought Freda's eyes open for a moment more, and she saw him rise again above the tossing waves, Clifford transformed into Neptune the sea god, riding a whale or a sea serpent towards her, a strong and magnificent guardian to accompany her on her voyage into the deep.

BLIND SUMMIT

Joe was standing bathed in light on the edge of a precipitous mountain-top. The heat of the sun soaked his body. The world lay at his feet – little golden fields and undulating woods; snug farmhouses with tiny sheep and cows; a city in the distance, its glass towers glinting intermittently as if they were signalling something to him in morse code. Then, finally, on the rim of sight, the sea – a great glittering sheet of light. Birds wheeled about the precipice: eagles, peacocks, even penguins swimming in the air. Next to him was Alan, his arm around his shoulder, weeping for joy. Over and over, Alan repeated the words

'It's beautiful, Dad! It's beautiful! I'd no idea it was like this! It's beautiful!'

Joe usually forgot his dreams. The few he could remember were nightmares – one legacy of his years down the pit. He would be hewing out coal with a toothpick while a foreman bellowed at him down a shaft 'You've not been meeting your quota, Joe Baxter – there'll be no lift to the surface for you tonight!' Then he'd hear the clank and whine of the lift going up, and knew he'd be in the mine all night. The taste and smell of coal dust was on his pillow in the morning after dreams like that, and in the bathroom mirror he was surprised to see that his face wasn't black.

But the dream about being on the top of a mountain with Alan, and Alan being able to see it all – that was the best dream, the happiest dream he'd ever had. It glowed in his mind when he woke up, like a dragon's hoard in a cave.

In the kitchen, they needed the light on to supplement the grey pallor of the day, and the windows were smeared with rain. But for Joe a kind of golden haze hung over everything. His happiness was so intense and unexpected that he had to share it with Maggie. Alan was still in bed, so he could speak freely.

'Maggie . . .'

'Uh-huh?'

She was reading the back of the cornflake packet in the glazed automatic way that she read it every morning. *The Yorkshire Post* and the *Sun* didn't come until after breakfast.

'I had this . . . beautiful dream last night.'

'Beautiful?' The word came back at him in inverted commas, like a rare butterfly on a pin. She looked at him over the top of the cornflake packet as if sheltering from something.

'Aye. That's the only way I could describe it. It were about me and our Alan.'

'Oh aye?'

'Aye. We was up a mountain. Together. And Alan could *see*. That were the best – Alan could see everything!'

Maggie shook her head slightly.

'Well, well!'

Then she lifted the teapot.

'It's gone nine o'clock. You'd better take him his cup of tea.'

Joe pushed Alan's bedroom door open with his foot. He cleared his throat. Alan hated being woken up with a start. You had to be slow, calm. Otherwise he'd be snappy all morning – maybe all day.

'Cup of tea for you, son,' Joe said quietly, edging forward into the gloom. The curtains were closed, because the noise they made being drawn back was a useful bit of the routine needed to coax Alan into wakefulness.

He put the cup down on the bedside table and pulled the curtains. The room was suffused with the feeble daylight. Alan's eyes were already open, looking uselessly his way.

'That you, Dad?'

'Aye. Cup of tea on t' table.'

'What's the time?'

'Nine o'clock. Just gone.'

'What day is it?'

'Er – Saturday. You'll be seeing Eleanor today?'

Alan snorted.

'No. Never.'

Joe mumbled something self-deprecatingly. Since Alan went blind five years ago, when he was fifteen, he was hyper-sensitive about inappropriate words and expressions. But you couldn't learn a new language, could you?

He got Alan's clothes laid out for him on the chair; Maggie usually did it the night before, but she'd been late back from the Friday bingo and must have forgotten.

Alan sucked at his tea cup, cooling the liquid with air on its way into his mouth. Joe was still so full of his dream that he couldn't help sharing it. Risky, he knew. He sat on the edge of the bed, wheezing a little as was usual at this time of day.

'Had a great dream last night, son. Lovely dream.'

Alan's pale face turned slightly towards him, puzzled.

'Oh aye?'

'Aye. It were you and me in it. We were on top of a mountain. It were all kind of bright and there was peacocks and eagles and all kinds of birds flying about.'

'Bloody hell!' Alan snorted.

Was he at least a little amused? Joe plunged on.

'The best bit though – the best bit – was that you could see it all Alan – tha' knows – the houses and the fields and the sea and all!'

He looked at his son hopefully. Had some little flicker of his own strange happiness filtered into this moment? At least Alan had not exploded.

Alan put down his cup of tea carefully on the bedside table, and lowered himself back into the rumpled nest of bedclothes. He closed his eyes.

'What the fuck's the use of *dreaming* you can see! I can see anything in the world when I'm asleep.'

The papers had arrived when Joe got back to the kitchen. While Maggie did the breakfast dishes he sat at the kitchen table and appraised her of the latest goings on in the world.

'Mad beast murders mother-in-law in bath horror.' He scanned the brief account. 'That's in America though.'

Maggie lit a cigarette and nodded, as if it were only to be expected.

There was nothing much. Then his eye was caught by an article entitled 'Miracle cures at holy mountain!' It was all to do with a place in Hungary where people with incurable ailments had been cured after climbing some hill or other. The article said that this mountain now joined a long list of places where such supernatural events were said to occur.

Joe read the article twice. He got the feeling that the reporter was not convinced by the evidence. But it got him thinking. That dream of his. It had been so extraordinary. He tried to re-enter it, but the gate was shut. Instead he sat wool-gathering about miracle cures. He imagined Alan waking up one morning shouting 'Dad! Mum! I can see! I can see!' Then he'd do his exams, get a job, marry – Eleanor would have to have a miracle cure too. They'd have children. He'd be a grandfather.

'Isn't he getting up then?' Maggie was slopping the dishcloth around the draining board. Peeling the potatoes for lunch would be next.

'No – I don't think he's out of bed' Joe replied carefully.

Maggie pointed her cigarette at him. A smoking gun.

'Joe – you should be firmer with him. He'll not get anywhere moping about in his bedroom.'

'It's a Saturday, love. He can have a bit of a lie-in.'

'He has a bit of a lie-in every day. He should come with me down to the butcher's to get our mince for dinner. Go and tell him.'

Joe pointed at the window.

'It's raining. He doesn't like going out when it's raining, does he?'

'Honestly!' Maggie went to get the potatoes out of the tiny pantry, her back expressing her disapproval at this laxity.

Joe sighed and went over to the window. A completely monochromatic scene met his eyes. Across their little scrap of a back garden were the grey backs of a row of council houses identical to their own. A grey dripping sky hung like God's dirty washing over the world. He looked with a practised eye at the puddle on top of the slightly concave rubber dustbin lid. Looked as if it might be easing off. He'd get his walk in.

Joe's heart was bad, and the doctor said he needed a bit of light exercise every day. On the other hand, his lungs were not too good either, and going out in cold damp weather set him coughing, sometimes for hours. He'd had to retire early from the pit because of his lungs, and it was a toss-up whether it'd be lungs or heart that would retire him early from life itself. He wasn't bitter about it, just a little scared. He was sixty-two now, and he still wasn't convinced there was a heaven in spite of a lifetime of Sunday sermons.

Anyway, the rain had virtually stopped, so he decided his heart could have its treat and his lungs could take their chances. He popped his head into Alan's room.

'Do you want to come out for a walk, Alan?'

There was no reply. Pretending to be asleep still. He carried on.

'I don't mind waiting while you get dressed – if you want to come.'

'No.'

'Oh. Righto then. Your mum's going down to t' butcher's later – you could have a walk then if you liked.'

'Aye. Ta ra.'

'Ta ra.'

He put on his cap and his plastic pac-a-mac in the hall, and revisited the kitchen. Maggie was peeling potatoes. Radio Two was on. She was happy.

'Do you want me to get the mince?'

It was a symbolic offer. The butcher's was her territory, but he knew she liked to be asked.

'No, I'll go later, love. There's some other things I want to get.'

'All right. Ta ra then.'
'Ta ra.'

Joe had a route. He turned left out of their front gate and walked to the end of Buttle Street. At the end, before crossing Huddersfield Road at peril of death, he always looked away to his right, where the colliery wheel could be seen over the roofs of the houses. It didn't spin around any more, but it was still there, a sort of memorial to thirty-five years of his life. Most of his life that was, when you thought about it, spent like a mole.

After Huddersfield Road he headed across the rec. The *wreck* more like. Why didn't the council knock down the graffiti-sprayed toilet block, which was permanently closed anyway? Why didn't they pick up the broken glass that seemed to sprout like a persistent weed around the kiddies' swings? The modest spire of St Mary's at the far corner of the rec caught his eye. He spent a minute in Christian activity, putting some of the glass into the bin.

When he was going past St Mary's, the priest, Father Duffy, was just emerging from the vestry door. He was an Irishman with a big red face. In his forties, Joe supposed. He was as fond of his pint of beer as any ex-miner and Joe sometimes chatted to him at the Feathers. He liked him – you always felt he had time to give you, never in a rush.

'Morning there, Joe!' Father Duffy hailed him with a wave of his hand. His fingers were like a clutch of Walls bangers. Raw ones.

'Morning, Father Duffy!'

'Taking your constitutional there, are you?'

'Aye. Er . . . do you have half a moment, Father?'

'Yes. Of course I do.'

Joe looked up and down the street. It was empty.

'I was wondering . . . er . . . what you thought of miracle cures, Father. Do you think there's owt in them?'

Father Duffy drew a packet of cigarettes out of his jacket pocket and offered one to Joe, who shook his head.

'Sorry. Of course, I was forgetting you don't any more.'

He lit up his own cigarette and blew out a small contribution to the surrounding greyness.

'What's got you on to miracle cures?'

'Oh – just summat I read in t' paper this morning. It were about some hill in Hungary where people were climbing up and getting cured of all sorts.'

'Well, Joe. I'll admit I'm a bit more sceptical than maybe you'd expect an Irish Catholic priest to be. I think there's an awful lot of nonsense about. I think the local tourist boards try to hype up these things. Mostly that's what I think these miracle cures are. Hype. Definitely.'

Joe nodded sagely. You couldn't trust the press, that was certain. Father Duffy took another draw on his cigarette, and then turned his left-hand palm upwards.

'On the other hand, you see, there are definitely exceptions. Most definitely. Lourdes, for example. Or Knock. Definitely. Now, I'll tell you a little story, Joe, that was told only last week to me by Father Reilly. Do you know Father Reilly?'

Joe shook his head.

'He's a parish priest over in Leeds there. Anyway, one of his parishioners is a deaf woman, and last year she made the pilgrimage to Lourdes and prayed that she would be able to hear again. Well, nothing happened. But a few months after she was back she had a dream. In this dream she was told that she had to go to a certain river. This was a place in Derbyshire that she knew very well. And if she bathed in the water there, she'd be cured. Well, she consulted with my friend Father Reilly, and he thought she might as well do it. Nothing to lose. In fact he offered to drive her there. This was in early May, and the water was as icy as hell itself apparently. She went in, up to her waist, turning blue with the cold, and suddenly she could hear birdsong! Now there's a miracle cure if you like Joe. She'd been deaf nearly all her life, and now she can hear as clear as a bell. Definitely.'

Father Duffy took half a step backwards, to assess the effect of this marvellous tale on his listener. Joe felt unable to provide pantomime amazement, but he tipped his cap slightly higher on his forehead and nodded.

'Well, there's a thing all right, Father Duffy. There's a thing.'

That night Joe had another dream. The Maggie of thirty years ago was standing waist-deep in a river. It was calm and quiet, and she was listening to birdsong. Her eyes were wide and shining. Then other sounds filtered in, like the different sections of an orchestra taking up a melody. The leaves started to rustle on the trees, and the water started to ripple and splash on the stony river-bed. Only the fact that she was smoking a cigarette rather spoiled the beauty of the vision.

Then the scene shifted, and he was standing with Alan on top of Blackmoss Tor. He knew that's where it was, because he'd climbed it when he was a young man, and used to go out walking in the Peak District on Sundays with Paul Harris and Roger Hunter. In his dream though, the Tor was a soaring pinnacle. Clouds floated down below like grazing ghost-sheep, nibbling the mountainside. Just as before, Alan was gazing in ecstasy at everything, exclaiming over and over 'It's beautiful, Dad! It's beautiful!'

In the morning he woke when Maggie got up from her side of the bed to go and put the kettle on. The dream was a beacon in his head, glowing, beckoning. Blackmoss Tor. Was he really supposed to try to heave himself and Alan up Blackmoss Tor in search of some miraculous event? On the one hand, he hoped not. On the other – well – he felt a flood of joy and hope sluicing into him. Was God giving him an almighty great hint? 'Get thi' selves up that hill and tha'll get a pleasant surprise!'

Although he had been a Catholic all his life, Joe did not consider himself quite the real thing. His weekly act of worship was basically a comfortable habit, like his cup of tea first thing in the morning, or his hour in the bookies on Saturday afternoon. It was just something he'd always done. One of life's main jigsaw pieces. But, on the whole, he *did* believe there was a God. He'd been inclined to think that He kept Himself to Himself, and didn't really meddle with people's lives too much. But – these dreams – and the newspaper article, and Father Duffy's story – could there really be such a thing as divine intervention?

Feeling a little mean-spirited, he addressed God in the interval before Maggie would return with their cups of tea.

'God – thank you very much for the dreams. And the signs. I wonder if you'd mind perhaps sending just one more sign, if you mean me to climb Blackmoss Tor with Alan? Forgive me for my weak faith.'

'What are you lying there mumbling about?'

Maggie had returned a little sooner than he had expected. He feigned a sudden start from sleep.

'Oh . . . what? What? Was I talking in my sleep?'

Maggie put his cup on the bedside table.

'I hope you're not starting that malarky again. You used to keep me up half the night with your chattering once upon a time.'

God's final signal came at mass later that morning. Sunlight was streaming uncharacteristically through the simple stained-glass windows on the south side of the church. Father Duffy was going through the liturgy off in a corner, to avoid being dazzled by the beam of radiance hitting the space in front of the altar. Joe's eye fell on an old copy of the parish magazine that someone had left in the pew in front. It was upside down, which was perhaps why he hadn't paid it any attention at first. But now he studied a small black and white photograph in the top corner of the front page. It seemed to show a line of people on top of a hill. Under cover of a general transfer from kneeling to sitting by the congregation, he nudged the magazine to face towards him. 'Parish Youth Group picnic in Derbyshire' it said. 'After a stiff climb to the summit of Blackmoss Tor (shown above), the party descended to the banks of Ladybower Reservoir for sandwiches and a game of rounders.'

Joe's heart leaped and he gazed in wonder at the sunlit church around him, as if God might actually show his face somewhere, just for a moment. He didn't. But it didn't matter. Joe was convinced, and he joined in the prayers during the rest of the mass with a fervour he'd never felt before. He left the church with a conviction planted in his heart as unshakeably as a huge slab of granite sitting out on the moors. He had to get himself and Alan up that bloody hill.

Now came the problems.

The next two weeks were not easy for Joe. Or for anyone else, he supposed, as more and more people got drawn into the scenario he was creating.

Maggie viewed it as little more than a suicide bid, in spite of respecting his motives.

'You'll end up dead before you're half way up, Joe. You can't even walk round the block without coming back coughing. I'm sure God doesn't want that.'

Alan refused to take the proposal seriously. He veered between outright ridicule and pretended acquiescence. The latter was probably the more trying.

'Dad . . . do you think we should carry tents when we go up Blackmoss Tor? In case we get caught out in darkness?'

'Er – possibly.'

'And we could take up a camping stove and provisions.'

'Well . . .'

'And my guitar. I could play that by the camp fire.'

'Alan . . .'

Then Alan would be hooting with laughter, hugging his sides. At least he was getting some pleasure, Joe thought.

Father Duffy was very keen on the prospect of a local miracle cure. The trouble was that he wanted to climb up Blackmoss Tor with them.

'You'll be wanting all the help you can get, Joe, getting up that great bloody hill there.'

'You're very kind, Father . . .'

'And it'd be as well to have a witness – if anything were to happen.'

'The thing is, Father . . .'

'I could actually say a mass up there. What about that, Joe? A mass on top of the mountain?'

'You're very kind. But the dream said it was just to be me and Alan. I don't want to go against the dream, Father Duffy.'

'Ah. I see. But are you sure, now? Definitely?'

But an unexpected ally emerged in the shape of Eleanor, Alan's girlfriend. She was a year or so older than him, and had been blind from birth. They'd met at the Institute about three years ago. At that time Alan was full of positive intentions. He was learning braille, he was going to do his GCSEs, interrupted when he went blind at fifteen. He was going to get a career going. Then it all petered out. He got discouraged, particularly when all his sighted friends were leaving school and not finding any work. What was the point of *him* trying, if there was no work around here for them?

Eleanor had stuck with Alan though, and now, after Alan

had told her about his Dad's crackpot idea, she called Joe on the phone.

'You know I don't believe in God, Mr Baxter, you'll forgive me for that . . .'

'Of course, lass . . .'

'But I just think it would be so good for Alan to have summat to aim at, summat to get him out of the house, doing summat.'

'Aye . . .'

'I'll try to persuade him, honestly, I'll try as hard as I can.'

'That's champion. If you could, that'd be champion.'

'I know what I'll say. Just give me a bit of time, Mr Baxter.'

Two weeks later, it was misty when Joe and Alan descended from the early morning bus at the National Trust car park off the Glossop road. There was no-one else about, and the bus driver gave Joe an odd look as he led Alan, cursing under his breath, gingerly down the step.

'Have a nice day!' the bus driver said, managing to convey that he thought this unlikely. Then the bus door whooshed shut, and the bus itself whooshed off into the grey murk.

Joe surveyed the scene. The car park hadn't been here in his walking days, and he couldn't honestly say there was anything familiar in sight. Only the first hundred feet or so of the surrounding slopes were visible. However, the weather forecast was good – early mist clearing to give a fine afternoon – so all they could do was set off and hope for the best.

Alan's feet scrunched on the gravel beside him.

'Do you want to keep your white stick out?' Joe asked.

'Aye. It'll warn t' fucking sheep to get out of my road.'

'Want some tea from the thermos?'

'No, I'm all right. I want a pee though. Is there anyone about?'

'No, not a soul.'

Alan unzipped and pissed in the middle of the car park. Joe stood back quickly, not to get splashed. While he waited, he could hear his lungs wheezing slightly in complaint at the moist cold air. Little did his lungs know what lay ahead. But otherwise he felt in good fettle. For a week, he'd been walking two hours a day, and he pictured his heart as a sturdy little pump, pumping efficiently to kingdom come.

Alan zipped up.

'Right then. Let's get on with t' bloody route march.'

Joe wondered, not for the first time, exactly what Eleanor had said to Alan. He seemed to have come round quite quickly to this mood of resigned stoicism. Indeed, he'd actually chivvied Joe to get it organised – 'get the bloody farce over with' – as he put it.

Joe unfolded his Ordinance Survey map. The path towards the summit of Blackmoss Tor went off from the north end of the car park, opposite the road. It was about four or five miles to the top, roughly. Sometimes the path cut across contour lines so close together that they almost merged into a single brown band. There were crags and tarns and bogs. The innocent little marks on the map added up to a bleak and inhospitable environment up there.

'What are you doing? Reading t' fucking paper?'

'Just checking the map, lad. Don't want to go off the wrong way.'

'Can't you see t' hill?'

'No. Foggy.'

'Bloody Hell! Blind leading t' blind then, eh?'

'No. I've got it sorted. Come on!'

He folded up the map and took Alan's elbow. They churned across the gravel to the far corner of the car park, and there was a little brown wooden post with a finger pointing into the mist. *Blackmoss Tor, Four and a Half*

Miles. A rougher, hand-painted sign said *Keep dogs on lead during lambing season.*

'Right, lad. T'path starts here.'

Immediately they left the car park the ground became uneven and stony. Alan prodded ahead with his stick and shuffled gingerly after it, while Joe steered him around the larger obstacles. He nearly turned his own ankle after a few minutes, he was that intent on Alan's progress. The dank air soon made them feel clammy in their cagoules, and their hair dripped moisture on to their foreheads.

'This is fucking jolly.' Alan offered, after about half an hour.

'Let's have half a minute.' Joe suggested. 'There's a big boulder just here. Lean back a bit . . . there. You can rest there.'

'Can you still see t' car park?'

Joe looked back through the murk.

'No.'

'How far do you think we've come? Hundred yards?'

'Come on, lad! We're not that slow!'

'Well, how far then?'

'I don't know. Half a mile maybe.'

'And what's t' time?'

'Half nine.'

'So we're doing what? Near on a mile an hour?'

'Aye. That'd be about reet.'

'Christ! Any slower and they'll put us on t' fucking map.'

Joe did some mental arithmetic. They should manage. Last bus back left at about seven. And he'd got Father Duffy's mobile in his back pack, for emergencies.

'Just call, Joe, if you're stuck up in the hills there. I can be there in an hour. No problem.'

Joe had the feeling he'd like to get a call. He was probably already planning a sermon about all this, and a starring role for himself wouldn't go amiss.

'Ready to go on then, lad?'

'Aye. Lead on, MacPuff.'

The next hour gave Joe plenty of opportunities for reflection on the wisdom of their enterprise. The ground got steeper and, where the path went across tussocky grass, slippery too. The fog seemed to be persisting. His lungs were wheezing like old bellows with holes in them, and the little pump in his chest was hurting like a hot stone pushed up against the inside of his ribs. But at least Alan wasn't complaining.

'Shall us . . . rest up . . . a bit here . . . Alan?'

They'd reached a shelf of land with a shallower gradient. Flat rocks were scattered about like dinner plates. Joe guided Alan to the edge of one of these, and they sat down.

'Jesus! You sound like a bloody accordion!' Alan offered.

'I'll . . . be . . . reet . . . in a . . . minute.'

'What am I going to do if you peg out here in't middle of bloody nowhere?'

'Father . . . Duffy's phone. In't back pack.'

'Oh, aye. The Flying Father. He'll come in by helicopter, will he?'

'I'll be all right. I'm . . . getting my breath back now.'

'Let's have a bit of grub. What we got?'

'Jam sandwiches. Cheese sandwiches.'

'Right. Let's be having them then.'

'Just a minute. Hold your horses!'

Joe worked the back pack off his shoulders. It wasn't heavy, but it occurred to him now that perhaps Alan should carry it. He was so used to doing everything for Alan that it hadn't crossed his mind.

After they'd eaten a couple of sandwiches and drunk some of the tea in the thermos, Joe thought the mist might be starting to thin out. Up above, somewhere, he now had the feeling that there was light trying to break through.

But standing up again too quickly made him dizzy, and he lurched against Alan, who was still sitting on the edge of their rock.

'What's up?' Alan said sharply.

'Nowt. Just stumbled a little.'

He stood until the world stopped spinning. His heart drummed.

'Can you carry t' pack, Alan? It's not heavy.'

'Aye. Strap us in.'

For the next hour, Joe's thoughts were almost exclusively about his own death. His heart and his lungs were already fighting him every step of the way, and now his brain joined in the general rebellion. *Give it up, Joe, for Christ's sake!* a little voice wheedled. *You'd be bloody stupid, killing yourself for a dream. That's what everyone's going to say at thi' funeral. Kidded himself he was inspired by God. Stupid old bugger!*

Twice he nearly said something to Alan, and choked it back. The growing light above the mist kept him going. It looked like there was sunlight up there, and it reminded him of his vision. He tried to concentrate on God. He was up there, waiting for them. Alan would be cured.

No.

He was shocked to find that he didn't believe it any more. This was the wild goose chase to end all wild goose chases. The revelation was so sudden that he stopped mid-step. He half-turned.

The next thing he knew, he'd lost his footing on a clump of wet grass. His guiding grip on Alan's elbow turned into a panicking grab.

'What the . . .' Alan yelped.

Then they were gone, slithering down the slope like two toboggans on their backs, slippery cagoules offering no resistance to the grassy slope.

Joe tried to get hold of something – a tussock, a rock,

anything – to slow down his descent. Finally he banged up against a big rock and lay breathlessly on his back, looking at the sky, waiting for God to take him.

He lay like that for an unknowable length of time. Then he heard a voice maybe twenty yards off.

'Dad! Are you all right?'

He heaved enough air through his lungs to fuel a reply.

'. . . Aye! . . . You?'

Then there was a sound he couldn't make out. It was either crying or laughing. Then it resolved itself. It was unrestrained hilarity.

'You bloody old loony! You're trying to kill us both, aren't you?'

Then Alan was off again, roaring with laughter.

Joe eased himself on to an elbow. He could see Alan a few yards further up the slope. Higher still, probably where the path was, his white stick was stuck into the ground at an angle, like an arrow shot from a bow. Carefully, he raised on to knees and elbows and went crab-like up to his son, whose laughing fit was just subsiding.

'Alan . . . lad. I think we'd mebbe best . . . give it up, tha knows.'

'You what?'

'I think we should give it up. Go back down.'

Alan's laughter had stopped completely. He didn't say anything for a few seconds.

'Are you hurting, Dad?'

'Just bruises. You?'

'No. I'm all right.'

There was another pause. Then Alan spoke again.

'I think we should go on. We must be over half way.'

Joe glanced at his watch. That was probably true. They'd been going nearly three hours. He sighed.

'Alan. I feel like a proper fool. I've dragged us up here because of a dream. It's just daft.'

Alan had some mud on his face. Otherwise it was paper pale.

'Dad. I *want* to climb to t' top. It's first time I've tried to *do* anything for years. Unless you're too sore, or tha ticker hurts or summat, I want to go on.'

Joe's brain was like a tumble dryer. Tumbling about in there were sudden pride in his son, fear of pushing his own frail old carcass beyond its limits, doubt about what God was up to (if He existed) and hope that some miracle could, after all, be on the cards. He was so confused he couldn't speak.

'Dad? Come on. Let's get back up to t' path.'

It was only about forty minutes later, in warm sunshine under a dome of blue, that they reached the top. Joe looked down at the shreds of mist still clinging to the valley floors and lower hillsides below. Visually, it was more like his dream than he could have dared to hope for, but instead of elation and joy, he just felt exhausted. He looked for somewhere they could sit down.

But Alan was excited. He got Joe to describe everything. They sat on a stone and got their cagoules off and basked in the unexpected warmth. After a while, Alan spoke hesitantly.

'Dad. Tha' knows . . . I'm going to do summat with my life. This is important, today. I know there won't be a miracle. I know I'll always be blind. But . . . anyway . . . what I want to say is . . . thank you, Dad!'

Joe put his arm around Alan's shoulder and Alan smiled at him. This was, after all, a kind of miracle. It felt as good as the dream. Better, because it was real.

'There's summat else,' Alan went on. 'Eleanor and me – we're going to get married, Dad!'

Joe squeezed Alan's shoulder.

'That's wonderful, lad! Wonderful news!'

*　　*　　*

A few minutes later, there was a sound of brisk footsteps behind them, and Joe turned to see a sweating, vigorous-looking young man arriving at the summit. He had a map dangling in a plastic pouch from a cord around his neck, a water bottle strapped to his waist, a back pack, and a general air of brisk efficiency.

'How do?' Joe said.

'Hey up! What a glorious view, eh?'

'Aye!'

The young man stood beside them for a minute, drinking from his flask. Then he consulted his map.

'You just walked up from the Glossop road car park?' Joe said, making conversation.

'No. Came from the other way, from the north. I'm doing six peaks today. Blackmoss Tor next.'

Joe cleared his throat to speak. Alan got there first.

'Tha what?'

'Pardon?'

'Where did thi say tha was going next?'

'Blackmoss Tor.'

'Alan . . .' Joe said, feeling a blush rising.

'Where the fuck are we now then?' Alan said sharply.

'Now?' the young man said, looking disconcerted. Joe thought he'd just spotted the white stick. 'Now we're on Holling Hill.'

'Oh,' Alan said.

'Er, and the Glossop road car park?' Joe said, worried about getting lost on the way back.

'It's that way. About three miles.' The young man pointed. 'Well, I'd better be going,' he added. ' Long way to go. Ta ra!'

'Ta ra!'

The young man strode off, and Alan started laughing.

'You old fool! You didn't even get us up t' right hill!'

Joe smiled. It didn't seem to matter all that much. 'Tell

thee what, lad, let's not let on, eh? To thi mother and Father Duffy and that.'

'Or Eleanor either . . .'

'Nobody.'

'Aye, all right, you old fraud.'

They laughed, and sat on in the sun's warmth, lost in their own thoughts.

THE SEVENTH EGG

Magnus held last night's whisky bottle at shoulder height, arm outstretched. Then he released it from his fingers to smash into the others at the bottom of the metal dustbin. The hens reacted as usual, setting up a gust of screeching and flapping in their sordid brutal enclosure. It was half past six. A bitter frosty sun was creeping on to the horizon. Magnus fetched the pail of cabbage leaves, carrot scrapings, crusts of toast and split teabags. Fumbling with icy hands he drew back the bolt of the splintery old gate and stepped into the hen run. The hens crowded around, squawking and jostling and pecking viciously at each other.

The mess flew in an arc from the pail and splattered onto the frozen mud and droppings on the ground. The hens rushed at it, claws skidding like ice skates, while Magnus stooped almost double to enter the low henhouse door and collect the eggs. There were seven. Delicately, one at a time, he started to put them into the deep pockets of his baggy tweed jacket. When he got to the last egg, from nowhere the fury welled up inside him like lava rising in a volcano. With all the venom and whiplash that his thin old arm could muster he hurled the seventh egg and then stood in bewilderment while the fury ebbed away as swiftly as it had come. He looked at the yolk dribbling down the henhouse wall. It felt like a small murder.

In the farmhouse Elizabeth lay huddled in the warm protective cocoon of her duvet. She watched the sun's first rays turn the thin bedroom curtain into a screen of light upon which the shadows of the willow tree danced. Her eyes traced imaginary routes along the limbs and arteries of the shadow tree. It had been her dawn game for as long as she could remember – since she was a little child. Then she heard the baby starting to cry and the milk in her breasts let down in an immediate surge. She threw off the duvet and got her feet half way into her slippers. She unlocked the bedroom door and went into the bathroom where they'd put the baby's cot because of the hot-water tank. Scooping up the tiny infant, she sat down on the linen box and put it to her breast. She whispered to it, confidingly: 'Rosie, I'm going to call you. Little darling Rosie.'

Bolting the hen-run gate behind him, Magnus turned his steps away from the farmhouse. He picked his way through the rusting carcasses of disused farm machinery that had collected in the derelict stable yard and passed through the gap between the buildings at the corner. The fields lay before him, flat and almost featureless. Fields that Magnus had wrestled with for a lifetime. His eyes narrowed in the bright low sunlight which bounced hard off the frost and dew. His nostrils dilated as he breathed in the cold smell of the earth. Scanning the spiky remnants of hedgerows and the solitary skeletal trees, it seemed to him that there might be an explanation for things out there, if he could only see it.

It was seven o'clock on Magnus's watch when he re-entered the house. Already the suitcases were in the hall. He went into the kitchen. The baby was in its carry-basket by the Aga. He thought it was asleep, but when he leaned over to look in, two eyes flicked open momentarily, disquietingly, before closing again. Tom was curled around the end of the basket. His tail lifted slightly as Magnus rumpled his ears, but he didn't get up. He was old too. Magnus poured his tea from the pot that waited on the Aga and settled into his chair to cradle the warm mug in his numbed fingers. He watched the second hand scurrying around the kitchen clock.

Elizabeth entered the kitchen two minutes later. She paused at the door, taking in the familiar shape of her father's back, the basket with the dog curled around it, the time on the clock. She said nothing, poured her tea, and sat in her own chair at the end of the long table. She hunched her shoulders and tucked her arms into her sides, as if it was necessary to occupy the smallest possible space in the room. She sipped her tea with bird-like dipping motions of her head. She glanced at him, his eyes still fixed on the clock. She waited for some kind of outburst of pleading or fury.

It was a quarter past seven. Magnus got down on to the floor. On his knees. Through the thin lino he felt the uneven old flagstones pressing on his knee-bones. All his joints ached. Tom got up from beside the basket thinking it was a game. Wagging his tail he panted and pushed up against

Magnus's chest. Magnus looked at Elizabeth, who stared blankly at him. He felt his tongue lying like a lump of steak in his mouth, immobile. He hung his head. There was no need to speak after all. It was enough to kneel. It was a silent offering of the last shreds of the dignity and bullying pride to which he had clung for too long.

Then Tom nosed into him again, and he lost his balance. He keeled over towards the Aga and put out an arm awkwardly to break his fall. His elbow buckled under him and his head jolted against the baby's basket. He lay on his back on the floor, his head inches from the woven cane of the basket. It rose beside him like a little wall, and on the other side the baby started to cry. Elizabeth towered overhead. For a moment he felt she was going to scoop him up into her arms.

Elizabeth reached over the sprawled figure on the floor and picked up her baby. She would feed it a little more and then change it. By then it would be nearly half past seven. She prayed they would come on time. As she carried the baby upstairs she sang softly to comfort it. The song her own mother used to sing to her: 'It won't be a stylish marriage/ I can't afford a carriage/ But you'll look sweet/ Upon the seat/Of a bicycle made for two.' The baby's cries turned to gurgling. She bent her head to kiss it, and thought for the hundredth time of how her father must have kissed her thus, on the forehead, as she lay as a tiny baby in his arms.

Tom licked Magnus's face. He pushed the dog gently aside, and looked up from the floor towards the black-painted irregular beams of the kitchen ceiling. His eyes found the nails driven into one of the beams, from which numerous keys dangled on pieces of string, like spiders. There was a key there that he was going to need. Slowly, joints aching, he rolled over on to his stomach and levered himself up with his arms. He felt dizzy at first when he got to his feet, but when the kitchen stopped circling around him he went to the nails and took the key to the gun cupboard. There would be no need for words.

When Elizabeth re-entered the kitchen with the baby it was twenty-five past seven. Her father was back in his chair, his eyes on the clock. Then she saw the twelve-bore propped in the corner by the back door, and the single red cartridge standing like a soldier on the table. She understood the wordless blackmail in an instant. It was how he had dominated her all her life. Until now. Now she was in charge. She felt like screaming at him: 'Do it! Go on – go out into the fields and do it!'

Instead she thrust the baby into his arms and said, 'Here – hold her until I go.' It was done in an instant, without thought. It was the first time she'd let him hold it. Taking the teapot and mugs to the sink she started to run water to wash up. From the window in front of the sink she looked out across the fields. One morning, one long ago morning, her grandfather, Magnus's father, had shot himself out there. It was an empty place – just a corner where three fields met, their sparse straggling hedgerows running together. Once there had been a dark stain there, under a heavy body. A loud report, a flurry of startled rooks, a dark stain. It was before she was born. A part of her childhood mythology. An accident. The gun and the cartridge were there to call up the old story. She looked at the clock. 'Come early! Come early!' she thought. 'Don't ever let me give way to him again!'

Magnus examined the baby. It lay quite still in his arms, eyes wandering unfocused over his face and on up to the ceiling. It would have a name in due course. Elizabeth and her mother would have it christened, officially or not. It could be a source of hope and joy, like any other child. He was glad Elizabeth had resisted his wishes. And her mother's wishes, once she found out. The image of the seventh egg came unbidden into his mind, dribbling its precious cargo of life on to the henhouse floor. He felt a wave of revulsion, followed instantly by a painful rush of love as he looked from one daughter to the other. His love was forbidden. Destructive. His love brought pain. He looked at the cartridge. Then at the clock.

The clock ticked like a time-bomb. It was twenty-eight minutes past seven. They might come early. Every second that his daughters stayed in the house was like gold dust trickling through his fingers. Why couldn't he hold on to those he loved? One after another they slipped away – his father, his wife, and now his daughter and the new one. He felt panic coming, and thought of the whisky in his room. His arms shook. The baby cried and Elizabeth turned, drying her eyes with the tea towel, and took it back. He put his hands on his knees but they wouldn't be still. They gripped his legs. The knobbly thickened joints of his fingers clung stiffly. His hands were like crabs. They might crawl up, attack. Sweat began to stand on his brow.

Tyres were on the gravel drive. An engine was turned off. Car doors opened and shut. The crabs clung on hard to his legs. His whole body shook. He needed a drink. Now. The doorbell rang.

Elizabeth put the baby into its basket. She looked down at her father in his chair, juddering, shaking, the white knuckles on arthritic hands clamped hard on his legs. She looked at the cartridge, the gun, the threat. She had to decide whether it would all end in whisky, as usual. The doorbell rang again. The door was open, but her mother wouldn't come in. Twenty years ago she'd said she'd never enter the house again.

Elizabeth decided. 'I'll come back, Dad. I'll come and visit you sometimes. I'll bring the baby.' Had he nodded? She wasn't sure. She picked up the carry-basket and went quickly through the hall to the front door.

Magnus stayed where he was, tracing the sound of their movements. Who would have come with his wife – ex-wife? The new man? Not new any more of course. Would he dare? He wanted to run into the hall, fall to his knees again, beg Elizabeth to forgive him, stay with him. But he also needed them all out of the house now, quickly, so he could stumble through the hall to his room. So he could tear open the cupboard door, grasp the neck of the bottle in his teeth and pour and swallow, pour and swallow until fire consumed his tears.

The bags had been carried from the hall. He heard the boot of the car slam shut. The baby crying. The front door shutting, gently, ever so gently. The car tyres on gravel, receding. Gone. Silence. Some rooks.

Later Magnus emerged from the house with the gun under his arm. In his pockets, instead of the eggs, were all the cartridges he could find. The sun was higher now, but his unsteady footsteps still rang out on hard frost as he made his way to the empty place where three fields met.

The deserted farmhouse resonated like a musical instrument to the shots, pair after pair of shots, that Magnus fired up into the empty winter sky.

Jessica and Jessica

The drive was boring, as usual. Jessica imagined a knife blade scything along, sticking out from the side of the car like one of those things on the picture of Boadicea's chariot. It cut off everything in its path at the height of her gaze. Lamp posts toppled. Trees became stumps. Car drivers in the slow lane lost their heads. Lorries were sliced in half. The whole of the hard shoulder was a mass of debris. It was still boring.

'Are we nearly there, Mum?' she said, knowing the question was an irritant, like scratching an itch that made the itch come back worse.

'Not yet.' Her mother's voice was patient. Too patient.

'Can we listen to the Spice Girls?'

'Again?'

'Yes. Go on.'

Her mother's left hand moved down to the cassette player. Slowly, like a patient python, it nosed the buttons. The music started. Jessica started to sing along, silently. At the end of each song, the motorway ahead applauded her, hurling white lines towards her, like bouquets.

Jessica was puzzled, but that was just normal now. Still, she tried to work it out. Mark was driving her somewhere. She remembered that she'd been told where, so she didn't want to ask again. In fact, she had a feeling that she'd asked only a couple of minutes ago, but the answer had immediately flown out of the car window to join the flock of forgotten information that circled in the sky above her all the time. Like buzzards.

'Mark . . .'

'Yes?' His voice was patient. Too patient.

'Never mind.'

She went back to trying to work it out herself. They were on a motorway. Going somewhere then, or coming back from somewhere. Where had they set off from? She watched her son driving out of the corner of her eye. He seemed very good at it. He'd turned out well, after all. She was proud of him, looking after her. Driving her to her destination, wherever that was.

At the motorway service station Jessica wanted to run in, to see if Daddy was there already. But she had to wait because Mum was wrestling with the crook-lock and the steering wheel.

'Come *on!*'

'There's no hurry. Car thieves love these places.'

'Do they?' Jessica looked about for men in stripy jumpers. Burglar Bill types. There were two men talking near the phone booths. Maybe they were car thieves.

'Right. In we go then.'

Mum took her hand. Squeezed it as they walked out of the sunshine and into the cafeteria. Jessica scanned the usual area by the window and her heart jumped like a dolphin. She sped through the sea of tables.

'Daddy!'

He stood up and she hugged into the warm smokiness of his jumper, looking up at him. All the lines in his face smiled down at her, and his eyes welcomed her back.

'Jessica! Hello, darling!'

They clung together for a while. Then her dad's body went a little tense, and Jessica heard her mum coming up behind her.

'Hello. Brian.'

'Hello, Jenny.'

'I'll get a coffee,' Mum went on. 'Jessica, do you want a coke?'

Jessica spoke into the jumper, a cowardly traitor afraid to show her face.

'Yes, please.'

Her dad detached her gently and sat her down opposite him at the table. They held hands across it.

'How's my girl been?' he said.

Jessica had been left by Mark at a table next to a man and a little girl. The little girl had fair hair and her face shone as she talked. She couldn't hear what she was saying. Mark arrived back at her own table with a tray. A cup of tea was exactly what she needed. She reached out a hand as soon as the tray was set down.

'Now, be careful, Mum! You know what these motorway service station teapots are like. I'll pour it for you.'

Jessica looked at the stainless steel pot. What *were* they like? Mark set out the cups on the tray, lifted the lid of the pot, stirred it with a spoon, put the lid down again, and started to pour tentatively. Tea washed down the side of the pot.

'Damn!'

'You've made a mess of that, Mark! You should have let me . . .'

'It's all right. I brought some paper napkins.'

He mopped and swabbed and she got her tea after a few moments. Mark stirred sugar into his. Over his shoulder she saw an extraordinary thing. Susie coming towards them with a milk shake on a tray. The last person she had expected to see.

'Susie! Fancy you being here!'

'Hello, Mum!'

Susie put the tray down and bent to kiss Jessica's cheek. She didn't seem in the least surprised at this extraordinary coincidence.

'Hello, Mark!'

'Susie.'

A brotherly peck on the cheek. Well, well. The whole family was here now. Apart from . . . Jessica looked at the vague shapes of people coming in or going out of the entrance. Where was Geoffrey?

'Your dad, Susie . . . is he . . .'

'What?'

They were both looking at her. Those two lines that made a 'V' over Susie's nose were faintly visible. Jessica realised that she was making some stupid mistake.

'Nothing.' She took a sip of her tea and smiled propitiatingly.

She saw Mark and Susie share a look. She said such idiotic things sometimes. She pictured the inside of her brain as a tangle of electrical wires. Some cack-handed electrician had got in there with a pair of pliers and severed half the connections. The iris she'd thrown down on to Geoffrey's coffin flowered briefly in her memory and vanished in a puff of dust.

'How are you then, Mum? Have you had a nice time staying with Mark?'

She could play that game. Just agree with most things. 'Yes, thank you. It's been lovely.'

'Good.' Susie took a long sip of her milk shake through a straw.

'Back to the land of the free then, for you.' This was spoken to Mark. But what did it mean? Mark didn't reply anyway. His shoulders moved up and down briefly, that was all, as if shrugging off a knapsack.

Jessica was trying to hear what the people at the next table might be saying. She wanted to tune in to a different frequency than the one used by her mum and dad. Theirs was a crackling, dissonant waveband. By leaning back a bit on her chair, she could get a mixture of the conversations. She breathed particularly slowly, like the yoga lady had taught her.

'You agreed two whole weeks! I've got the time off work!'

'It's only a day, Brian. I need to take her shopping for new school uniform.'

'Why couldn't you have done that before now, at the start of the holiday?'

'Has she been wearing that dress all the time, Mark?'

'Of course she hasn't.'

'Because it's supposed to be for best.'

'Have you happened to notice that nine-year-olds grow bigger almost as you watch, Brian? She'll be bigger in two weeks' time.'

'That's ridiculous. She's not a . . . a . . . vegetable!'

'I let Mother choose what she wants to wear. Don't I, Mum?'

'What?'

'It's not ridiculous. She grows out of clothes very quickly.'

'I said I let you choose your clothes, Mum.'

'I should bloody well hope you do. Who else should choose my clothes?'

'Ssh! Mum!'

'Your fault, Susie, for bringing up the subject.'

'She'd be dressing up for the Lord Mayor's show every day if she was given the chance.'

'It might be only a day, but it completely messes up . . .'

'I've not had any problem . . .'

'. . . for the end of the holiday. We were coming back from Cornwall on the Saturday. Now you want . . .'

'Mark . . . she's got to be kept with her feet on the ground. Not imagining she's off to meet the Queen every day.'

'. . . and I've already paid for the Friday night.'

'I did mention before that I would have to get her uniform.'

'But you never said it had to be . . .'

'She's hardly mentioned the Queen all the time she's been with me.'

'One whole week!'

'That was what we arranged. Why do you say it like that?'

'Why can't you consult me, Jenny?'

'I could consult you if you were a reasonable person who you could make reasonable arrangements with.'

'You're always wanting to snip off a day here, a day there!'

'That's not true!'

'It's all right for you! Why don't you try it for a month?'

'You know I can't do that. The travelling . . .'
'. . . with your job. I know.'
'I can't have her for longer. This is old ground.'

Jessica was picturing the Queen. As she'd looked at that wedding the other day. A model of elegance and grace. She needed a pee.

'Susie – I'm just going to the bathroom.'

'You see where it is? The yellow sign?'

Jessica nodded and set off. She couldn't see a yellow sign, but she had a memory of this place. She knew her way about here. She nodded at the lady clearing away trays.

'Hello! How are you, Margaret?'

The lady looked puzzled, but she smiled back. That was Margaret, who used to live two doors down on Bank Terrace. She was ageing gracefully. But it was a pity she had to do a job like this, and so far away from home.

The yellow sign swam into view. Jessica's hand moved automatically in search of a penny in her handbag. But she hadn't even got a handbag. She stopped dead for a moment, then remembered that you didn't need pennies any more.

Jessica was finding it harder to screen out Mum and Dad. It was bad enough hearing the one-sided telephone conversations they had, but hearing both sides was even worse. She hoovered up the last droplets of coke with her straw.

'Can I go and look out of the window over there?'

They looked at her, as if surprised to find her present.

'Which window?' her dad said.

She pointed.

'Don't go out of sight then,' her mum said.

At the window she looked out at the service station's little playground. Some children were on the swings, moving with an easy rhythm from one point of altitude to the other, back and forth. They looked like they were having more fun than she was. Behind the swings something painted bright red caught the sunlight. They'd added a roundabout since she'd last been here. No-one was using it. She turned her feet round and round, now facing her parents, now facing out of the window. Round and round in a circle, not back and forth. An old lady – the old lady who had been at the next table – appeared to be looking at her. On the next rotation she was walking towards her. Nearer on the next turn. And now standing, smiling at her. She was quite small, for a grown-up. Smiling.

'Hello, dear! That's a pretty dress!'

'Thank you. So's yours.'

'It is, yes. My best dress. What's your name?'

'Jessica.'

'Jessica! Well, well. You'll never guess what my name is!'

The old lady's face had given it away.

'Jessica?'

'Well done!'

'There's one in my class at school as well.'

'I suppose there are hundreds of us, dear. Thousands.'

Jessica wondered why the old lady was talking to her. Perhaps she didn't want to sit down at her table either. She seemed nice.

'Have you got brothers and sisters, dear?'

'No.'

'I have a sister. But I haven't seen her . . . oh, for years.'

'I'd like a sister. But my mum and dad aren't going to have any more children.'

'Why ever not?'

'They don't live together.'

'Oh dear. Children are so important. My children are over there. My little boy and my little girl.'

Jessica glanced over at the table next to her parents.

'They're grown-ups.'

'Yes. They are now. But they didn't used to be.'

'Do you all live together?'

'I'm not sure. No, I don't think so.'

Jessica looked out again at the roundabout. The sun glinted from it. There was still nobody using it. It was a shame.

'There's a roundabout there.' She pointed it out to the old lady.

'Do you think you could take me out to it, if my mum and dad will let me go?'

'I should think so.'

Jessica went back towards the force field around her parents' table. She didn't tune in to the words, but observed their hand gestures and their faces. At the next table too, the old lady's children looked like they were arguing.

'Mum, Dad, can I go with the old lady out to the swing park? To go on the roundabout?'

Her mother looked at her, and she pointed towards the old lady.

'That old lady there?' her mum said.

'Yes, we were just talking by the window.'

Her dad craned up slightly in his chair, like a giraffe going after a leafy branch.

'I can see the roundabout from here.'

'All right,' her mother said. 'Don't go out of sight though. We'll be out in a couple of minutes.'

Outside it was warm. Jessica trod gingerly across the woodchipped surface behind the little girl. The cries of other children on the swings were like seagull voices. She remembered a beach, years ago, in the sun.

The roundabout shone, brilliant red, reflecting sunlight. The little girl had perched on one of its radiating bars, smiling.

'Will you give me a push?'

Jessica grasped the curved end of the bar with both

hands. There was much less resistance than she expected. The roundabout began to move, soundlessly, gracefully. She took two or three steps, then gave a final shove, being careful not to fall as she let go. The little girl went past her four, five, six times before slowing to a halt.

'Do you want to get on?' she said. 'I can get it going and then jump on as well.'

Jessica glanced back at the service station building. Well, she could do what she wanted, couldn't she? Although she imagined Mark and Susie would disapprove. She climbed on to the platform of the roundabout and gripped the bar firmly.

'Not too fast!'

Jessica pushed the roundabout for a full circuit, then jumped on next to Jessica. They grinned at each other.

The swings, the car park, the service station building, the motorway itself over a hedge, lorry tops blurring by. Everything circled around the still point of Jessica's vision. She laughed with the novelty of it, the remembered novelty. Then two figures appeared in front of the building. At the entrance to the swing park. Walking towards them past the swings. Standing right next to the roundabout.

'Mum! What on earth are you doing? I thought you were going to the loo?'

Mark.

'You'll make yourself sick!'

Susie.

The roundabout had slowed to a halt anyway. They helped her off on to the woodchip, which heaved like the deck of a ship at sea.

'Oh, stop making a fuss. I was just having a bit of fun.'

Jessica saw her mum and dad appear at the gate of the swing park.

'Come on, Jessica!' her dad called, cheerfully. She loved

that note in his voice. Her mum was already smiling her special brave-at-parting smile. The nice old lady was starting to move off, one arm linked with her daughter's. She waved with her free arm.

'Goodbye, dear! Nice to have met you!'

'Goodbye!' Jessica replied, waving back. She stayed for one more moment on the bright-red roundabout, imagining being old.

HOUSE OF STRAW

In the burgeoning darkness, the feeble lights of Mossburn flickered through the drizzle. Folk were drawing their curtains and poking their coal fires into life. The bell over Mrs McHogg's General Stores tinkled for the last time as a late customer was hustled out.

The hills rose on all sides of the town, plump spongy pillows filled with water, where sheep tore at the drenched grass and oozing burns glinted in the last of the daylight. To the north, a little road snaked out of Mossburn and up towards the hills. Not the main road – that followed the valley floor towards Maffit – but a muddy, narrow unnoticed little lane with dry-stone walls. It was signposted 'Law Farm and High Law'. It twisted through gently tilted fields full of sheep and cows, and then hitched itself more steeply through a leafless wood until it attained a sort of plateau. Here Mossburn's lights were lost to sight, and the road ran past Law Farm and then up again to a higher ridge where High Law reservoir was cupped in a fold of the land. There the road ended.

Lights were on in Law Farm. Helen was in the low-ceilinged kitchen. Its mean little windows faced down the darkening road towards where it disappeared into the wood on its descent to Mossburn. Drizzle was drifting in wind-blown sheets against the panes. The wind never stopped blowing across this exposed shelf of land. Helen cursed the rain and the wind together under her breath as she drew the curtains against the murk.

She had broken off from feeding Rachel, who was five months old. Rachel lolled in a sort of low chair made of cloth slung across a tubular metal frame. Just now she was making it rock back and forth with vigorous kicks of her legs, screaming at the interruption to her meal.

Stuart, who was four, was at the enormous kitchen table, painting. His efforts were visible on sheets of paper scattered across the pitted wooden surface. Mostly aeroplanes, improbable monsters, and houses with smoke billowing out of dozens of chimneys. He bent forward over his work, his mouth open and his eyes unblinking in an expression of tranced focus. Then he leaned back slightly and spoke without looking up.

'Mummy! Come and look!'

'Just a minute, Stuart. Let me finish feeding Rachel.'

Helen perched again on the chair beside Rachel and spooned slop into the gaping mouth. She thought of a mother bird bringing worms to its young, the nest filled with squawking desperate beaks. What was daddy bird doing in the meantime? Her gaze drifted to the telephone, an old-fashioned black one on a special shelf clumsily tacked on to the wall. In the month that they'd spent at Law Farm it hadn't rung once. She was sure it must be faulty. John claimed that whenever he tried to ring her, it was engaged. This was not impossible – Helen had got into the habit of ringing her mother almost nightly, and sometimes during the day as well. But she should get it checked.

It had been her husband's idea to rent this old farmhouse in the Scottish Borders. He was Scottish, and he wanted his children to grow up with Scottish roots, so it was best to move north from London before Stuart started school. Helen had wanted to buy somewhere in Edinburgh, or at least near it, but John had grown up on a farm. He wanted the children to experience the country life. Helen had finally agreed when he'd suggested renting this place for a year only. They'd give it one year, to see if they could 'acclimatise'. Only it seemed to be Helen and the children who were doing all the acclimatising. John was kept busy by work in London and the States, and he'd only spent a couple of weekends up at Law Farm since they had moved in October. Now it was late November, and Helen felt the resentment building up layer by layer as the days dragged along. Her daylight hours were consumed by the children, which was all right in itself. But there followed endless evenings of isolated tedium, reading books or the newspaper, or watching the TV. She felt, as she frequently said to her mother on the phone, in exile. It was her mother in fact who had first used the word 'marooned', and without actually saying anything specific, she gave Helen the impression that she thought John had let them down. Of course, Helen's father had let *her* down, and continued to do so. He had suffered a stroke, and she was virtually a full-time nurse to him.

When Rachel had eaten enough, Helen put her near the radiator and turned Radio Three on. That usually sent

Rachel to sleep. It sounded promising – something sombre with cellos. Stuart had left his painting and wandered off somewhere. Absent-mindedly Helen started to tidy up his things.

One of his pictures took her attention. She stared at it, unable to connect it with her son. She looked around the kitchen foolishly, as if an artist might be concealed somewhere in there. It was nothing like anything else Stuart had ever done. A portrait, roughly executed with strong confident brush strokes. A portrait of a rather flabby-faced young man with untidy hair and a vacant expression. Utterly mystifying.

'Stuart! Come here a minute, darling!'

Stuart appeared at the doorway, holding a few pieces of brightly coloured duplo in his hands.

'I've just been looking at this picture you've done. It's . . . it's very well painted, dear! Who is it?'

'My friend.'

'Your friend?'

'Yes.'

'Is it someone you've seen in Mossburn?'

'No.'

'Someone you've met at Mrs Minter's – Barbara's?'

'No'

'Well . . .'

'Bye!' Stuart was off again. The pieces of duplo were evidently aeroplanes, from the noise he made. Or perhaps spaceships. Helen looked again at the painting, an alien intrusion. She put it away in a cupboard, as a curiosity to discuss with John when he finally showed his face.

The next day, Helen went down to Mossburn early. It was a Thursday, the day she left Stuart with Barbara Minter, a childminder she'd found through a card in a shop window. Barbara had a four-year-old girl herself, and Helen thought it was no bad thing for Stuart to have a little company of his own age. Although she had some reservations about the Minter way of doing things.

After Barbara Minter's, Helen went to Mossburn General Stores. There were problems here too. The concept of self-service had not yet penetrated to this backwater of the retail trade. Also it was a monopolistic concern, owing to the fact that the nearest alternative was in Maffit, fourteen miles away. Mrs McHogg, the ancient proprietress, was therefore at liberty to dispense with the finer points of charm when dealing with her customers. Helen always entered the shop with a sense that her status as a newcomer, and an English one at that, marked her out for a particularly flinty reception. Even the baby in its sling didn't soften Mrs McHogg's heart.

'Tea, did you say?'

'Yes please, Mrs McHogg, a box of teabags.'

'We've only the loose.'

'Oh. Well, I'll take a box of that please, Mrs McHogg.'

'A'm tae save these for Mrs Harris.'

'Couldn't you just spare one?'

'Och weel – you can have a quarter pound. A' suppose she'll no miss that.'

Helen girded her loins for the next request. 'Have you any fresh fruit today?'

Mrs McHogg looked at her as if she had sprouted ass's ears. 'It's Monday the fruit comes.'

'I see. Well, may I have some tinned peaches?'

'A'll have tae get ma wee ladder out for them.'

'I'm sorry.'

Mrs McHogg set off with pained resignation for the dark corner where she kept her stepladder. As she manoeuvred it noisily into position, the bell over the street door tinkled. Helen turned to see who was coming into the shop. Standing on the threshold, his head nearly touching the door lintel, was a great tousle-headed boy. He was staring straight at Helen with mouth agape, his heavy-lidded eyes fixed intently on her face. She tore her own gaze away and looked down at the counter in front of her. Her hand reached out of its own accord, touching the wooden surface, testing its solidity. This was the boy in Stuart's picture! Unmistakably. And he was staring at her as if he knew her. She heard a sort of inarticulate rummaging in his vocal chords, as if he were trying to find some word in there, but he was cut short by Mrs McHogg from the imperious height of her stepladder.

'What do *you* want, Simon? Well? Dinnae stond letting a' the cauld in! Come in or get awa' wi' ye!'

There was a pause. Helen looked again towards the door. Simon backed out into the street, still staring. He pulled the door closed behind him, and stood for a moment longer gawping through the glass, like a fish shut out of its aquarium. Then he was gone. Helen realised that her fingernails were digging into the palms of her hands, and unclenched her fingers slowly. She spoke to Mrs McHogg's back, as the proprietor wearily descended from on high.

'Who was that, Mrs McHogg?'

'That? That big tumphie? Simple Simon. Have ye no seen him stravaiging aboot the toon?'

'Er no . . . but I think . . .' What could she say? Her four-year-old son had painted a portrait of him? Her train of thought was ended by a tin plonked on to the counter in front of her.

'There ye are – peaches!'

Helen cursed inwardly. 'Oh – I'm sorry – that great tall boy standing at the door and staring at me distracted me. Could I have three tins, please?'

Mrs McHogg's facial expression suggested that she was mentally re-creating the savour of neat lemon juice. With infinite reluctance she headed back towards her stepladder, muttering something about people who wanted to own every peach in the town.

Helen thought about this encounter with the boy for the rest of the day. She took the painting out of the cupboard to look at it again. Surely Stuart must have seen this Simon boy sometime, and carried away a mental image of him in his head, like a photograph. Could Stuart have a photographic memory? Like that autistic boy she'd once read about in the paper, who drew buildings?

At four o'clock that afternoon, she went to collect Stuart from the drab little harled council house where Barbara Minter lived. It was already getting dark. As they drove up the road towards Law Farm, Stuart became quite agitated, looking out of the windows into the huddled trunks of the wood.

'Mummy!'

'Yes, Stuart, what is it?'

'Nothing. I saw something.'

'What, in the trees?'

'Yes.'

'What was it?'

'I don't know. Are there bears in the wood?'

'No, there aren't any bears left in Scotland.'

'Where did they go?'

'Oh, they all ran away when people came to live here.'

'I thought *people* ran away from bears.'

'Not always. Bears aren't as fierce as people.'

Once they were in the house, Helen put Rachel into her cot for an hour. She'd nodded off in the car, and there was no point in trying to fight it. When she came downstairs, Stuart was in the kitchen, staring at nothing in particular.

'Mummy!'

'Mmm?'

'Mummy! Simon's coming.'

Helen looked hard at him. 'What did you say, Stuart?'

'Simon's coming. He's coming up our road.'

'Who's Simon?'

'I don't know. I painted him.'

Helen went to the window and peered out into the almost blackness. She could just see the road, but there was nothing moving on it. Then she recoiled from the window with a gasp as a pale moon of a face loomed into the pane. She drew the curtains with a sweep of her arm. Waited, heart thumping. Two, three, four seconds. Then there was a knock on the door. Stuart looked up at her.

'That's him. He's here now.'

Helen was frozen to the spot. The moment stretched, and she heard a few spits of rain start to tap at the window. Then the knocking at the door was renewed.

'Mummy . . .'

'Sssh!'

'He *knows* we're here, Mummy.'

'Go upstairs, Stuart. Quickly.'

'But Mummy . . .'

'Go *on!*'

Stuart reluctantly set off up the stairs. Helen waited until he was out of sight, then went down the short stone-floored passage to the back door. She opened it a crack. The boy was standing very close, towering above her. The rain was starting to come down hard, and water was running down his big pale face. She spoke sharply, no nonsense:

'Yes? What do you want?'

His eyes were glued to his feet. He mumbled so low that she could scarcely hear him.

'It's . . . I'm . . . I've come to see . . . I . . .'

'What is it you're saying? I can't hear you.'

That silenced him completely. They stood for a moment, as the rain turned into a torrent. Helen opened the door a little wider. He was like a dumb animal standing there, like a cow in a field, dripping and steaming.

'You're soaking wet! You're the boy I saw at Mrs McHogg's shop, aren't you?'

'Yes, I'm Simon. I've . . . I've come here . . .'

Suddenly another voice chimed in, right behind Helen. Stuart had crept down the stairs again.

'Mum . . .'

Helen spoke urgently over her shoulder:

'Stuart! Get upstairs, now!'

Stuart reluctantly retreated. Simon's face had lit up though. He raised his eyes to meet hers for the first time.

'I . . . I've come . . . ask if . . . to ask if I can play with Stuart?'

'Do you know Stuart?' Helen said brusquely.

But his head went down at that. She tried again, more gently.

'Have you spoken to him? Do you know Barbara . . . Mrs Minter? In Mossburn? How do you know Stuart's name?'

But it seemed all too much for the boy. He stood there, thoroughly befuddled, water running off the end of his nose. He sneezed, felt in his pocket for a handkerchief, failed to find one, and wiped the back of his hand across his nose and mouth. In a flash of understanding, Helen suddenly saw him for what he was – a little child in a great big body. He was cold, wet, awkward. She opened the door wide.

'Come in! Come on – come into the kitchen. I'll put the electric heater on and you can get warm and dry.'

Simon shuffled along behind her into the kitchen, and she sat him down at the table. She passed him a towel and told him to dry his hair, but he was so hopeless that she took the towel off him after a moment and started to rub it herself. She tried questioning him again.

'How do you know Stuart?'

'I just do.'

'I see. You just do, do you?'

Simon positively cowered under the towel. She heard him whisper something.

'Pardon?' she said.

He spoke again, barely above a whisper. 'Please . . . don't . . . don't be cross!'

'I'm not cross. I'm just . . . puzzled. I mean . . . don't you think you're a bit big to be wanting to play with a four-year-old? You've finished school haven't you?'

There was silence under the towel. Helen tried her gentle voice again.

'Do you go to school?'

'Didn't like school.'

'No? Well . . . do you work? Have you got a job? What do you do?'

'Play.'

'Pardon?'

'Play. And walk around.'

'And do you live with your parents? Your mummy and daddy – do you live with your mummy and daddy?'

'Mummy . . .'

'I see. In Mossburn? Your mummy lives in Mossburn?'

'Yes.'

And then, for no reason that was apparent to Helen, he began to cry. Great heaving sobs that shook his whole frame. Helen hesitated, then put her hand on his shoulder. He seemed so helpless.

'All right, Simon, all right. Come on.'

She got hold of a box of tissues and passed him one.

'Here – wipe your nose.'

Just then, the kitchen door creaked open. Stuart's face appeared around the edge.

'Stuart! I thought I said you were to stay upstairs!'

'I wanted to see Simon.'

Simon's sobbing was abating. He looked up with interest when he heard Stuart.

'Hello, Simon! Do you want to play with my cars?'

Simon spoke through suppressed sniffles.

'I've got a garage for my cars.'

'I make garages out of bricks. Mum . . .'

'Yes?'

'Can me and Simon have the bricks?'

'I think Simon had better go home now.'

'Oh Mum! Please!'

Then Simon took it up.

'Please . . .'

'Please . . .'

'Please, please, please . . .'

They were giggling now, getting silly. Helen gave in. Simon seemed so harmless.

'Oh – all right then. You can play with the bricks.'

Three days later, she rang John. He had been in Los Angeles for the last few days. Fixing up some media deal or other. Lynchpin of the British film industry that he was. Or thought he was. She was weary of his absorption in it all, weary of his absence. He claimed to have tried to ring her, but the phone had never gone. There must be a fault with it.

John's news was that he had another trip to the States coming up immediately, and he wouldn't be able to come north for at least two weeks. Helen was furious. To punish him, she told him all about Simon:

'Stuart's got a new friend. He's about six foot three and eighteen years old and his name's Simon. No, I'm not joking. He's simple-minded, and he likes to play with Stuart. He came to the house last week, and now he comes every morning. What? Oh – they run around, play silly games. No, I know that's what you'd do. But you're never here, are you, John? So if he goes berserk with an axe one day you'll be able to read about it in the papers, won't you? Right! Well, if you want any say in the matter, you'd better bloody well come and live here!'

She slammed the phone down. She was steaming. No way was he going to strand her in this god-forsaken hole and have an easy conscience about it. If she could give him nightmares about his family being butchered, so much the better.

The next Thursday, she dropped Stuart down at Barbara Minter's for the day as usual. The wind whistled through the bleak little council housing scheme and scattered bits of litter. An ice cream wrapper fluttered against her boot as she waited for the door to open. Ice-cream for God's sake! Who was eating ice cream in this climate? The door opened, and Barbara's face appeared, exhaling smoke. Behind her in the house a television was on, and an infant was wailing somewhere. Barbara didn't open the door wide enough to suggest that Helen might step in.

'Och, hello, Stuart! Come on, there's a cartoon on the telly!'

'I'll pick him up at four as usual then Barbara . . .'

'Aye, that's fine. Cheerio the noo.'

Stuart slipped past Barbara Minter's ample figure and into the house. He always seemed happy to spend the day there. Watching telly and eating chips, from what she could gather. Helen spoke quickly, before the door could shut.

'Er . . . Barbara . . . there was something . . .'

'Aye?'

'Do you know a big lad in the village called Simon?'

'Simple Simon?'

'Er, yes. That's what they call him, is it?'

'Och aye – he's nae too clever.'

'What do you know about him?'

'He's made friends with your wee Stuart, hasn't he?'

'Yes. Sort of.'

'Stuart tells me he plays with him in the kitchen and round the garden at your hoose?'

'Yes, he does.'

'I thought I'd seen him once or twice heided out on your road up the hill.'

She took a deep drag from her cigarette and leaned out confidentially from her doorway like a lobster poking out from under its rock. Her advice came in a thin stream of smoke with little puffs of italics.

'I'd no let *him* in ma hoose! Who kens what's going on in *his* heid?'

'That's why I wanted to ask . . .'

'A big strong laddie tae' imph? Built like a tree!'

'Do you know where he lives?'

'It's one o' they grey wee hooses on the Maffit road.'

'Have you heard – well – anything bad of him?'

'Och no – no *yet*! But he's only been in Mossburn a wee while. A year or two mebbe. Lives wi' a big fat woman – his mither I suppose. They go tae the kirk every Sunday, but they dinnae talk to anyone, like. Mebbe she's a bit the same way as him – ye cannae be too sure to look at her.'

There was a sudden shriek from within the house. Barbara raised her eyes skywards.

'Och! I'd better see wha's happening! I'll see you later Mrs Foster.'

The door was shut. Helen returned to her car, where Rachel gurgled with pleasure to see her.

Things carried on in the same way for another week. Helen was starting to get used to having Simon around the house. He and Stuart would spend hours at the kitchen table together messing about with paints. They were on exactly the same wavelength.

'More red, Simon . . . more red lines. Yes, that's it! Now
– blue. Blue sky . . .'

'More bluer. Lots of blue. Sunny . . .'

'That's the sky and . . . that's the sun . . .'

'Do it shining.'

'Shine, shine, shine, shine . . .'

'That's sunny!'

Then Simon leaned over and started adding to Stuart's
painting.

'What's that, Simon?'

'Big cloud coming. Big black cloud.'

'Lots of black. Shall we do rain?'

'Yes . . .'

'Rain, rain, rain . . .'

Then they were splattering water everywhere, giggling
like mad. Helen intervened.

'That's enough now! You're getting silly and making a
mess.'

'Can we play in the garden, Mummy?'

'Yes, if you put your coats on.'

'Can I take Stuart up the lane to see the horses like
yesterday?'

'Horsies! Horsies!'

Helen let them go. It would be all right as long as they
didn't pass beyond the gate at the brow of the hill, where
she could still see them from the window. The two of them
clattered out into the little stone-floored hallway and started
getting into their coats and boots. Helen started to clear up
the litter of paintings on the table, then stood stock still.

It was another painting like the one Stuart had done
before. Another of those extraordinary portraits. It was of
Stuart and Simon holding hands. So utterly different from
all the other childish daubs that they'd done. She called out
into the hallway.

'Stuart! Simon! Who did this?'

She carried the picture out to them. They glanced at it without much interest, struggling into boots. Simon spoke.

'We both did.'

'Both of you?'

'Yes.'

Stuart piped up.

'I drew Simon and Simon drew me. We're holding hands. Come on, Simon, let's hold hands to see the horsies now!'

And then they were off at a run, holding hands, happy as Larry. Rachel started to cry in the kitchen, deprived of the sight of her mother for more than thirty seconds. Helen shut the back door and went back to her. She stood at the window that looked up the lane, and watched the boys galloping away Simon running in tiny little steps so as not to leave Stuart behind. She glanced again at the strange painting, then back to the two figures, one so huge, the other so tiny. She recognised with a new pang of misgiving just how close they had become.

A couple of days later John, her husband, appeared, unannounced, in the late afternoon gloaming. He hadn't been able to get through on the phone. Susan's relief and Stuart's delight were cut short when he announced that he had to get back to London the next day. When Stuart had gone to bed and Rachel was asleep too, they had a row. John had brought news. He had acquired a small flat in Fulham – not big enough for all of them – and that was going to be his base from now on. The return to Scottish roots apparently was now postponed. Where the bloody hell did that leave her Helen wanted to know. And the kids? Were they to be completely abandoned? No, John would visit whenever he could. It was a busy time coming up. But he'd be with them for Christmas at least, in a month's time. They could rely on that. Helen was so furious she wouldn't let him share her bedroom. She made up a bed for him on the sitting-room floor, in front of the embers of the dying fire. Then she cried into her pillow over the embers of their marriage.

Later, she dreamed of Simon. He was standing on a hilltop with Stuart, looking down at a curious house made from straw. John was sitting in his car nearby, wearing a wolf's head, and Simon was pointing at him and saying to Stuart: 'He'll huff, and he'll puff and he'll blow your house down! He'll huff, and he'll puff and he'll blow your house down!' She woke up, and thought that she'd remember the dream in the morning. But in the cold dawn it was gone, and so was John.

It was a foggy morning, unusually still for that exposed place. When Stuart discovered that his father had gone, he retreated into the sitting room to watch television with his thumb in his mouth. Helen went out to the back step to chop some wood for the fire. The chill moist air got into her bones, and she swung the axe hard to keep warm. The splintering impacts came back as muffled echoes from the surrounding hills. Pausing in her work, she discerned a dim form lumbering through the fog across the fields. As the shape became clearer, like a whale surfacing from under-water, she saw that it was Simon. She wondered vaguely why he was coming from the hills like that, instead of up the road as usual. When he arrived, she took him in to Stuart, but he hardly looked up, so he came back outside with her and asked if he could help chop the wood.

Helen knew he was too clumsy to entrust with an axe, so she declined his offer of help. But he was so desperate to be useful that she sat him down in the kitchen with a bowl of potatoes to peel for lunch. She gave him a scraper rather than a knife, but five minutes later he was rushing out to her, crying.

'I've cut my thumb! Ohhh . . . it hurts!'

'Oh Simon! How have you done that, you silly boy? Let me see . . . oh dear . . . let's run it under the cold tap. Come on!'

In the kitchen, Simon stood sniffling back tears as Helen put his hand under the tap and then rummaged in a drawer for tissues and sticking plasters.

'Here we are. Right. Sit down here next to me. Put your hand out. Let me dry it, Simon! Come on – I'll do it gently. There. It's a clean cut.'

She peeled the backing off the sticking plaster and stuck it down over the small gash in the fleshy part of his thumb. Then he started sobbing in earnest, as if torn by some deep-seated grief.

'Simon! What is it? Here, hold my hand. There! There! What is it?'

'Stuart's daddy isn't coming back is he? I'm so sad! I'm so sad!'

'Oh, Simon! How do you know that? Oh dear!'

And then Helen was trying not to cry too, because suddenly she thought Simon was right. John wasn't coming back, not at Christmas, not at all. They sat there hand in hand, gradually pulling themselves together. Helen stood up at last.

'Come on, you big baby! Cheer up! Come on!'

Luckily Stuart came in then. He at least seemed to have brightened up a bit.

'Come on, Simon! Let's play hide and seek in the garden!' he said.

Helen got Stuart into his boots, and out they went. She stood by the kitchen window, watching. Stuart was hunting round while Simon crouched behind the big oak tree in the garden. Simon was giggling to himself with excitement, a little four-year-old boy in a great big body.

When she was in the police station, that was how she described Simon to Inspector Leach. Like a four-year-old child whose body had grown too big. She had conceived an instant loathing for Inspector Leach. Everything he said seemed to insinuate that he knew you were trying to hide something from him. He had a face like a weasel. The big policewoman who brought the tea was nicer. She had given her a sympathetic look, at least.

Inspector Leach was leaning forward now, fixing her with his narrow little weasel eyes. She drew deeply on her cigarette, smoking being a habit she had reacquired in the last twenty-four hours.

'Now, we have to go over this one more time, Mrs Foster.'

'I've done nothing wrong!'

Inspector Leach raised his eyebrows. 'Nobody here has suggested that you have, Mrs Foster. But I want a record of your statement – you can start the tape recorder now, WPC. Keddie.'

The big policewoman nudged the microphone a little closer and started the machine with a click. Then she went back to her chair in the corner. Leach continued.

'Later this recording will be typed out for you to read and sign. Now, one more time please, Mrs Foster. From the beginning. Just as you told me when I came out to the house.'

Helen spent a few moments hauling the chaos of memories into a chronological line. She searched for the right place to begin. 'Yesterday morning . . . yes, yesterday . . . Simon arrived as usual, about half past nine. It was very mild – almost like a spring day. Anyway, he looked hot and uncomfortable, as if he'd been running. He and Stuart went out into the garden to play and I stayed in the kitchen with Rachel.'

'Did you often let Stuart and Simon play out of your sight?'

'They weren't out of my sight. I could see them out of the kitchen window. Why are you trying to make me feel guilty?'

'Just establishing facts Mrs Foster. No need to get upset. Go on, please.'

'At about ten o'clock I put Rachel in her cot for a snooze. She's still only little and she sleeps a lot.'

'How old is she?'

'Five months.'

'You've not suffered any symptoms of this "post-natal depression" sort of thing?'

Helen bridled. 'What has that got to do . . .'

Inspector Leach interrupted. 'Facts, Mrs Foster. Any relevant facts.'

She drew on her cigarette for calm. 'No, I haven't.'

'You'll perhaps give us your doctor's name?'

'Doctor Hilary White, Sevenoaks, Kent.'

'Thank you. Go on, please.'

'After I'd put Rachel down, I went out into the garden to look for them. They weren't there. I called out: "Simon? Stuart? Where are you?" There was no reply. I listened. I remember . . . in the silence . . . I could hear the sheep tearing at the grass. I wondered if they could have gone up the lane to look at the horses. But I could see the lane was empty all the way to the top of the hill. I went back into the house. I checked every room. I was getting frightened. I fought down horrible images rising in my mind. All the suppressed fears a mother has . . .'

'What sort of fears Mrs Foster?'

'I don't know . . . accidents . . . awful things . . .'

'Things to do with Simon, Mrs Foster? A big strong boy, a bit funny in the head . . .'

'Yes . . . some things . . . I wasn't easy in my mind. I mean . . .'

'And yet you let him play with Stuart, what – every day?'

'What are you saying, Inspector Leach?' Helen felt anger welling up again. The cold hard weasel eyes held her own, mesmerising her. 'Just come out and say whatever it is you're thinking.'

The eyes turned away to the barred window high in the wall behind her. She could see the bars reflected in his pupils.

'Facts, Mrs Foster. Merely interested in all the facts. So, you couldn't find them in the house. Where *did* you find them?'

'There's an old derelict barn behind the house. I'd forbidden them to play there because it was all filthy and splintery. I went up to the gap where the doors used to be and I could hear whispers. I thought they might be hiding from me as a game. But when I looked in, I could see them in the gloom there, completely absorbed in what they were doing. Simon was sitting cross-legged, with his back towards me. He'd taken his shirt off. Stuart was kneeling behind him. They were both serious, and whispering, whispering quietly. I couldn't hear what they were saying. I took a step closer. On Simon's back – his back was very broad and white – Stuart had been drawing. He had a stick of my lipstick. I took another step closer. It was another of those . . . extraordinary . . . pictures . . .'

'Another?' Leach was leaning forward now, eyes popping, scenting prey.

'Stuart and Simon painted together. I could show you the pictures.'

'Go on.'

'It was like . . . some other pictures they'd done. It was a portrait. It sounds crazy, I know, but even in lipstick on Simon's back it was definitely a portrait . . . of me. I was crying in the picture, and underneath . . .' She stopped and fumbled for a cigarette, lit it. Hoped he wouldn't notice. '. . . crying. So I screamed out . . .'

'Just a moment, Mrs Foster! You said "underneath". What was underneath the portrait?'

This was nothing to do with this Leach. Why had she mentioned it? 'Just . . . letters. Some letters.'

'Does Stuart know his letters?'

'Some of them. Not all of them.'

'Did the letters make a word, Mrs Foster?'

'I'm . . . it wasn't clear. I'm not sure.'

'You must tell me the truth, Mrs Foster.'

She hated him. This was not a matter for the police. This was her own private business. But he had her on his hook.

'I'll tell you. It's not important. There was a D, and an I, a V, an O, an R . . . Stuart was just starting another letter when I screamed out "Stop it!" and ran into the barn, and snatched Stuart up in my arms. Simon stood up at once. He towered over us, a great white half-naked hulk. I backed away. I spoke without looking at him. "Get away from here!" I said. "Get your shirt on and get away! And don't ever come near us again! Do you hear me? Never speak to us again! Go!" Simon burst into tears, and then of course Stuart started up as well. I think I was crying myself by the time I'd carried him back into the house and locked the door.'

'Did your little boy say anything about what they were doing?'

'He just said "But Mummy – we were only drawing! Simon told me what to draw." He was sobbing, and it was hard to tell what he said exactly. I held him close, and tried to quieten him. I held his face against my shoulder so he wouldn't see, and went to the window in the back room upstairs that overlooks the barn. Eventually Simon came out, buttoning his shirt up. It took him ages, he was so awkward. He didn't look towards the house. He kept wiping his cheeks and nose with the back of his hand. At last he set off along the lane, up towards where the horses were. I don't think he knew where he was going or what he was going to do.'

'And how did you feel towards him at this time? Were you angry, Mrs Foster?'

Helen thought back to that moment, watching Simon disappear, holding Stuart to her shoulder while his sobs died down. 'I felt sorry for him. Sorry for the little boy inside him. But I felt angry too – angry at whatever he had been telling Stuart. And angry with his mother. Why was he coming to us for love and attention? To a family of strangers? Why was he walking away now into the hills, instead of back along the road to Mossburn, to his mother?'

The door opened and a policeman came in with a tray of tea things. He put it on the table and went out again. The big policewoman got up from her chair but Leach waved her back.

'I'll be mother, shall I?' He smiled grimly and poured tea for the three of them. Then he lit a cigarette, and carried on. 'So – what did your little boy say later?'

'He kept saying "I want Simon to come back!" Over and over. He asked what they'd done wrong. Of course I couldn't answer him very well – I didn't really know *what* they'd done wrong. But I just knew that I had to stop whatever it was that was growing between them. It was too . . . I don't know. It was as if there was some kind of bond between them, as if Simon could open some sort of doorway into Stuart's mind. It frightened me.'

'And the word "divorce" – did Stuart know what it meant?'

'No, I don't think so.'

'Why do you think it was that particular word that was being written?'

'I . . . I don't know.'

'Mrs Foster – we have to know everything that led up to . . . last night.'

This weasel Leach. What business was this of his? But she

had to answer him. 'My husband is away a lot. Simon . . . Simon knew that things weren't right.'

Leach looked incredulous. 'You discussed your marriage with this boy?'

'Not discussed . . .'

'You confided in him?'

'Not confided.'

'What word would you use, Mrs Foster?'

'He just . . . seemed to know, that's all.'

'Mrs Foster, were you having a relationship with Simon?'

'A what? A *relationship*? Do you mean did I go to bed with him? Good God! This is crazy. Are you seriously saying that?'

'We have to consider every possible fact that may relate to what happened, Mrs Foster. Could you answer my question?'

'Yes, no . . . I mean . . . Good God! He was a child! He was mentally a four-year-old!'

'But not physically.'

'I want to have a lawyer here.'

'No need, Mrs Foster, no need. There will be no charges against you. I'm just trying to get to the bottom of this. That's my job.'

Helen lit up another cigarette. Calmed herself with a deep drag of smoke. 'There was never any question of anything like that between myself and Simon.'

Leach nodded, as if she had jumped through a hoop to his satisfaction. 'Very well. That answers my question, Mrs Foster. Shall we go on? The events of last night, please.'

Helen drew at her cigarette. She didn't want to go through it all again, but this tenacious Leach was like an angler reeling in a fish. She made herself go on.

'By last night, it was getting thundery in the distance. At about eight o'clock, when I went out on the back step to get some wood for the fire, I could smell the rain coming nearer.

I checked that all the windows were shut tight, and read Stuart his bedtime story. He wanted the story of the three little pigs and the big bad wolf who comes to blow down their houses of straw and wood. I would have chosen a more comforting sort of story after the unpleasant events of the day, but that was the one he wanted. When I'd tucked him up and turned on his night light, I went downstairs and poured myself a good scotch. Then I tried to ring John – my husband – but he was out. Thunder was rumbling closer when I put the phone down, and I could hear the first heavy raindrops on the roof.'

Helen closed her eyes for a moment and sucked in the smoke. She pictured herself again, going from room to room in that desolate farmhouse, feeling already the certainty that it would never be a home for the whole family, that John would never come to share any of those rooms, that they would leave the place as soon as she could fix up some sort of alternative.

'I went down to the kitchen, and I was running the taps and gathering crockery to start washing up when I heard the voice. It was outside the back door. "Mummy! Mummy!" the voice went, "Let me in!" I stood stock still, holding my breath. It was Simon. "Let me in, Mummy! It's raining and I'm getting cold and wet!" Then there was a knocking at the door and a shaking of the handle. "Mummy! Please Mummy!"

'I went along the stone passage to the door. I was horrified at the thought of him out there, like a little child lost in the night. But I knew I had to be firm. Who knew what he might do, if he were deranged enough to think I was his mother? I spoke sharply through the door: "Go home, Simon! Go home to your mother! Go home right now or I'll call out the police and they'll come to take you away!" '

'There was a short silence on the other side of the door,

then I heard Simon beginning to sob. "Please! Mummy! Please let me in! Please!" It broke my heart to hear him.

'I kept saying through the door "Go home! Go home!" and Simon seemed to stay there forever, crying, and rattling the knob. Finally he went quiet. I went up to the spare bedroom, which looked out over the back door, and there was still just enough light to make out where he was. Thank God, he was going back towards the road.

'I was jumpy all evening after that, not surprisingly. Every little sound made me start. Rain kept falling, sometimes heavily, and the rumbling of thunderstorms crossing the hills kept shaking the window panes. I went to bed early, and fell into a shallow sleep, full of anxiety.

'In the middle of the night a loud clap of thunder woke me up. I looked at the luminous dial of my alarm clock. It was half past one. Just as I settled my head back on to the pillow I heard a creak on the stair. I went rigid. It's ridiculous, but I wanted to pull the sheets over my head and hide. Then I thought of the children.

'I called out "Who's there?" There was no reply, but as I strained to hear something, Stuart's voice came to me. It sounded as if he were singing something, very faintly, out on the landing. I got out of bed and went to my bedroom door. There was Stuart, in his pyjamas, just coming up the stairs. His eyes were open, but glazed over. I realised he must be sleepwalking. He stopped at the top of the stairs, and now I could hear what he was singing:

> "Humpty Dumpty sat on a wall,
> Humpty Dumpty had a great fall,
> All the King's horses and all the King's men
> Couldn't put Humpty together again."

'I called out very softly to him: "Stuart? Are you awake?" but he started his song again at the beginning, walking slowly towards his bedroom. He climbed into his bed and pulled up the blankets around him, still mumbling

". . . All the King's horses and all the King's men
Couldn't put Humpty together again."

'Then he turned his face into his pillow, and straightaway he seemed to be in a deep sleep. I went back out onto the landing. I wondered what Stuart had been doing downstairs. I was frightened. I called down. "Simon? Simon? Are you down there?" There was no answer but the thunder and the rain. I called again, louder: "Simon? Are you in the house, Simon?" Again, there was no reply. But the house felt different. I started to go down the stairs. Somehow I knew there was something down there. I got down to the dark hall. Nothing there. I went to the kitchen door, pushed it open. Flicked on the light.'

Inspector Leach's eyes were boring into her. The policewoman, Helen noticed, was sitting forward on the very edge of her chair. She stubbed out her cigarette, which had grown a long tail of ash in her fingers.

'The first thing I saw was a litter of felt-tip pens strewn on the floor and the table. There were papers with drawings all over the table. In the dark, in his sleep, Stuart had been drawing. And writing – using the alphabet he only half-knew. Words like "Mummy", "Simon", and – there it was again – "Divorce". Then I saw one big picture. The colours were mainly black and red. There were ugly rooks circling in cloudy skies. There was a house made out of straw, leaning and derelict. In the garden of the house was a tree. And hanging from the tree on the end of a rope was a heavy body.

'I stared and stared at the drawing. I tried to understand. As the thunder rolled lower and lower into the distance I finally realised what it might mean. I fetched my heavy raincoat from the hook in the hall, and got my boots on. From the broom cupboard I took out the big torch, and I got the carving knife from the kitchen drawer. I hauled the aluminium stepladder from under the stairs, and went to the back door. I unlocked it, and went out into the pouring rain. Simon's body was swinging from a branch of the oak tree in the garden. I cut it down. His body fell on to the grass.'

She looked at Inspector Leach, as if he would somehow be able to help. He turned his eyes away for the first time.

'I was too late, you see. I should have let him in, out of the rain!'

Through the sudden assault of her tears, she heard Inspector Leach speak to the WPC. 'You can switch off the recorder now, thank you.'

The funeral service took place four days later. Helen left the children with her mother, who had come up to help look after them while she packed up the house ready for leaving.

There weren't many people in the kirk, and Helen identified Simon's mother easily enough by her solid build. She was sitting in the front row of course, but she wasn't wearing black. Perhaps she didn't have a black dress.

At the end of the service Helen waited by the door. She didn't know what she was going to say. But Simon's mother approached her with a wan smile.

'Mrs Foster?'

'Yes.'

'How do you do? I'm Simon's aunt. Who he lived with.'

'Oh . . . I'm terribly sorry . . .'

'Aye. He was a lovely laddy!'

'But I thought he lived with his mother?'

'Oh dear! I really should have visited you, when Simon first started spending time at your hoose. But I don't have a car you see. I tried to ring, but I never got through.'

'There was something wrong with the line. No one could ring me.'

'Oh dear. Listen – I live just around the corner. Have you time to have a cup of tea with me? I've something to show you.'

It was a small house for two such big people to have shared. After their cup of tea, the aunt took Helen up to Simon's little bedroom. It had a window looking out to the steep hillside at the back. The aunt rummaged in a drawer for something while she continued the story she had started downstairs.

'Aye . . . well, as I was saying, when he was four, his father went off and left them to live in Canada. He was never any good, that man. Now my sister, God save her, she'd always been – well – a bit weak in the heid to be honest. Now when, you know, her man – and they were never marrit by the way – when he went off, that sent her completely . . . you know . . . doolally. She was aye greetin' and hoping he'd just be back for her any day. She couldn't understand, y'ken? It was a' too much. Anyway, she couldn't look after Simon properly, and . . . well, to cut a long story short, she ended up in an asylum and Simon ended up with me.'

'But he told me all along that he lived with his mother, like I said.'

'Aye, well . . . that was just Simon. He never accepted it in his own heid that she'd been taken away. She died years ago – when he was eight – but he's always talked as if she were still around. Just gone out to the shops, or visiting a friend, y'ken. Something like that.'

The aunt had found what she was looking for – a big envelope – and shut the drawer. She sat down on Simon's bed, and looked up at Helen.

'When he first told me about you, he called you his mummy. He was that daft, I didn't pay too much attention. Maybe I should have.'

She opened the envelope, and took out a sheet of paper.

'Here we are, here's the picture. He did this a long time ago, but I kept it because it was that good.'

As soon as Helen looked at the picture it was familiar. It was just like those strange paintings Stuart had done, first on his own, and then together with Simon. Crude in some ways, with rough brush strokes, but such clear unmistakable images for all that. There was a line of people, holding hands. Herself, and Stuart, and a baby, and another little boy that might have been Simon when he was younger. A bright-yellow sun shone down on them all from a blue sky. Simon's aunt was watching her face. 'That's you, isn't it, Mrs Foster? You and your weans.'

Helen nodded. She couldn't speak.

'He did that when she died, all those years ago.'

Then they were both crying, arms awkwardly around each other's shoulders, side by side on the bed. The sun came out and made a little square patch on the wall, investing the faded colours of the old flowery wallpaper with fresh life and vigour.

When Helen got back to the farm, her mother was standing by the kitchen table. She looked up sharply when Helen entered the room. She held a piece of paper in her hands. Helen noted the mess of paper and paints on the table.

'Helen – just look at this picture of Stuart's I've found. It's quite extraordinary.'

Helen took the picture. There was the line of figures again – herself, Stuart, the baby, and Simon. Just the same as Simon's picture. A bright-yellow sun shone down from a blue sky. Before she could react, or feel anything, Stuart himself came running in. His face was happy for the first time since Simon had "gone away".

'Mummy! It's sunny outside. Will you take me to see the horsies?'

Helen put the picture back on the table without a word. Then off they went up the road to see the horses, and the winter sun sent their shadows dancing along the ground before them.

CUL-DE-SAC

A pine coffee table for the sitting room. That's what it all started with. A very simple objective. Where could I buy a small pine coffee table? Balancing Yellow Pages on my knee, I phoned the Pine Emporium.

'Coffee tables, madam? Yes, we have coffee tables in a variety of shapes and sizes.'

'Where exactly are you?' I asked.

'Are you coming by car?'

'Yes.'

'Just drive down MacMahon Road. We're on the left at the end, just before the park. You can't miss it.'

*   *   *

I set off in an optimistic mood. Since I'd moved into the flat I'd been putting coffee cups down in odd places such as the floor, the mantelpiece, the window ledge. I needed some system, a bit of order. I looked forward to my coffee table. To sitting in front of it and lowering the cup, or mug, into its proper place. Next to a newspaper, or a magazine. Probably on a place mat – I'd have to get some of those too. Leading a neat, orderly existence. So different from the way I'd carried on before going to the hospital.

MacMahon Road was familiar at the top end. There was a butcher's I'd used to use on the corner. But it was a very long road, and it became less familiar the further I drove down it. Its commercial instincts also became less and less certain. At the top, butcher's, baker's, newsagent's, video-hire shops. Half way down, shops that looked like good ideas but weren't – hand-painted furniture, book exchange, model boats and planes. At the bottom end, junk shops, launderettes, shops with desperate-looking people standing at their doorways. And, especially, 'To Let' signs. The bottom end of MacMahon Road was not thriving. It was not a promising setting for a Pine Emporium.

'Just before the park,' the man had said. I drove past a flat expanse of grass traversed by paths. Some leafless trees were forcing themselves upon the landscape. This must be the park. Which meant I'd gone too far. I'd envisaged the Pine Emporium as a large and welcoming place, possibly with its own car park, bustling with excited newly-weds eyeing up pine wardrobes. Perhaps serving free coffee to its customers. Its locale seemed to make this unlikely, especially as it was possible to drive past without seeing it.

MacMahon Road was clearly coming to an end a couple of hundred yards ahead, where there was a T-junction. A huge building with blank brick walls, possibly a warehouse, barred the way implacably. There were no yellow lines here. I decided to park and walk back.

There wasn't a lot of traffic on the road. In the park a gaunt old man was walking a thin mongrel and a fat old lady was walking a fat dachshund. They crossed paths without a nod, even the dogs ignoring each other. Perhaps they used to be married.

Beyond the park I walked slowly past the shop fronts. 'You can't miss it,' he'd said. The desperate owners of the shops observed my movements. I felt conspicuous. My skirt was too short, or too long. My jacket was too bright, or too tight. I was wearing too much make-up, or too little. There was something wrong.

There was also no sign of pine. Even at walking speed. The nearest thing was a timber merchant, signposted down an alleyway. You could hear the sound of a buzz saw, as if a gigantic bee had flown in there and become trapped. I decided I would make enquiries here, on the basis that wood would form a bond between businesses.

At an open double door at the end of the alley, I stopped and looked into the workshop. In a warm golden haze of sawdust, the workers wore brown overalls. They were old, mostly. I cleared my throat and they saw me. One of them approached, white moustache at the ready. The others stopped working to watch.

'I wondered if you could help me? I'm looking for the Pine Emporium.'

He took off his thick dust-filmed glasses in order to think. He looked nonplussed. 'Pine Emporium?' he said, as if considering a miracle or a vision. 'Just a moment please, madam.'

White moustache consulted with his fellows. Some shaking of heads and some nodding. Hands pointing to all parts of the compass. A tendency to drift off back to work. He returned.

'We think it's up MacMahon Place. Carry on up the road to the first turning on the right. That's MacMahon Place.'

'Thank you!' I said. He nodded, and walked me to the entrance of the alley.

'Up there!' he pointed unambiguously. 'Up there and turn right.'

The first turning to the right was called Stubbs Lane. It was a narrow lane which turned a sharp corner after about thirty yards. I went along it. On either side there were tall stone-built tenements. The ground-floor windows all had dirty net curtains, or blinds. Turning the corner revealed more of the same, terminating in a cul-de-sac. I turned round to head back to the main road.

There was a youth in a black leather jacket standing half way along the lane. He'd either come out of a doorway after I'd passed, or he'd followed me in from MacMahon Road. He'd got his hands in his pockets, and he was leaning against the wall, looking into space. He was so still that you would have thought he'd been there all along. Like a chameleon.

I had to pass him. He turned his head as I approached and gave me the look that women hate. The one that starts at your face, travels down as far as your knees, then back up to your face again. I set my eyes out of focus, staring blankly ahead of me as I passed him. I heard an intake of breath, sensed a slight movement, felt panic, quickened my pace.

'You're looking for the Pine Emporium?' he called after me. His voice was too old for his body.

I stopped and looked back. He had almost no hair. A blank face.

'Yes. How do you know?'

'Heard you asking.'

'But I didn't . . .'

'See me. No. But I heard. Do you want me to show you?'

I didn't want his company. Not his or anybody's. I just wanted to be alone. In a pine emporium.

'Is it near here?'

'Quite. But you need local knowledge.'

Again his eyes flicked down across my body. I willed him to shrivel up and die. Spontaneously combust, leaving just a little heap of ashes. But he persisted in existing.

He detached himself from the wall while I hovered uncertainly.

'Follow me,' he said, and headed back into the cul-de-sac.

'There's no way out down there,' I protested.

He spoke over his shoulder. Flatly, matter-of-factly. 'Yes there is. It's a short cut.'

I followed him at a little distance. I was ready to turn and run. Or scream. There must be people behind these tattered net curtains, like spiders sitting in their cobwebs. I was in a public place.

The young man reached the end of the cul-de-sac and vanished into the wall. Then his hand reappeared, and waved at me to follow.

Only when I was right in the corner at the end of the cul-de-sac could I see the alleyway which lay between the two sets of tenements. It was more like a tunnel, with an arched entrance The young man was already making his way along it, his shaved head bobbing in the half light like an egg shell. I let him get even further ahead, then followed warily. Why was he helping me? How had he heard me asking the way?

The alleyway twisted and turned. Every time I came to a corner I half-expected my guide to be waiting for me with a knife in his hand. But he was always well ahead, bobbing along without a backward glance.

Finally we emerged into a small enclosed square. It was like one of those unexpected and secretive piazzas you come across in Venice. But ugly. The buildings around it looked like warehouses, or factories. There was a scum of old cardboard boxes and litter around the edges of the space. At each corner was an alleyway, like the one we had come through. Too narrow for cars.

The young man went towards the alleyway diagonally opposite our own. He turned briefly.

'Wait there a minute!'

Then he was gone.

A minute. Two minutes. Five minutes. I paced up and down. All right, he hadn't mugged me or indecently assaulted me. But was he just a malicious prankster? Why had he left me here, in this horrible square? I looked at my surroundings closely. Blank brick walls gashed with illegible graffiti. Small blank metal doorways in recesses, silted up with rubbish. And silent. Not a sound from the surrounding city came in here. Nor birdsong, nor wind. It was like a vacuum, which nature abhors.

As I paced up and down, I felt an oppressive claustrophobia pressing in upon me. My chest felt constricted. The air in this square didn't contain enough oxygen for proper breathing. It brought back the memory of my room at the hospital, with its door locked at night. Blank walls, scarred with prints of flowers, always flowers. Bright, garish, intimidating flowers like admonitions: 'Be cheerful, be cheerful, be cheerful . . .' At least there were no flowers here. But the bright colours of the graffiti were like flowers too. I had to get out of here.

It was then that I realised I didn't know any longer which was the alleyway I'd come in by, or which was the one the young man had vanished into. The four corners of the square looked identical. I peered into all the entrances in turn. Each one was the same, a dim stretch of blank-walled passageway, turning a corner after about twenty yards. I picked one at random, and walked quickly along it. It twisted and turned like the one I'd come along before, but eventually it ended in a tall gate with iron bars. The gate was fastened with a heavy chain and padlock. But I didn't want to go through the gate anyway. Because beyond the gate was another square like the one I'd left behind, a blank litter-filled space with alleyways at each corner.

I went back and tried a different alleyway. Again it snaked its way through high indifferent walls until it reached a barred gate. I leaned against the bars and looked through.

The interior of a vast warehouse stretched away into the distance. Pine furniture stood in serried ranks like a huge silent army, waiting for orders. Wardrobes, beds, cupboards, bookcases, kitchen dressers, tables – and coffee tables. Quite near to me I could see dozens of coffee tables, exactly the sort of coffee tables I'd pictured for my flat. They were perfect.

I tried the padlock which held the gate shut. It was firmly locked. I called out.

'Hello? Hello? Is there anybody there?'

My voice sounded small in that huge space, like an irrelevant fly buzzing on a window pane. I tried to shout as loud as I could.

'*Hello! Hello!*'

There was a movement somewhere in the pine forest. A rustling of paper. Then someone came into view from behind some wardrobes, holding a newspaper. A young woman, in some kind of uniform. She walked unhurriedly towards me, folding the newspaper. She had terribly short hair. She looked just like the young man in the leather jacket. A twin sister.

'Yes?' she said, not coming nearer than ten yards from the gate. I pointed at the coffee tables.

'I'd like to buy a coffee table. For my flat. Could you let me in?'

She laughed. 'What? Through there? You can't come through there!'

'Why not?'

'Not allowed. You should know that.'

Why should I know that? I felt a flush of anger suffuse my face. 'This is ridiculous. I've got money in my bag, and I want to spend it. Are you turning away a customer?'

She laughed again. 'Oh no, we never turn a customer away! We're obliged to take everyone who comes.'

'Well stop arsing about and let me in then.'

Her face hardened. 'That's enough of that sort of cheek. Now go back and have a lie down. The door will be unlocked at the usual time.'

I felt tears of impotent rage starting to come into my eyes. I blundered back along the alleyway into my square. Even with blurred, watery vision I could see that it had diminished. It had a ceiling. Paintings of flowers where the graffiti had been. A bed. I lay down and waited for morning to come.

Lost/Lust

I would appear to be rooted in solid soil. I'm sitting in the sunlight of a summer evening in my garden, shaded slightly by our apple tree. My wife Claire and our children are playing catch with a tennis ball. I would appear to be reading the newspaper.

But my eyes are unfocused on the print. I feel as if I am on a journey in endless space, peering through a porthole at unknown nebulae. This feeling comes over me often now. A feeling of being lost. It has its beginnings in events many years ago, when I met my first girlfriend, Alice.

*   *   *

I was sixteen, fuelling my courage with cider at the annual school disco. A friend pointed out a girl to me, sitting at a table with her friends. She was called Alice, he said, and had asked him what my name was. As I looked over at her a strobe light twitched on and the room began to pulse between black and white, carving zebra statues frozen in attitudes of frenzy out of the hot darkness. The girl Alice tossed her head and turned towards me, her long mane of zebra hair settling back on to her shoulders in a series of strobe-sculpted snapshots of crystalline grace. I felt lust for this equine creature, a desire so urgent that my shyness could not prevent me from acting. I stumbled over to her table, and shouted something that was lost in the music. But she smiled, and followed me to the dance floor where we gyrated amidst the crowd, all conversation made impossible by the pounding beat. After a while I shouted again, and she followed me to a dark corner. Alice looked at me and tossed her mane, releasing a sudden assault of scent. Lust gripped me again, and I found my mouth drawn towards hers by an undeniable gravitational force. She closed her eyes and so did I. We collided in blackness, like planets pulled from their own orbits. Our mouths docked in a sliding slack-jawed Cherry-B and cider-flavoured tussle. Our tongues we kept to ourselves. We were, after all, only sixteen.

When we began to meet in daylight, uninfluenced by alcohol, I found that Alice was tall and slender, like me. Her legs in particular were thin, and her feet turned slightly outwards, which gave her a vaguely duck-like gait. She had long, light-brown hair, and regular, quite attractive features. But she had reproachful eyes, even then. To me, she was the personification of femininity, a planet hitherto beheld in the distance, wondered at, unreachable. Now I could feel its contours, hear its thoughts, bask in its possession. Only gradually did she become a person to me. I began to consider myself in love.

We were a couple until we left school, and we took it for granted that our long-term future was to be together. We went to different colleges – I to Leeds to study medicine, she to art college in Birmingham – but we saw each other every weekend. For me though, after a year or so, there was a gradual sense of decline in these meetings. They evolved into a numbing routine, filled increasingly by Alice's talk of jobs, houses and babies. By the time I was twenty, I was beginning to doubt whether I wanted to be tied to Alice for the rest of my life.

I might have drifted on, uncertain of what to do, but for a decisive turn of events. My parents announced a move to America. My father was being offered a five-year contract there. I was smitten with envious excitement, and after long and complicated enquiries about visas and qualifications, I found out that I could gain the opportunity to continue my studies there. I hardly hesitated.

Alice crumbled like a broken wall when struck by the news. I had forced myself to tell her in person, but could not have prepared myself for the extremity of her reaction. She cried beyond all possibility of comforting, cried as if it were a madness which would never release her. I waited until finally she slept through sheer exhaustion. Then I left.

The trickle of painful, tearful letters went on and on. For two years I struggled to bury my guilt in the deepest, darkest place I could find. Eventually, once the letters finally stopped, I had buried it so deeply that it could only surface rarely, in troubled dreams.

I live in York now, with my wife and three children. Claire is a teacher, and we married twelve years ago. In the time we've been together, Claire and I have gradually fallen out of love. We've become a working unit, a cooperative for bringing up the children, whom we do love. We don't talk about it. It's too threatening to acknowledge it – we just get on with life. I'm a doctor – a surgeon – and have attained a degree of recognition in the medical world by pioneering certain micro-surgical procedures. The extra hours I've had to devote to research, and writing up and demonstrating my discoveries, have not assisted the smooth running of our marriage. We sleep in the same bedroom still, but in twin beds. We might have sex once in a while, if we've been at a party and had a few drinks. But it's unusual. We're a typical couple, in many ways.

A year ago, a little before my fortieth birthday, I was in London for a conference, and I found myself in an unexpectedly restless frame of mind. London was made for restlessness that summer. There was an extraordinary warm wind scurrying through its streets, and the weather reports said that it came from far in the south, bringing with it grains of sand from the Sahara. There was a sort of hazy yellowness about the air, and the windscreens and paintwork of vehicles acquired a thin film of dust.

I gave my paper on the first morning of the conference. We were in a strange echoing auditorium where my voice seemed to set up a rush of sound in the domed roof, as if a flight of birds was up there, searching for the way out. But when I looked at the faces of my audience I saw no sign that anyone else was disturbed by the phenomenon. I found it hard to keep going, reading my words mechanically, unaware of their meaning because I was preoccupied instead with their metamorphosis into birds as soon as they left my lips.

At lunchtime I was kept busy with discussion about my paper, and gratified by numerous expressions of enthusiasm and appreciation. I took my place in the body of the hall afterwards, to hear the next presentation. It was on a topic quite closely related to my own, but as I listened, the birds resumed their flight, and I found myself drifting away into thoughts and feelings which seemed as random as movements of the warm wind which could still be sensed even indoors. As I sat there in a trance of birds and currents of air, I gradually became aware of a tremendous urge to get outside. As soon as the paper was concluded, while clapping was sending sharp pistol-shot echoes around the dome, I got out of my seat and out into the afternoon heat. I walked quickly away from the conference hall, knowing that if I hung around near the door, someone would engage me in conversation. I didn't know where I was going, but I loosened my tie with a sense of impatience and stuffed it into my jacket pocket. I slackened my pace after a few hundred yards, and for an hour or so I strolled the streets at random.

It was four o'clock, and the pavements were busy, but without that ant-like frenzy which characterises the period when work has just finished and people strike out for home. My thoughts were unfocused. I suppose it's been such a rare thing in my life to be alone, completely alone, that I don't know what to do with myself when I am. I felt as if an invisible puppeteer had just released my strings, but, like Pinocchio, I had a residual mischievous will of my own. In that hour of wandering about before returning to the conference for the teatime seminar, I began to feel a sort of freedom. It was partly attributable to my sense of a job done – my paper had been delivered and well received. But it was also to do with anonymity, with the feeling of being dissolved and absorbed into the faceless multitude in a city far from home.

As I sat, half-listening to the final paper of the day, my vague feelings began to coalesce around a simple idea, a simple small rebellion. Tomorrow I was going to miss all the conference proceedings, and just head off into London, like a piece of driftwood carried on the currents of a river.

That evening served to do two things – it increased my impatience, and revealed to me something of the nature of my sense of restlessness. After the conclusion of the day's business, I found myself swept up into a group of my colleagues and, in a fog of medical chatter, deposited in a corner of an Italian restaurant in Soho. My companions were mostly older than myself, and were earnestly intent on dissecting the day's proceedings. Frequently I fell out of the conversation and looked, as if through a high impenetrable wire fence, at lively animated groups at other tables, at couples sharing subdued intimacies, at the waiters making jokes between themselves and flirting with the women customers. What in particular took my eye on a number of surreptitious journeys was a woman seated with a couple of her friends directly opposite me. She was petite, about thirty years old with black hair. Her face was very thin, but fascinatingly appealing. Her features composed themselves into endless expressions of delight, horror, amusement, disgust and surprise as she talked with her companions. I became preoccupied with watching her. I knew that she was out of my reach, that I would never speak to her or even meet her eyes, but this impossibility fanned the flames of my impatience. I almost reached a point where I felt I would stand up and astonish both my medical colleagues and the woman herself by walking across to her table and saying to her: 'You are the most beautiful woman I have ever seen. Please accept my invitation to join me for lunch tomorrow.'

The notion of such an absurd act filled me with cringing embarrassment, but its converse, sitting and sipping my coffee, distractedly nodding to a conversation about bone-marrow transplantation while she paid her bill and left my sight forever, filled me with a sense of cowardly self-loathing.

But the incident, or non-incident, had caused my sense of restlessness to take shape and solidify. I found that I was gripped by the unfamiliar, or at least indistinctly remembered, emotion of lust. When the black-haired woman had gone I found myself looking around for other attractive women to watch.

At the end of the evening, we left the restaurant and headed back towards our hotel in a group. At the lurid doorway of a sex cinema, framed by pink light bulbs, a girl in a short spangly skirt pouted and beckoned to us. Some joke was made and we hurried on. At that moment I decided that what I would do the next day was seek out a prostitute.

I had never been to a prostitute before, but I had often seen their cards in London phone boxes. French lessons a speciality, or curvacious young lady seeks attention. After breakfast I returned to my hotel room and waited until my fellow medics would all be settled down for the first session of the day. Then, feeling as if I were being watched, I went out to a phone box near the hotel to collect some of these cards. I took them back to my room and after much hesitation, I made a call. The woman who answered was friendly and business-like, and we quickly made arrangements to meet at a tube station entrance.

An hour later I emerged from the precipitous escalator tunnel and passed through the ticket barriers. I picked out the woman immediately. She had her back to me, but I knew from her description it was her. She was wearing a blue tee-shirt and short black skirt. She carried a blue shoulder bag. Her hair was shoulder-length, copper-coloured.

For a moment I hesitated. I was about to take a step into unknown, shameful territory. Something that had only existed inside my own head as a powerful but vague impulse was about to take shape and form. Another human being was involved. It seemed too real. I stood stock still, uncertain of what to do. Then she tossed her hair back and seemed to look at her watch. The movement of her hair as it settled back on her shoulders had a crystalline slow-motion grace that fired up my lust, blotting out every other consideration. I moved forward, like a fish being reeled in, hooked. The hooker turned as I spoke, my words sounding ridiculous, formal: 'I believe you're waiting for me?'

She was turning, turning, the object, the object-to-be of my lust. Turning, as her face turned towards me, into a human being. A living, real, human being. I gasped 'No!' as our eyes met, locked, widened.

'Oh my God!' Her face crumpled into disbelief or shame or horror. I felt as if I had stepped off a cliff and was plunging downwards. 'Alice! I can't believe this. Alice?'

We stood like window-dummies, two feet apart, plunged into an invisible turmoil that shut out everything around us. The rushing passengers, the litter blowing in the warm wind, the noise of traffic outside the tube hall – it all fell away into a distant world.

Alice broke the silence. 'Andrew? Was it you I spoke to on the telephone? Oh, if only I'd known.'

What could I do? I felt paralysed by the situation, unable to regain any sense of control over what was happening. The coincidence seemed so overwhelmingly apt, so clearly fated to confront my new infidelity with my old guilt, that I felt in the grip of some supernatural force. And my old guilt was fiercely, suddenly redoubled. Why was Alice reduced to this? Alice, whom I'd once loved, whom I'd always hoped would meet someone else, be happy, raise a family. Why was she doing this? And then there was my own sense of shame, which brought a sudden rush of blood to my face. What would she think of me now, wanting to buy sex? A trick, a john, a punter.

Alice recovered her speech before I did. 'Andrew – you're

grey!' I looked at her gratefully. Tried to smile. Looked at the lines on her face, under the make-up. She tried to smile too. 'Do you . . . do you want to come with me? For a coffee? My place is just around the corner.'

I nodded. We walked, side by side, along the busy main road outside the tube station. There was a street market. Reggae music blasted out at intervals from the stalls, mingled with the cries of the vendors. It meant we didn't have to speak. After a hundred yards, we turned off into a side street, immediately leaving the hubbub behind. Tall Victorian tenements made a dark cool canyon of this side street, and to my ears our footsteps rang out like thunderclaps to tell everyone to look out of their windows. Alice indicated a door with green paint peeling away from its surface, and unlocked it with a familiar movement of her head to clear the hair from her eyes.

We climbed a flight of stone stairs past two landings until we reached a door with Alice's name on it. Just her Christian name. We still hadn't spoken since we left the tube station. She opened the door and we went in. An old woman poked her head unexpectedly into the hall.

'It's all right, Jenny. I know this gentleman. You can take a break for a bit.'

Not meeting my eye, the old lady brushed past us with her copy of the *Sun*, and left the flat.

'The maid,' Alice said. 'My protection.' She led the way into a sitting room, quickly gathering up some girlie magazines off a coffee table and throwing them into a drawer.

'Sit down,' she said, indicating a settee. 'I'll put the kettle on.'

I sat on the settee, looking around the room. There was nothing personal about it. Some of the furniture looked as if it had come from the cheapest self-assembly kits while other pieces were obviously battered relics gleaned from second-hand shops. The pictures on the walls were prints of flowers in plastic frames. There were one or two dusty plants. No books. A radio. A small television.

The window veiled with net curtains a view of rows of identical windows across the street. I listened to Alice moving about in the kitchen, and wondered what we were going to talk about. An absurd cowardly desire just to get up and run away, through the door, down the stairs and off, came over me. But guilt held me in place, this time. Guilt, and something else. A mixture of curiosity and something better – concern, I might call it. A belated emotion, since I had smothered my concern for nearly twenty years, thinking I would never meet Alice again. Thinking that somehow, somewhere, she would have got along just fine.

Alice came back in with the coffee. 'Still one sugar?' she said. I nodded. She spooned in sugar and handed me the mug, then sat down opposite me on the only other chair, a kitchen chair.

'So, what brings you to a prostitute?' she said neutrally, taking a sip of her coffee.

'It's something to do with this weather, this hot weather.' I felt like an idiot as soon as the words were out.

'Aren't you married?'

'Yes. I am. I . . . don't live in London.'

'No. You live in York. Thirty-four, Ploughdown Road, York.'

This simple statement hit me like a whirlwind. I was thrown into the air, disorientated. 'How do you know where I live?'

'I wanted to know. Then. It was ten years ago you bought that house. I didn't actually know if you were still there now. At that time I was thinking of approaching you. But not later.'

'Why were you thinking of approaching me? Why didn't you?'

'I was in some trouble. Heroin. You were a doctor. But I got out of the trouble for myself.'

'Are you still . . .'

'I've been clean for five years.'

'But then, why . . .'

'Why am I a hooker?'

'Yes.'

Alice lit a cigarette. 'It's a long story. It started with smack. But now – well, why are you a doctor?'

'To help people I suppose.'

'I do that. And you're well paid?'

'Yes.'

'So am I. And you can have a nice house, and look after your family, and afford to use London prostitutes?'

'I've never been to a prostitute in my life.'

'Don't bother to seem respectable in my eyes.'

'It's true. This . . . you . . . it would have been the first time.'

Alice laughed then. It was a genuine laugh, but brittle. A new kind of laugh, that she must have acquired in the many years I hadn't known her.

'Your first time! And you got me! Do you think fate is trying to tell you something?'

'I don't know what to think. I was on some sort of fantasy trip. Escapism. Trying to scratch a kind of itch.'

'With a human scratcher.'

I felt worse and worse. She took another pull on her cigarette. A nervous, long drag. She seemed to be more in control of this situation than me, but the strain was showing in her slightly trembling fingers.

'I'm sorry if I'm making you uncomfortable, Andrew.'

'Let's not fight, Alice. I . . . I've felt guilty about what I did to you all my life.'

'Guilty or sorry?'

'I couldn't do otherwise at the time. It was just something that happens to human relationships.'

'You stop loving people? Like your wife?'

'It wasn't just as simple or as sudden as that.'

'It seemed sudden to me. One day you came and said you were going to the States. For several years. And I wasn't invited.'

Guilt was smothering me like a blanket. I wished I hadn't come to Alice's flat. What good was this doing either of us? I tried to gulp my coffee quickly, and burnt my tongue. Alice leaned forward, scrutinising my face.

'Poor Andrew. I shouldn't remind you of all this, should I? Painful memories. How's your wife? Is she still a teacher?'

'Just started going back part time. She stopped . . .'

'For the children. I know. I've got children too.'

'Have you? I'm really pleased, Alice. You always wanted a family, didn't you?'

'I said I'd got children, not a family. Their father was a complete bastard. I haven't seen him for years. I don't want him to have anything to do with them.'

'I'm sorry. How old are they?'

'Eighteen. Twins.'

Something seemed wrong. My children were much younger. My mind grappled with numbers. 'Eighteen? But . . . you're thirty-nine, the same as me, aren't you?'

Alice just nodded once. She pulled on her cigarette and leaned back to exhale, eyes narrowing in the thin stream of smoke. She watched me.

I was in quicksand, sinking. Eighteen – thirty-nine – she had them when she was twenty-one. When we were *both* twenty one. The unspoken question hung, absurdly melodramatic, in the air between us. I made myself speak it.

'The twins – am I their father?'

Alice stubbed out the cigarette. 'Would it make any difference now if you were? They've grown up now. You've missed all that. And they think their father is dead. Which he is, to all intents and purposes.'

I stood up, too agitated to stay still. I walked to the window, then back to Alice.

'Alice – all those letters – you never said anything about being pregnant, or children. How do I know you're not just making this up? Is this your idea of revenge, after all these years. A cruel joke?'

Alice looked at me. Her face was white. The voice was little more than a whisper. 'How dare you call me fucking cruel!' She stood up and fetched her handbag from the kitchen. Rummaging, she found a small wallet, and pulled out of it a photograph of herself with two teenage boys. I studied their faces for any trace of familiarity, without success. I could see Alice in them, but not myself.

'You would have told me, Alice, in your letters. Why wouldn't you have done that?'

Alice looked straight at me. Her eyes were surgical instruments of rebuke, cutting into me without anaesthetic. 'Because if you wouldn't come back to me for my own sake, I didn't want you back at all.'

'Alice – that was wrong! How do you know what my feelings might have been? You didn't give me a chance!'

'I begged you to come and see me!'

Tears were coming into my eyes. The room was a sub-aqueous, dissolving world. 'I didn't know! I thought it was best to make a clean break.'

'So did I, in the end.' She put the photographs back into her wallet. Looked at her watch. 'I'm meeting another trick in twenty minutes. You were only booked in for half an hour, Andrew.'

I dabbed at my eyes with a handkerchief, uncertain of what to do. Alice spoke very clearly. 'I want you to go now. I've said too much.'

'No – you've not said enough. I can't just walk away. Not now.'

'I don't need you, Andrew. Not now.'

'What are their names? The boys?'

'Philip and Richard.'

'How do they . . . what do they need?'

'Nothing from you. They're doing fine. Their father would be proud of them.'

'You can't go on like this . . .'

'Like what? Doing this?' Alice pulled a face. 'Getting too old, am I? Oh, don't worry, I have no illusions. If you're not supporting a drug habit and you can stay out of the clutches of pimps, you can make a lot of money at this game. I'll be able to retire in about five years. Build a new life somewhere – a nice place, where the boys can visit. Perhaps I'll be a grandmother one day.'

'But what do they do? Are they at college? Do they work?'

'No more questions. It's time to go, Andrew.'

I pleaded with her to tell me more, but Alice just shook her head. The only words she would speak were 'It's time to go.' I found myself being ushered out of the flat. She walked down the steps to the street door with me. It felt like I was going down into a deep well, from which I would never escape. Alice held the door open, and I stepped out mechanically, desperately thinking of some way to establish a connection, find out more. Alice read my thoughts.

'Don't bother ever coming back here, Andrew. I'll be moving somewhere else quite soon. You have to keep moving around, or else the neighbours tell the police.'

'Can't I at least give you something? Something for the boys?'

'I don't need anything from you now, Andrew. Goodbye!'

She shut the door. I looked at the patterns on its green peeling surface, searching for a country I could recognise in the outline maps of bare wood fringed with flaking paint. Alice's footsteps receded up the stone steps inside. When I could hear the sound no more, I understood that I was completely lost.

Like a piece of driftwood I somehow found my way back to the tube station, past the the street vendors and their stalls blasting out a jumble of noise. Everything was ghostly, insubstantial, and empty. What burned with reality inside my head was the edifice of the life I hadn't led, the family I hadn't had, the mistake that I'd made, and the guilt that would sit on my shoulder and chatter in my ear like a familiar for the rest of my days.

So here I am, sitting, as I said, under the apple tree in my garden. A year has gone by, and I've kept my grip on this life I lead – my work, my marriage of collaboration, my children. Here comes my youngest daughter now, running up to tell me something. I prepare to slip back into my world. But still at times it seems provisional, uncertain . . . only one of many possible lives which I could have led on this wandering planet.

A Golden Thread

I wash and sew and clean for Señora Madison, and in return she gives me a little money – a very little, always apologising – 'You deserve double this, Juanita. I'm so sorry.'

'It's all right, Señora Madison,' I always reply. 'Your English lessons are my real pay.'

I want to speak good English because it will help me in my career when I leave college. I am going to be a successful film actress. Señora Madison always speaks to me in English, although her Spanish is excellent, if rather old-fashioned. Sometimes I wonder if the English she is teaching me is of the same vintage. Señora Madison is eighty.

The washing and mending and cleaning don't take up much of my time anyway. Señora Madison has seven long skirts and seven cotton blouses, worn in strict rotation. In winter she uses one of her two cotton jumpers with buttons at the front – 'cardies' she calls them. Most of the time she sits at her window, watching the aeroplanes coming and going like great roaring grey birds. The airport is only three kilometres away.

Her apartment is very small and very easy to clean, since she has almost no possessions. All of the walls and ceilings are white, and when the sun strikes in through opened shutters, then sharp black shadows join us and mimic our every movement on those blank surfaces.

There are no ornaments except for two black and white photographs on her dressing table. One shows a handsome man with a fine dark moustache and a piercing gaze which follows you about the room. He is posing stiffly in a suit in front of a broken column at some archaeological site or other. That is Carlos, her dead husband from Madrid.

The other picture shows a young woman in spangled tights and a plumed head-dress like a peacock's tail. It is taken from below, and the woman is balancing easily on a tightrope, holding a long pole with a small round weight at either end. That is Señora Madison, at a time when she was Señorita Madison. She went back to her maiden name when her husband died.

Señora Madison's English lessons are always the same. We start off with me reading some article to her from *The Times*. Raoul fetches her a copy about once a month from the airport bookshop. She listens to me with her head tilted slightly to one side, like a bird listening for worms, and pounces on any mispronunciation. Then we have a little conversation in English, which always turns ultimately in the same direction. Towards the past and her fame as an acrobat and death-defying tightrope performer. The path to her past may twist and turn unexpectedly through a thicket of other topics, but it's always going to lead to the same place.

When we get there, Señora Madison always tells me the same things with the same words. Her dull eyes almost sparkle as she dredges up this ancient history with relish and gusto. I've never been certain if she thinks it's all new to me (her short-term memory is quite imperfect) or if she just doesn't care, as long as I continue to sit and listen. When it's time for me to go she returns to the present moment as if she's coming to a funeral. Her crest falls.

I retell her stories to Raoul, and he adds his own little comments until we are clutching each other in helpless hilarity on my mother's sofa. My mother goes to bed early and reads magazines on Friday and Saturday nights when Raoul comes around – to give us a little privacy, she says. But she can hear every word, and sometimes when we've forgotten she's there, her voice floats like a ghost through the wall 'What was that about Señora Madison's admirers in Paris, Juanita?'

I have no idea at all how Señora Madison got the impression that I didn't take her stories seriously. Oh, I believed her that she was an acrobat and so on. But she exaggerated everything. To hear her talk, she was the queen of tightrope walkers, the toast of the profession. Confidante – nay, mistress – to half the crowned heads of Europe, who flocked to her performances and visited her dressing room afterwards in droves. The hat stand at the door groaned with crowns. I kept my face composed and stored it up for Raoul.

But one day she looked at me severely when we sat down at the table beside the window for my weekly 'lesson'.

'I wonder, Juanita, if you appreciate how famous I once was?'

'Of course, Señora' I replied demurely.

'Because I now lead a quiet life, you perhaps think I exaggerate?'

'Not at all!'

'I *chose* to lie low for a while, Juanita. The pressure, the adulation, the endless exercises and training . . . it all became too much for me.'

'That's understandable. It must be hard to stay at the top of such a profession.'

'It is. And I wouldn't settle for lower standards. But now I'm ready again for the challenge.'

She fixed me with those pale watery eyes of hers and waited. I didn't know what she wanted me to say. Her words didn't seem to make any sense. Ready for what challenge?

'Oh yes,' I said, hoping to buy time and get a little more information.

'Yes. I am ready for the world again, Juanita. Tomorrow I will begin to train again. My public has been deprived for too long.'

'You're . . . you're going to . . .' I faltered.

'Walk the tightropes of Europe. Yes, my dear Juanita. The yawning chasm of the future will be spanned by a single golden thread. I will walk that thread.'

I must have looked like a goldfish, gulping open-mouthed.

'You must help me, my dear. *Will* you help me?'

My mind had raced into Doctor Sugero's surgery, where I was explaining to him that Señora Madison had gone mad. That was the only sort of help I thought I could offer her. But I nodded blandly.

Señora Madison's crinkled road map of a face folded happily into a smile.

'I knew you would, my dear. And, who knows, you may find yourself in the limelight too. An association with myself will do no harm to a budding talent such as yours. You may meet all kinds of influential people.'

Then she pushed her chair back and stood up as straight as an old thorn tree on the edge of a sea cliff. She reached towards the ceiling with her fingers splayed out. The sun almost shone through the thin parchment-like flesh. The shadow on the wall behind her looked far more substantial.

'I am ready to soar like an eagle!' she said.

Neither Raoul nor my mother were in favour of resorting to Doctor Sugero, for different reasons.

Raoul anticipated more evenings of hilarity on the sofa: 'Give the old lunatic her head, humour her; let's see what she gets up to!'

My mother's motives were more pragmatic: 'You'll only upset Señora Madison, if she finds out you've been running about saying she's gone mad. And then where would your wages and your English lessons go? *I* can't afford to send you to college if you don't earn a little money too.'

The next time I visited Señora Madison, I joined her in a whole series of contortions remembered from her acrobat days. She stretched and bent her old body this way and that, and I copied her. She was not discomposed by the failure of her limbs and torso to deliver the goods.

'It's bound to take a little time to loosen up, after so many years of laziness!'

She insisted however that I should push myself – 'a lithe young thing of sixteen!' – and that night I could hardly sleep for my aches.

This went on for three weeks. Señora Madison must have been doing her exercises conscientiously every day, because at each weekly interval I could see the improved strength and flexibility in her body. On the sofa, Raoul enjoyed composing items for the local paper. 'Octogenarian to run marathon!' for the sports pages, and 'Old lady with renewed vigour seeks able-bodied young men' for the personal columns. I heard my mother tittering through the wall at that one, although she maintains a front of prudishness at all times.

On the fourth weekly visit after Señora Madison's initial announcement of the resumption of her career, I finished my cleaning duties and came to the table for my English lesson – supplemented nowadays with a course of exercises – to find a small pile of bank notes heaped up. It was not, however, a reward for my services.

'I wondered if you could do a small piece of shopping for me, Juanita, dear? Down at the ships' chandlers at the harbour?'

Ships' chandlers? What on earth were they? But it became clearer.

'I want you to buy me a length of ship's rope – best quality, medium weight – about forty feet long. Do you think that's enough money?'

I counted the pile of notes.

'I don't know, Señora. I've never bought rope.'

'Well, come back if it's not enough and I'll get it later. I'm saving up, each week.'

Señora Madison received a small pension from the state. Her husband had been a civil servant of some kind – not an archaelogist as I had at first assumed from the photograph. I knew the amount, and tried to imagine 'saving up'. She must have been going without food.

'What do you want rope for, Señora?' I asked, naturally enough. I had an unpleasant premonition, and was proved correct. Señora Madison motioned me to her window, which looked out across the narrow street towards the identical window of Señor and Señora Penata, who owned a bakery down below.

'You see the little railings outside my window, Juanita?'

There was a small ornamental balcony outside the window with railings. Pots of geraniums occupied it.

'Yes.'

'And over the street – about thirty feet away – Señora Penata's?'

'Yes.'

I didn't listen very carefully to the rest. I was too busy thinking about how I could possibly stop her.

I decided to secure a breathing space by taking the money but not seeking out any rope-sellers.

There was a sensation in our neighbourhood that week when a person fell out of an aeroplane into someone's back yard. A stowaway or an illegal alien or someone of the kind, trying to hide in the wheel compartment. They must have dropped out as a plane took off and roared over our roof tops. Since it happened in the hours of darkness, nobody knew anything until the householder – Carlos Pereira, who is a waiter at the Excelsior – opened his door in the morning and found his dog standing guard over the body.

It had made a small human-shaped crater in the packed earth of the yard and I went to see it, like everyone else. It hardened my wavering intention not to buy a rope for Señora Madison.

But my courage failed me the next week when I turned up, ropeless, at her door. Instead of reasoning with her, as I had intended, I found myself paltering out excuses for not having carried out my errand. She pursed her lips slightly, more in an expression of determination than anger.

'I could go down to the harbour shops myself. How frequent is the bus?'

Señora Madison hated to go out. She looked at me. I crumbled.

'No . . . no. I'll go this afternoon, Señora.'

'So she's got the rope?' Raoul said, the next evening.

'Yes,' I replied.

Raoul painted a vivid picture of Señora Madison prancing back and forth along the line stretched out above the street while the local urchins peered up her long skirts. I felt he was being unnecessarily cruel, and my mother was quiet too, on the other side of the wall.

'What's the matter?' he said at last, when he finally realised that he was giggling unaccompanied.

'I don't know. I feel it's my responsibility to stop her being stupid.'

I assumed, I don't know why, that Señora Madison would proceed no further without my aid. But Señor Penata had cheerfully assisted in the rigging of the line. It was common in our neighbourhood to sling clothes lines from house to house and to use broom handles or long sticks to hang and retrieve the more distant linen. He had, he said later, only commented that such a strong rope would probably outlast the houses themselves.

Her death was as sudden and comprehensive as that of the aeroplane man. Although she fell from a relatively modest height, she succeeded in landing on her head, and snapped her neck. Like the aeroplane man she had fallen silently at some time in the night, and only at dawn was the body found. I imagine she was trying to perfect her technique in private, determined to appear utterly professional on her first public appearance.

Raoul had no more jokes to make on the subject. My mother looked as if she shared my feelings of guilt. After all, she had discouraged me from speaking to Doctor Sugero.

There were no relatives at the funeral. Just ourselves and an equally remorseful Señor Penata and his wife. Afterwards, in the absence of anyone else's interest, I took possession of Señora Madison's two photographs.

I look at that image of the dazzling, confident tightrope walker. It makes me feel better. I was fond of Señora Madison, and I think that a moment of terror as she fell in the darkness to an instant death was probably not the worst fate for her. After all, it saved her from having to face the chasm of the future in the knowledge that she would never cross it on her golden thread.

Hairpin Bend

The road bent back and forth like a paper clip, doubling and trebling on itself, hanging on to the edge of the land with the blue lava of the Pacific down there on the right, waiting to drag you in. Davis beetled his Volkswagen lazily around the curves. There was no hurry; the road was clear. He was on his way to San Francisco, meandering down northern California, taking his time. He was on holiday for a month. He might never go back to work, the way he felt right now. He might just drive for the rest of his days, on these lazy highways.

It was good to get away from things. Breaking up with

Cathy had shaken him up. He couldn't concentrate in the office. He broke up a chair one day. Ordinary grey swivel chair. Smashed it to bits. Cut his hand ripping out the metal springs from the inside of the damned thing. A long vacation was the boss's idea. He could do his mental repair work in the car, mulling things over, looking for the silver lining. Maybe that was the silver lining down there, that line of white where the ocean met the land? It made him feel good to see it anyhow. Swing, wing, gliding along. He hummed a sort of a tune. Swing, wing, gliding along. The sun was warm; it was a great day to be out. Great. Life was just great, wasn't it?

'Eureka' the cardboard sign said. The cardboard sign was being held out by a man standing on the edge of the road. He was on a tight bend, where Davis had to slow right down. The man was tall and thin, with long black hair and sunglasses that looked like a fly's compound eyes. He was as thin as a stick. Thinner. Davis had slowed down to a stop fifty yards past him before he had realised he was going to give the guy a lift. It just grew out of his new feeling of peace and calm. Also, he wouldn't mind a bit of company, just for a while. He'd been on his own for a week and Eureka wasn't too far ahead – maybe thirty miles.

The black-haired man reached the car, and Davis leaned over to pull open the passenger door for him.

'Hi! Appreciate it,' the man said as he climbed in. His long limbs squashed up against the dashboard.

'That's fine,' Davis said. Then he put the car into gear again and pulled off.

'My place is about ten miles this side of Eureka, but it's easier just to write "Eureka".'

'Sure.'

The man folded his cardboard sign as small as he could make it. It wouldn't go into the pockets of his checked lumberjack zip-top. None of them. Eventually he put it on the floor at his feet.

'I'm Mickey!' he said. 'Squeak! Squeak!'

Davis half-turned. 'Squeak?'

'Mouse – you know. Kind of a little joke. My friends call me Mickey Mouse. Some of my friends.'

'Oh, yeah. My name's Davis.'

'Pleased to meet you, Davis. I was stood on that bend for near on an hour before you came along. Road's awful quiet today.'

'Yeah.'

Mickey wound the window down on his side of the car, and put his elbow out.

'Mind if I have the window like this?'

'No problem.'

'You on holiday?'

'Yep.'

'Must be nice. I been up here to see my lawyer.'

'Your lawyer lives near that bend on the road?'

'Sure – well, a couple of miles away. He's got a beach house.'

Davis waited. He knew he only had to wait.

'My lawyer's a pretty smart guy. Trouble is, he wasn't home.'

A shriek caught Davis's attention. Seagulls were gathering around a rocky point off to the right, on the edge of the Pacific. They were circling and screaming. In a minute their razor-sharp bills would dive into a shoal of fish. They'd hit like a hail of bullets. What if something came at you like that, out of nowhere, out of the sky, tearing the life out of your silvery little body?

'I needed to see my lawyer because the state is trying to say I'm not insane. And if I'm not insane, I don't get my invalidity paychecks any more.'

'You're insane?'

'Certified insane, yeah. I don't need to work.'

Hitch-hiker strangles VW vacationer. Mad Mickey croaks car owner. A writer of *National Inquirer* headlines got to work inside Davis's head.

'So . . . why does the state think you're not insane any more?'

Last squeak for Mouse's victim.

'You don't work for the State of California in any capacity, do you Davis?'

'Nope.'

'Well, the truth is, I never was insane. But I came back from 'Nam pretty shook up, and I couldn't stick with anything, you know. I'd hold a job for a week, two weeks, then I'd wake up one morning and I couldn't do it any more. Sometimes I'd just break things apart, I was so mad inside. So I read up about invalidity benefits and I decided the best thing would be to go insane.'

That made more sense than going in and destroying a grey swivel chair, Davis thought.

'So – how did you do that, exactly?'

'Well. I started out by stealing some chickens. Then I plucked those chickens and stuck the feathers all over my body like I was some sort of big chicken myself. Stuck 'em on with glue. Then I just lay there in my room awhile until they came and found me. Took them three days. I said I was a coward for the way I acted out in 'Nam, and this was my punishment.'

'That must have made a pretty good start.'

'Yeah. It was a little obvious maybe. But they're very understanding here about Vietnam vets. They know we'd got shook up a little. A couple of doctors got me certified so I could settle down without having to worry too much about getting a job.'

'Did they know you weren't really insane?'

'I don't know for sure. I mean, I never let on I was

faking it, and if they thought I was faking it, they never said so.'

The road was straightening out a bit. The Pacific came and went off to the right. Sometimes there were some low hills in the way. There were more trees – mostly twisted cypress or thorn – buckled by the winds and spray.

'So you're on vacation, huh, Davis?'

'Yep. A whole month's vacation.'

'Where you headed?'

'San Francisco.'

'You been there already?'

'No – you?'

'Sure, a few years back. Golden Gate Bridge . . . Chinatown . . . Oakland . . . Bart . . . You know what "Bart" is?'

'Nope.'

'Bay Area Rapid Transit. Kind of a subway train thing. So are you in a hurry to get down there?'

'No hurry at all. I'm just taking my time.'

'Why don't you stop off at my place – it's right off this road in a few miles? Sit in the sun and smoke a joint.'

'I might just do that.'

It was one of those mobile homes that could never ever be mobile. Any effort to move it would shake it to bits. It was a few hundred yards off the highway, surrounded by a big area of scrub thorn and some dwarfish pine trees. Not too far away you could hear the sea smashing its fist into a cliff. Davis got the ice box out of the car and opened them a couple of beers while Mickey went inside and brought out a small bundle of newspaper. They both sat down on the step of the mobile home and Mickey carefully opened the folds of the paper and set about making a joint with the dried-up leaves of cannabis inside.

Davis sipped his beer and smelled the sea spray in the air. This side of the mobile was sheltered and warm. Mickey lit the joint and took a couple of long drags. Then he passed it to Davis, and he took the smouldering tube between thumb and forefinger and inhaled a slow deep pull of the sweet-smelling smoke. Pleasure rushed tingling into his chest and his head and his limbs. Then the wave retreated, leaving a wash of calmness. Mickey grinned at him.

'Good weed, huh? That's from Oregon.'

'It's good, yeah.' Davis shut his eyes, feeling the warmth of the sun on his face and the brightness of it through his eyelids. He was grateful to Mickey, bonded in this simple moment of happiness with him. For the first time since Cathy had gone he felt peace inside him. Deep peace. It lasted maybe a minute. Then he heard an engine.

A motorbike came bumping along the rough track from the highway, invisible through the scrub until it was almost upon them. It was a hog, a ground-hugging machine with ape-hanger handlebars. The rider lay rather than sat on it, his spiky red hair resting against a tall backrest topped by a Maltese cross.

'Oh shit!' Mickey muttered as the bike came into view. 'Oh shit!'

The biker skirted around Davis's parked beetle, scanning it with raised eyebrows. Then he drew up to the step and turned a wide cold smile on to Mickey. He had a face that was nicked with small scars like a football field with small wedges of turf kicked and hacked out of its surface. He had the coldest eyes Davis had ever seen. He switched off his engine, but stayed sitting on the bike.

'How you doin', Mickey Mouse?'

'Okay. You?'

'Well – I had a long ride over here. Four hours. You get my letters?'

'Letters?'

'Sure. Letters.'

'Nope. I didn't get no letters.'

The biker turned his gaze to Davis. 'How you doin?'

'Fine.'

'Friend of Mouse's?'

Mickey butted in. 'He just gave me a lift, that's all. We were just . . .'

'Being dopeheads. I can see that. Well, pleased to meet you . . .?' He raised his eyebrows.

'Davis.'

The biker leaned forward and shook his hand. It was like letting a snake crawl over your skin. 'Pleased to meet you, Davis. I have a little business to discuss with Mouse here, if you don't mind.'

Davis made to get up, but Mickey put his hand on his shoulder. 'You stay right here Davis. Ain't nothing private.'

The biker turned his cold eyes on Davis. 'But maybe you've got a long way to go, and you mustn't let us hold you back.'

Davis looked at Mickey. He was white, but he didn't repeat his request for Davis to stay. The whole scene felt bad; it had gone from a blissful moment of peace and calm to a bad scene in a flash. Who was this motorcyclist? What 'business' did he have with Mickey? Davis didn't want to know. He drained his beer and stood up.

'Well – nice to have met you, Mickey.' He didn't meet Mickey's look. Then he nodded to the biker, and walked back to his car. He felt uneasy turning his back on the spiky red-haired man with the cut-up face. He was the kind of man you kept in your line of view. He got into the car, fired her up, and reversed into the open ground in front of the mobile. He turned the car around and drove back the few hundred yards of track to the highway. Before he was out of sight, he stuck his head out of the open window and waved. Mickey and the motorcyclist remained motionless, watching his departure, like a freeze frame at the end of a movie.

*   *   *

He drove for twenty minutes. Was it the dope that had made the scene seem so bad? On the empty road Mickey's white face and insect eyes appeared. Davis blinked, and the spiky-haired biker took Mickey's place, hovering so vividly in his mind's eye that he seemed to be stuck on the windscreen. Should he have stayed? He pulled in at a small diner in Eureka, and ordered a coffee.

He looked through the window at the street with its line of hoardings for motels and Kentucky Chickens and Taco Belles. He looked at the formica table top and his hands resting beside his coffee cup. Cowardly, guilty hands. Biker says scram; Davis ducks out. The fun of driving to San Francisco had vanished like a block of ice thrown into a furnace. He felt torn by curiosity, guilt, indecision. How could he go on with his carefree holiday in this state of mind? He drained his coffee, paid the waitress ('Have a nice day, sir!') and headed back north, the way he had come. Every mile of the road a voice in his head – probably the headline writer – was telling him to turn around and get on with his life. Davis dices with Destiny. Davis heads towards definite deep shit.

When he got to the turn off to Mickey's place, he drove beyond it and parked in the pine trees a few hundred yards on. Then he made his way quietly on foot back towards the vicinity of the mobile home. As he approached, he could hear the roar of a motorbike revving and braking. The surf-laden breeze carried the sound louder and softer as it gusted, but it didn't sound as if the bike was going any place. It must just be driving around and around. As he got nearer still, he could hear excited whoops and shouts on top of the noise of the engine. He stopped. His stomach was twisted in a tight anxious knot. He wanted to forget this. But it was too late to go away now. He had to finish it.

He worked his way through the scrub and trees until he was right behind the mobile, with its flaking green paint and pock marks of rust. What if he was seen? What possible explanation could he give for creeping around here? What if the biker had beaten Mickey up – or killed him even? The roar of the motorbike continued, going around and around the open space on the other side of the mobile home.

Fear almost stopped him breathing as he lay down flat on the ground, and wriggled on his elbows into the space under the corner of the mobile. Almost afraid to look, he peered out.

From here he could only see the wheels of the motorbike going by. The bike went quickly past where he was, then seemed to hit something out of his line of view, which slowed it down. The rider whooped at this point, then circled around to repeat the process. Davis withdrew from his position and made his way to the other corner of the mobile home, where he would be able to see more. Slowly, moving as quietly as a spider, he pulled himself forward inch by inch until he could see.

He almost cried out when his gaze was met by that of the red-haired biker, who was lying on the ground thirty feet away. His eyes still had that hard, dangerous glare. But his mouth hung open, and his body lay twisted in a pool of dark blood. Each time the motorbike hit the torso, the head jerked upwards as if the body were coming back to life. Then it slumped back into the dirt as the wheels scrambled over and Mickey circled around for another run, his long black hair flowing behind him, his naked body daubed with blood.

As Davis sneaked away back towards his car, the sound of Mickey's whooping grew fainter, until it was lost in the screams of seagulls and the pounding of the sea.

Way later, Davis saw the lights of San Francisco up ahead under a sky which was beginning to hint at dawn. Behind him lay a long dark road. He'd been thinking a lot, driving through the night. He wasn't going to go to the police about what he'd seen. They'd find out, or they wouldn't. Only God knew if a man like Mickey should be punished. Only God knew what he'd seen or done in Vietnam.

Now he felt tired but unexpectedly elated. Somewhere around Ukiah he'd found himself singing the unbidden words 'It wasn't me, oh no, it wasn't me!' to the tune of some forgotten pop song. At first it seemed obvious what the words meant – he was alive wasn't he? By Santa Rosa it had dawned on him that the song had a different meaning. He remembered how he'd ripped the guts out of that swivel chair. The blind, insane rage that possessed him then. Paddling his toes on the edge of a sea of darkness. But near Eureka he'd found what it was like further out in that deadly sea, how even a nice guy like Mickey could find himself way out there, buffeted by waves of madness. As he drove over the Golden Gate Bridge, the black waters of the bay rippling harmlessly beneath him, Davis felt surer than ever that he was headed for dry land.

After the Party

I've not stopped drinking since the night of the party. This piss-awful blue-label vodka – they should pay you to drink it. The distillery's in Nasijek, along the valley, but it was closed down last year. Not because they'd been poisoning the local populace for a century or more, it was just that the workers had all pissed off – more important things to do I suppose. Luckily I'd laid in stocks, just in case.

There's been no work done around here either, not since the party. I've thrown slops to the pig, but that's about it. Now the frosts have stopped, we should be turning over the fields for the sowing. I said as much to Maya, my wife, but she doesn't care. More pissed than me – just lies there, grinning.

Yesterday at dawn I had a hell of a fright. I'd stumbled to the door from wherever I'd been sleeping, woken by the light, and everything was flooded! There was a sea where my fields had been. Then I realised it was a thick white mist coming off the ground. It was high enough to hide the tops of the new trees at the end of the east field. Gradually, I became aware of some sort of movement above the surface of the mist, a long way off. It got clearer – a kind of waving snake-like line. Clearer, and closer – Jesus Christ! It was a sea serpent! It had a long neck and a small head, and it was coming silently and steadily towards the farmhouse.

I was in a cold sweat, I can tell you. I couldn't move or speak. Like a nightmare. Then I managed to find my voice. 'Maya! Maya!' I yelled, as if she was my mother who would come and wake me up. The lazy cow couldn't be bothered to shift herself, but the sea monster stopped moving and looked straight at me. It must have been about a hundred yards away. Then it turned and ran away, and I recognised that it was a giraffe! I could hear its hooves – do giraffes have hooves? – splattering the mud of the field. Then the splattering turned into clattering. It must have reached the Nasijek road. I lost sight of it, and the sound of its feet diminished to nothing. Stupid thing must have turned north, because the next thing I hear is an explosion. Every fool knows that the road north is covered in mines.

It was only the bang that made me certain it wasn't just a vodka giraffe. It must have come from the zoo at Vinkivci. Christ knew what else might have got out – lions and tigers probably. I went back indoors to get my bottle.

Anyway, that was yesterday. This is definitely the second day after the party, and now it's dawn again, as far as I can tell. Sky's just a grey blot, but it's light enough to see outside. I may be pissed, but I'm ready to give the men their orders. Where are the idle pissheads? Their bikes are all here, leaning in a line against the wall of the barn.

Every morning they ride out on these bicycles from Kasalje just before dawn. I often see them coming – the land's completely flat going that way, and you can pick out their bicycle lights in the dark, like little twinkling stars in a line. Not that they all set off together, but they must meet up on the road sometimes, by chance.

There's three of them. There's Streten, who's older than me even, with a face like a wrinkled-up old apple. He's a cheerful one, full of jokes, even though he's had a hard life. One of his boys was killed last year, but he even made jokes about that. Said he'd be building a barricade around heaven, to keep his father from coming in and ordering him around as usual. His favourite son too – the youngest.

Then there's Vojin. Strong as a boar. Big sloping shoulders. Bit of a reputation in Kasalje as a ladies' man. Sometimes he's at the barn well before dawn, sleeping in his clothes on a hay bale. Never been home all night I suppose. No family – lives with his mother, who doesn't know half of what he gets up to.

The last of my three musketeers is Relya. Intellectual. That's what some of the other farmers call me, just because I've a few books in my house. But Relya is cleverer than me. He's never without a book. Carries one around in his pocket and sits and reads while he eats his bread and cheese. You never know how to take him. He'll say crazy things with a straight face, and then make the most ordinary comments with a lop-sided grin like he's winding you up. He gets on some people's nerves that way, but we're all used to him. He's got a nice family – they all come out for the harvesting when we need them.

I ring the bell on Relya's bike. It makes a rusty churring sound. Did they leave their bikes here after the party? But surely they wouldn't have walked home? Too pissed to ride? I'm uncertain again whether the party was last night or the night before. But then the giraffe was definitely yesterday. It's no use having a watch, with this vodka.

Could it be that I'm late, and they've set to their work without waiting for orders? They know what's to do as well as I do, after all the years they've been working for me. Yes – something tells me they'll be clearing out the ditch that takes water from the stream into our pond. That gets choked up with stuff every winter. Not that it's a job anyone likes doing – back-breaking work – but I have a feeling they might be there. I set off in completely the wrong direction. One minute I know what I'm doing, the next I'm off in the clouds. They really ought to shoot the people who made this vodka.

Anyway, I about turn and head for the ditch. In the event, I do find one of them there. It's Vojin. The ditch is dry, because it's still blocked up nearer the stream. But I can't believe it's a good place to sleep. He's lying in there like a great hummock, curled up like a baby. I shout down at him to wake up. 'Vojin! Come and help me muck out Boris!' Boris is the pig. But Vojin's out for the count. It takes a hell of a lot of vodka to stop Vojin; he's so big. I feel I should get him out of the ditch, but I couldn't possibly shift him on my own. I seem to remember seeing him in the ditch before, but I'm confused about whether it was a long time ago, or just after the party. I sit down for a moment to think.

That was some event, that party. Fireworks like you've never seen! The whole sky lit up. Went on and on – an all-nighter. Maya, me, Streten, Vojin and Relya, we all hit the bottle together. They didn't want to leave. Relya's family was away on holiday to Split or somewhere. Vojin's mother was away at her sister's. Streten was a widower. So none of them had any big reason to want to go back to their own houses. Vojin got talking about some girl he wished was with us. But then she was married, so she'd be partying with her husband instead. Vojin was drinking like a fish. But I've got crates of this stuff.

We were totally out of it by the time the crowd from Krusnica turned up. We'd reached that stage when we'd run out of energy and were just slumped about, hardly even talking. We were watching the fireworks over Kasalje, mesmerised. But when the Krusnica lot arrived we got a second lease of life.

They were a wild bunch. I knew one or two of them by sight, from market days. Most of them were strangers though. Naturally I was anxious at first, but they just seemed to want a good time. They livened us up all right. They dug out the record player and we had some dancing. They hit the blue-label even harder than we had. I saw one guy – big red-headed man nearly the size of Vojin – down a whole bottle in a oner. That would kill some people.

We drank to keep up with our guests. Maya went to heat up some soup. She was the only woman at the party, so she was loving it. She'd been whirled around the room to the music until she was dizzy. What if she was sixty-five?

There was a hell of a big bang over at Kasalje while Maya was off heating the soup. We all rushed out of the door to look – except for one or two who had passed out. There was a big fire – too big for a bonfire – somewhere in the middle of the town. Must have been an accident. We watched it for a bit. I heard Relya getting into some stupid argument with the Krusnica lot. They all went back inside, shouting, and I went behind the barn. I thought I'd have a piss. Let them calm down a little. Whatever happened, I never got back into the house. I must have passed out somewhere – in the barn I think. I think I remember lying with my cheek on rough straw, hearing more shouting from the house. Although that could just have been a dream.

I leave Vojin in the ditch. Streten and Relya are obviously not turning up for work. My vodka bottle's nearly had it, but there's more inside. Even those bloody fish from Krusnica didn't know I had a cellar full of the stuff. They turned the house upside down. Even pulled my poor old books off their shelves. Pure mischief – they couldn't have expected to find vodka behind my books.

Maya should sort it out. I've got work to do out here. I go in and shout at her, not for the first time: 'Maya! Maya! Get this place sorted out!'

But she just lies there on the kitchen floor, grinning.

THE PRIEST OF
TEPICOAPAN

P adre Sebastian hunkered down behind the dry-stone wall. The low evening sun behind him cast his shadow grotesquely long and thin against the pale loaves of stone which concealed him. He was a black vengeful spider, hot in his cumbersome cassock. He was in good time.

On the hillside behind him, tinkling goat bells made languid music. Cicadas added their notes too, from the long brown grass of a dry gully off to his left. He was aware of these tranquil sounds, but their calm was at odds with his mood. He had prayed that God should provide him with thunder and lightning, not an evening like any other. But God often let one down.

The priest risked a look over the top of the wall. The cemetery on the other side was empty except for Herminio, the grave digger. The glint of his shovel could just be seen, as it rained showers of earth up into the blue sky. Padre Sebastian craned up another foot. Yes – beyond the far wall of the cemetery the mourners could now be seen. They were winding up the road from Tepicoapan in a thin black line, preceded by the coffin. And in the coffin – by far the best place for her – was Luisa Emilia Obregón.

Padre Sebastian loaded two red cartridges into the barrels of his shotgun. Then he leaned the gun against the wall and, reaching down, grasped the lower hems of his cassock to twist them up between his legs and tuck the cloth into his leather belt. It was important that he should be able to run unhampered if necessary. Squinting through a chink in the wall, he observed the little procession enter the cemetery by the bottom gate. Fat Padre Felipe from Machiza was in charge, unctuous religiosity and sweat dripping off him in equal measure as he overtook the coffin and led the way to the grave. Herminio, the grave digger, scrambled out of the pit with alacrity, as if reborn, and Padre Felipe waved him away with the silver crucifix he carried.

Then, as the coffin bearers turned towards the grave, Padre Sebastian saw Pablo for the first time. It was unmistakably him, even after twenty years. He wore a suit, and his face was red from the exertion of carrying his mother on her final journey. She had borne him into the world, and now he bore her out of it. A lock of black hair fell forward into his eyes, as it always had done. For a moment, Padre Sebastian regretted what he was going to have to do. As the bearers reached the grave side, he cocked the hammer of his shotgun.

Pablo had not been to Tepicoapan since he was a child. His mother's death had brought him back like a ghost to its dusty streets, surprised to find that he still made footprints in the ground of a world he had departed so long ago. His parents had sent him away to school in Mexico City when he was seven, where he lived with his grandmother in her big house in the suburb of Coyoacán. They always came to stay at his grandmother's for the school vacations. There was plenty of room, and they enjoyed the change, they said. But gradually he had come to feel, without much caring about it, that they were keeping him away from Tepicoapan.

It was just a *pueblo* like any other – a jumble of white houses clustered around a plaza. The church was the only building of any distinction, with its facade covered in a diamond-patterned motif, and little stone figures of angels and cherubs and saints cropping up at every architectural opportunity. The facade terminated in a roof with the outline of a coat hanger, topped by a cross, and to the left was an ornate bell tower. Pablo stood before the church for a while. It seemed like a building he had visited in a dream, familiar and eccentric.

As he walked around the village, only the smallest of changes could be discerned: the *almacén* on the corner of Calle de Obreros had reinvented itself as a 'supermercado' without becoming one iota larger or more comprehensive in the range of goods on its gloomy shelves. Television antennae had sprouted from every roof top, and there were even a couple of satellite dishes, but the inhabitants of Tepicoapan, it seemed to Pablo, might as well have been privileged to observe life in some corner of the Andromeda galaxy as to know what went on in Mexico City 300 miles away. How could it have any bearing on the lives they led here? Everyone seemed old. The friends of his parents, who clutched him in bony embraces of sympathy, gave him the feeling that Tepicoapan was no more than a waiting room for death.

Pablo had never expected his mother to die at all, least of all in Tepicoapan. She was a forceful, proud woman, who would have wished for a larger stage for her demise. She had always talked of its being only a matter of time before she and his father moved to Mexico City, to begin 'real' life. But Ignacio Obregón, although deferring to his wife in most things, had never given in to her wish to leave Tepicoapan. The compromise had been the long school holidays spent at Pablo's grandmother's house in Mexico City. That way Luisa Emilia got enough of city life for her husband's peace and quiet. And they continued the habit long after Pablo finished school, and his grandmother entered her eighties, as vigorous as ever.

The manner of Luisa Emilia's death had been strange. A poisonous snake had somehow found its way into her bedroom and bitten her on the foot. Ignacio spoke to Pedro that evening on the telephone, and reported that her leg was bloated and covered in purple blotches. Neither of them had anticipated that this condition would rapidly spread to all parts of her anatomy, finally dispatching her the next day at about the time that she would normally have been preparing lunch. The snake itself was never seen by anyone else, and among those who did not personally hear Luisa Emilia's vivid description of its attack, there was some disinclination to believe in its existence. No-one could remember seeing a snake before in Tepicoapan.

As the mourners gathered around the freshly dug grave, Padre Sebastian rose unseen from behind the wall, thirty yards away, and levelled his shotgun at the coffin.

'Stop!' he shouted, and they turned and saw him. There was an outbreak of panic, whose most extreme manifestation was the instant prostration of Padre Felipe on the ground. He lay with his face in the dust, his silver crucifix held aloft to ward off evil. Pablo's father, Ignacio, was one of the few who kept his head.

'Padre Sebastian!' he called. 'What on earth are you doing?'

The voice that replied was tight, like a clenched fist. 'Take the box and bury it at the town dump! That witch shall not rest in holy ground!'

Padre Felipe spoke from the ground. 'Padre Sebastian! Be reasonable! Señora Luisa Emilia was one of your congregation for more than twenty years! Of course she should be buried here!' He ventured to get up on to his knees. 'Think of the upset you're causing Ignacio and their son Pablo!'

For answer, Padre Sebastian fired a blast over his head. The noise seemed to fill the entire sky, and fandango birds burst screaming from the eucalyptus trees beyond the cemetery wall. Then, as the birds vanished, the loudest sound in the whole world was the sound of Padre Sebastian cocking the hammer for his second barrel.

Padre Felipe led the rush for the gate. Pablo and the other three coffin bearers swayed uncertainly under their burden, but held their ground. Ignacio too stood like a rock amidst the black retreating tide of the other mourners. Then he opened his arms in appeal and began to walk towards the priest. 'Padre! Sebastian! How long have we known each other? Be reasonable!'

The shotgun pointed at his chest. It shook a little. Padre Sebastian hadn't expected this.

'Come no nearer, Ignacio! Your wife was not a true member of God's Church. Satan sent the serpent to claim her as his own. She cannot be buried in hallowed ground. I told you not to bring her here! But no, you went sneaking around to Machiza to get that fat pretend-priest Felipe to come and do your dirty work!'

As Padre Sebastian talked, Ignacio advanced steadily and calmly, step by step. He was only twenty yards away now, his eyes fixed on the priest's in dumb entreaty.

Pablo called out, his voice quavering. 'No, Father! Leave it! We'll do as he says!'

But Ignacio kept walking. He spoke: 'Come on, Padre Sebastian! I know what this is all about!'

'Stop, Ignacio! I don't want to hurt you!' Padre Sebastian felt the fires of hell. Thou Shalt Not Kill. The shotgun wavered, pointed down towards the ground at Ignacio's feet.

'Please – put the gun away, Padre, and let's talk.' He kept walking. He was only five paces away. Padre Sebastian closed his eyes and squeezed the trigger. The gun jumped bruisingly against his shoulder, and Ignacio dropped to the ground with a cry.

Pablo darted forward, abandoning the coffin, which slithered out of the grasp of the other three bearers and tipped into the grave, landing upside down with a thump. Padre Sebastian opened his eyes, stood horrified for a moment, then scurried off like a black beetle along the edge of the cemetery towards the village.

Ignacio looked up at his son with a grimace. 'The crazy bastard shot me in the foot!' He waved his hand towards the grave. 'Let's finish burying your mother, then you can carry me to Doctor Ortiz to get the pellets out.'

The coffin fitted so snugly into the hole that Herminio had dug that it was impossible to right it. So they had to settle for Luisa Emilia being buried upside down in holy ground, and threw symbolic handfuls of earth on the coffin's base. Padre Felipe could complete the blessing later, and they would ask Herminio to enlarge the grave, so that Luisa Emilia could be the right way up for the feast of the Día de los Muertos, when the whole village came to eat and drink by candlelight with their dead.

Pablo and the other bearers took it in turns to carry their new burden piggy-back down the hill to the village, where

Dr Ortiz, who had been one of the mourners, was just taking a brandy in his sitting room.

'What a business!' he muttered as he set to work removing the pellets from Ignacio's foot. 'Your family is cursed below the ankle Ignacio. Your poor wife is the first person to be bitten by a snake in living memory in Tepicoapan, and now you – the first person in Tepicoapan to be shot in the foot!'

Pablo was helping himself to the doctor's brandy. 'Where has that crazy priest run off to?'

The answer came in the form of an incessant pealing of the church bell. It rang and rang while Dr Ortiz laboriously extracted pellets and dressed the foot. Fortunately Ignacio had been wearing his thick black leather boots, and the wounds were not too deep. Dr Ortiz lent him a cane walking stick, and the three of them made their way out into the plaza, where a majority of Tepicoapan's inhabitants were gathered, gazing up at the church tower. The bell could be seen swinging like a mad thing through the arched opening at the top. At street level, the church doors were bolted shut, and Don Guillermo, the mayor, was hammering furiously against the wood. Two policemen from San Mateos were leaning against their police car nearby, smoking cigarettes.

Eventually the bell stopped, and people took their hands away from their ears. It had always had a hideous cracked tone. Don Guillermo took advantage of the calm to roar at the church.

'Padre Sebastian! Open the doors immediately! This is Don Guillermo! I *order* you to open the door!'

High in the facade of the church a little wooden shutter opened. There was a tiny window up there, hardly big enough to get your head through. The barrel of a gun poked through the opening, and a shot was discharged into the air over the plaza. The pigeons that hung about all day on the roofs rose in a panic and flew stupidly in circles before descending again. The people of Tepicoapan reacted similarly, running pell-mell along the side streets that led away from the plaza, before returning more slowly to the corners. They huddled excitedly there while the younger men of the community demonstrated their machismo by peeping out into the plaza and reporting what was happening.

Meanwhile, the mayor and the policemen had flattened themselves against the church doors, immediately below the window. The barrel of the gun was withdrawn, and after a while the face of Padre Sebastian appeared at the little opening. His features were in darkness, but his eyes caught and reflected the dying light of the sunset, so that they gleamed like red marbles. Then he poked his head out slightly, like a tortoise, and delivered some observations in the loud declamatory voice he employed for his sermons.

'Get back to your homes and pray, impious and fallen people of Tepicoapan! I know your tricks and schemes. I know of the bombs you make in your bread ovens! I know you want to blow me up! Well – I will defend Mother Church to the end. I have guns and ammunition, and food enough to outstay all your malice! Now go – back to your homes and pray for forgiveness!'

The face withdrew, and the barrel of the gun reappeared. This time it pointed downwards, towards the centre of the plaza. The voice of Padre Sebastian came in slightly muffled tones from inside the window. 'Those of you who are at the church door – get away now, before I shoot!'

The mayor and the policemen consulted briefly. It appeared impossible that Padre Sebastian could manoeuvre his shotgun to a suitable angle for firing straight down at the church door. Then the barrel of the gun was withdrawn and a bony hand with a revolver waved out of the window above them. They scurried off to the nearest of the side streets. Where the hell had he acquired this arsenal?

Night was beginning to close in quickly now, and it was difficult to see very much. There was something of a festive atmosphere. People regaled each other with stories about the priest. In the space of half an hour, the mild eccentricities he had exhibited for years were recounted and embroidered upon, while his antics in the cemetery just a short time before grew to mythical proportions. According to some eye witnesses, he had brandished the very snake that had killed Luisa Emilia. Others spoke of volleys of shots which it was a miracle anyone had escaped.

Pablo and Ignacio withdrew from the crowd to go home. As darkness fell, and it appeared that no police assault on the church was to take place, people were beginning to drift away. Pablo felt that he had underestimated Tepicoapan. It had, after all, the capacity to surprise.

His father was philosophical. 'He'll come out in the end. However much food he's got in there, he can't last forever.'

They settled down for their own supper. The maid brought a salad with lettuce, tomatoes, eggs and avocados. Also freshly baked *bollos*. Pablo poured some wine from a cool earthenware jar and waited for her to disappear back to the kitchen. Now that he was alone with his father for the first time since the shooting, he wanted some answers.

'What in God's name did Mama do that upset Padre Sebastian so much?'

Ignacio broke open a *bollo*. 'She was a good woman . . .' He looked intently at the crumbs of the crusty bread and began arranging them on the table with his fingers. 'This was supposed to be a day for mourning her, for remembering her. And then all this happens!' The crusts made a rough cross.

Pablo felt again that emptiness in the pit of his stomach which he had experienced when he first heard of his mother's death. It was true – they'd forgotten about her in the midst of all this craziness. He felt his eyes begin to prick, and quickly took a drink of wine.

Ignacio sighed. 'Padre Sebastian and Mama fell out. A long time ago.'

'Why?'

'It was nothing much. He wanted to interfere in our affairs. He got ideas in his head. Thought God told him things . . .'

'What was it to do with?'

'Well – it's not important. He probably forgot how it started himself.' Ignacio was rearranging the crusts, mechanically, into a circle. 'For more than twenty years she's been going to mass, taking communion from him. But he'd never speak to her or meet her eye.'

'If he gave her communion, why couldn't she be buried properly? What's his reasoning?'

Ignacio winced at a twinge of pain from his foot. Then he smiled wanly and put a finger to the side of his head. 'I think Padre Sebastian has lost his reasoning.'

Don Guillermo was not prepared to wait until Padre Sebastian ran out of food. For years he had felt himself the target of many of the priest's sermons. The pride of the affluent was one of Padre Sebastian's favourite topics. He would rail against those who eschewed the simple country life in favour of living in sinful cities. But even worse were those who polluted the country with city ways – with unnecessarily lavish houses, tennis courts and Mercedes cars. Don Guillermo had a big house on the Ixtapal road, a tennis court and a Mercedes. He glowered at the preacher during these passages, which occurred every four or five weeks. But, as mayor, he could hardly go to church in Machiza instead of Tepicoapan.

So Don Guillermo had not been slow to see the silver lining in the present turn of events. Padre Sebastian could hardly remain parish priest of Tepicoapan after this gun-happy episode. The sooner the situation was resolved, the better. Don Guillermo had read that a tactic sometimes used by the United States army in siege situations was to bombard the enemy with constant noise, depriving them of sleep. This seemed to him an appropriate technique to bring to bear here. From a chance remark of the priest's, Don Guillermo knew that he hated Mariachi music. The remark had been passed when he had himself been enthusing on his large collection of Mariachi music, which he enjoyed on the best hi-fi sound system that he had been able to afford.

The people of Tepicoapan were therefore suddenly awakened at about midnight by a blast of trumpets as a scratch band of Mariachi players rounded up by the police on Don Guillermo's orders swung into action. They had been positioned out of the line of fire from the church window, but as close to the church as possible.

'Aye, aye, aye, aye! Canta y no llores! Por que cantando se alegran, cielito lindo, los corazónes!'

Inside the church Padre Sebastian was pacing up and down the central aisle with his rosary beads, praying a lengthy penance for shooting Ignacio. He knew he hadn't killed him, but he could have done. He had come within inches of losing his eternal soul. He glanced at the lurid painting on the south wall, where sinners were barbecued by little red figures with horns. Beside the picture, Christ looked out at him from his glass case, and his painted eyes were reproachful. That look made the priest's mind whirl with doubt. He felt as if he'd acted correctly, in blind obedience to the will of God – like Abraham, or Moses. Hadn't the sign been quite unmistakable? Satan had sent a serpent to claim Luisa Emilia for his own. No-one else in Tepicoapan had ever been bitten by a snake. How then could she be buried in holy ground? It would be blasphemous. Why couldn't everyone see it as clearly as him? But all the villagers were in league against him – they'd never seen Luisa Emilia for what she was, and now they wanted a

Christian burial for her. He felt as if the church was a vessel of purity in a tossing sea of wickedness. The people of Tepicoapan had shown their true colours today, and he must somehow reveal to them the truth, the light of Christ. He must be a steadfast mariner, steering for calmer waters. He was trying to think of some practical course of action when the first blast of Mariachi trumpets shattered the calm of the church. Now what? Were they holding a fiesta of devilry out there? Triumphing over the retreat of God's representative to the last bastion of the church? Where were the pure in spirit, who should rally to his cause? The image of Pablo as a child came unbidden to him, chin lifted as he sang as sweetly as a nightingale in a dark forest. Suddenly, he halted his pacing and stood stock still, transfixed by a luminous idea.

It was the hour before dawn. The Mariachi band had long since laid down their instruments. Once Don Guillermo had retired to his elegant home, which was over a mile from the village, they quickly succumbed to the appeals of the pyjama-clad residents around the plaza. With the yawning acquiescence of the policeman in charge of the operation, they came to an arrangement to start again at first light, before Don Guillermo would be likely to appear.

Since Padre Sebastian was considered to be under siege, no-one thought to mount guard against a sortie. So when a shadowy figure slipped out of the back door of the church into the narrow Paseo del Virgen and hurried the two dozen yards to the house on the corner with Calle Orsino, there was no witness.

In a bedroom on the ground floor of the house, Daniel Ortesa was asleep. He was seven, and sang in the choir on Sundays. When he was awakened by Padre Sebastian's torch shining in on his face through the open window, he was in a dozy and suggestible state.

'Come on, Daniel!' Padre Sebastian hissed. 'Look lively now, or you'll be late for choir practice!'

Daniel sat up reluctantly. 'But I'm in my pyjamas, Padre!'

'Never mind – slip on a dressing gown and meet me at the door to the vestry. Don't bother waking Mama!'

Daniel was rather in awe of Padre Sebastian, and dared not turn over and go back to sleep, as he wished he could. So, moments later, he whisked out of his house and ran, dressing gown flapping, to join the priest in the Paseo del Virgen and enter the chilly vestry at the back of the church. It was strange that there should be a choir practice in the middle of the night. And that the rest of the choir was not present. But Daniel had only attended two choir practices before, and perhaps every third practice took place in the dark. Everything about Padre Sebastian and the church was a puzzle anyway. He had recently had his first holy communion and eaten a piece of God's body. Much to his relief, it turned out to be just like a piece from an ordinary *bollo*. However, this raised a whole series of questions about the nature of God ,which he was afraid to ask. Daniel imagined a great bread oven high above the stars, where God was baked. But who baked God?

As dawn broke, Sergeant Martinez was shepherding the protesting Mariachi players along Calle de la Vaca Sagrada towards the plaza. They had slept badly on the floor of the sergeant's living room. The muttering band passed by Ignacio's house, and Pablo and his father both woke out of uneasy sleep at the disturbance. They met in the blue-tiled kitchen.

'More of that blasted Mariachi music any minute now . . .' Ignacio complained, stumping around with the aid of his walking stick while Pablo prepared coffee.

But instead, minutes later, the early morning hush of the village was pierced by a sweet high voice. Its source was hard to define at first, because it seemed to fall from the sky to fill the whole place. It was as if one of the pigeons that strolled on the roof tops had decided to sing a hymn.

'*Padre nuestro que esta en el cielo!*
Sanctificado sea tu Nombre'

As the voice continued, people with houses on the plaza looked cautiously out of their windows. Others gradually identified the source of the sound and gathered at the corners of the streets leading into the plaza. Ignacio and Pablo threw on coats over their pyjamas and joined a group of listeners.

The tiny shuttered window high in the church's facade was open, and little Daniel Ortesa was giving the performance of his life. It was a bit nerve-racking, to be singing alone and so publicly, but 'Padre Nuestro' was his favourite hymn, and Padre Sebastian said it was fine for him just to keep repeating it.

The piping words made a forgotten chord resonate in Pablo's mind. He remembered the cool dark interior of the church filled with his own childish treble. He remembered Padre Sebastian's face in the thin white light from the window behind the altar, smiling, encouraging, and above all, happy. He began murmuring the words aloud. Ignacio took his arm.

'Padre Sebastian loved your singing. He used to say you were so pure in spirit that your voice was like a mountain stream.'

'I remember . . . a little.'

Ignacio paused. He hadn't meant to tell him, but now it seemed to him that Pablo might as well know what was at the bottom of this business. He went on:

'He thought God had marked you out for the priesthood. We talked, he and I, of your going to the seminary school at Hiquila.'

Padre Sebastian's face, rimmed with white light, smiling. Pablo remembered.

'I remember, one day, he asked me if I wanted to be a priest. I said yes.'

'And you told your mother, didn't you? Because a week later she was full of her plan for sending you away to Mexico City to school. Padre Sebastian never forgave her.'

'Was that what started it all? Me?'

'He said God had chosen you, and she had defied him.'

Poor Padre Sebastian. Pablo wished he could have been the saint that the priest had imagined. He would have liked to have made something of himself – something more than a bank official in Mexico City. But then again . . . he would miss the money, and the girls. Nevertheless, drawing strength from a deep well of memory and feeling, he began to sing louder. His voice was still good, and he enjoyed singing on the rare occasions he went to church. He heard his father join in too, then the people who stood nearby. Little by little, the rest of the village began to sing, quietly at first, but gradually the sound swelled as if an invisible choir had occupied all the streets and houses of Tepicoapan.

'Hagase tu voluntad asi en la tierra
Como en el cielo!'

Pablo and his father were the first to enter the plaza, and taking courage from their lead, the other villagers followed. The plaza was filled with dishevelled people in hastily thrown on garments or pyjamas. They sang with faces uplifted to the window where Daniel led the hymn, his face illuminated by the dawn sun as it shone full on the church facade. Many of the villagers saw with their own eyes how the two stone cherubs in the recesses to either side of the little window glowed as the sun reached them, and moved their lips to sing too. Don Guillermo arrived in his Mercedes at the edge of the plaza, and tried to get the Mariachis to strike up, but by now they also were devoutly roaring out the words of the hymn, and would not be deflected.

Padre Sebastian stood in the centre of his church. The

building was a lighthouse, and the singing welled up around it like the sea. The words of the hymn lapped at its walls in a cleansing, healing tide of faith. Jesus was watching him from his glass cabinet. His wooden painted eyes told him what to do. Laying down his shotgun and pistol on one of the wooden benches, the priest of Tepicoapan walked to the doors. He drew back the bolts and turned the enormous key in its lock. Then he threw the doors wide open and walked out into the plaza to rejoin his flock and to embrace Pablo and Ignacio in a gesture of acceptance, contrition and forgiveness.

FIRE DEMON

I was in Mexico City on business. It was my second visit there, and I knew a small bar just outside the Zona Rosa where I could have a quiet drink without being deafened by Mariachi trumpeters or pestered by prostitutes. I just wanted a peaceful solitary drink. You could sit at a table and get served, but sometimes the waiters had tunnel vision, so I went up to the bar.

'Una cerveza, por favor,' I said to the barman. I don't speak Spanish, but I can get this request out. The barman opened his mouth to speak, and I added 'Tecate' before he could begin his exhaustive list of Mexican beers.

He turned and rummaged in his fridge, and I noticed that an old man seated further along the bar was staring at me. When I got my beer, I headed for a table, and to my annoyance the old man came over and drew up a chair without a word. His features were angular, and ravaged by stormy experiences, alcohol, or both. His eyes were large and unblinking. Presumably he had overheard my imperfect Spanish accent, for he addressed me in English.

'I hope you won't mind me joining you for a moment, but I wondered perhaps if you were a visitor here?' His English was only slightly accented, and his voice was like a rustling of dry leaves.

I cursed inwardly, taking him for one of these bar-propping old soaks who seem to be distributed, one per bar, around drinking places the world over. I travel quite a lot, and I know the type.

'Yes, I'm just here for a short time,' I said, without enthusiasm.

'Declan Martinez,' he said, offering his hand, which I took reluctantly. It was bony, but gripped my own strongly, too strongly. His haunted eyes held my gaze. I didn't give him my own name. After a moment, he spoke again.

'Irish mother, Mexican father. A wild and tempestuous sanguinary concoction! How old would you say I was?'

I had got my hand back by now, and took a gulp of my beer. His opening conversational gambit threw me a little. 'Sixty?' I hazarded, thinking that I erred on the polite side.

'Fifty!' he replied, with some satisfaction. 'I've had a life that would add years to anyone's appearance.'

He took a sip of his own drink, still holding me with his eyes, and it was then that it dawned on me that I was going to hear about that life. All of these people seem to have a story to tell. I was the helpless wedding guest, and this Ancient Mariner had me squarely in his sights. I looked at my nearly full glass of beer, and resigned myself to the inevitable, praying only that it might be short. But, just like Coleridge's wedding guest, my indifference was turned to horrified fascination by the tale I was told. For my companion was both a priest and a murderer, and had reasons of his own for acquainting me in particular with his story.

He did not offer any more small talk. He asked nothing about me, or my reasons for visiting Mexico. He simply launched into his narrative, leaning forward slightly and speaking quietly but distinctly. His eyes were almost constantly on my face, as if he feared that he would lose me before his tale was told, and had to hold me there by hypnosis. His told his story without hesitations, and in such a way that I felt he must surely have written it down once, and that now he was reciting it perfectly from memory. It went like this.

When I was seventeen, my mother was found to have cancer. It was too far advanced to be treated, and within weeks of the discovery she was in hospital, where they gave her pain killers. My father had to carry on with his work – he was a diplomat – so the maid and myself ran the household as best we could, and looked after my sister, who was only seven at this time. My father visited the hospital after work. He seemed to come home later and later as the weeks went by. Of course I thought he was at my mother's bedside. I was devoted to my mother. She was a saint.

I visited her every afternoon as soon as I finished school. She had a room to herself – one of the privileges our money could buy – a cool room with light-blue walls where I'd sit for an hour, sometimes holding her hand, and tell her the events of my day. I remember everything about those afternoons: the hospital trolleys echoing in the corridor outside her door; the smell of the eucalyptus tree outside the open window; the rasping sound in her chest when she breathed; her hands as white as the crisp linen on the bed.

In the evenings I distracted my sister, Nuala, while the maid got supper, and when it was bedtime I told her stories I could remember my mother telling me. She went to see Mother early in the mornings with my father, who then took her to her school.

I saw very little of my father at this time. He was working all day and was out all evening at the hospital. Then came one night when he didn't come home. My sister and the maid went to bed earlier than me. I was sitting by the fireplace reading stories by Edgar Allan Poe, and had frightened myself enough to want to wait up until my father came in. Eleven o'clock came and went. Half past. The distant, constant, hum of the traffic on the Periferico faded to the separate sounds of occasional vehicles. I heard an owl in one of the gardens. Midnight was silent.

I picked up the phone and dialled the hospital, ward twelve. The night nurse who answered knew my voice. She was sometimes on in the afternoons when I visited. Was my father still there? No, he hadn't been there at all that evening. I thanked her and put down the phone. I went up to bed, but couldn't sleep. Where could my father be until this hour? At one o'clock I heard the fumbling of keys at the front door. I had left my bedroom door ajar, and this is what I heard:

'Sssh! Sssh! We should have gone back to your place!' My father was speaking in an unsteady whisper, modulating to a hoarse croak.

'But you promised to show me your house!' A woman's voice, louder, a bit tipsy.

'We should have gone to your place I say.'

'But I told you! My sister – la vaca – is staying. Have you forgotten? And there's only one bed. Do you want to share the bed with a cow as well as me?'

'If the children heard us . . .'

'They're in bed asleep. Besides, what's the problem? You're a widower now – almost.'

'It's too soon. They must get used to the idea slowly, gradually, after . . . the death. It could take months. Let's go to a hotel.'

'Not again! I told you I'm not having some receptionist looking at me like I'm a whore. It's the middle of the night. I'm staying here or you can drop me off at home.'

'No – I need you now. Tonight, with me.'

'Fine, then fix me a drink and we'll go to your room.'

'This isn't sensible. The children . . . I must take you home very early, before they wake.'

'OK. De acuerdo.'

I heard their footsteps along the hall. Laughter and clinking of glasses in the kitchen. Stealthy movement up the stairs. My parents' bedroom door opening, then clicking shut. It was a heavy door. I heard no more.

How can I describe my feelings? If my mother had been a religious idol, a madonna of purest alabaster, then it was as if my father had hurled it upon the earth and was smashing it into poor, bleeding fragments. I pictured her in her cool blue hospital room, moonlight falling on her pallid pain-drawn face. I was overwhelmed by a mixture of pity for my abandoned innocent mother and a burning hatred of the man who could cast her aside so callously in her final days. My feelings for my father were already ripe for the reception of the hatred which now flooded into me. His neglect of me and my sister had always seemed a natural function of his long working hours, his frequent absences abroad, and a character naturally humourless and unbending, unsusceptible to childish enthusiasms. Added to this, my progress through adolescence was marked by those confrontations not uncommon between children and their parents. But whereas my mother retained my love and respect, indeed inspired it, by her

221

willingness to allow me to reach my own decisions and make my own discoveries, my father instead invited angry words and mute disobedience by his uncompromising rule-making. He was, therefore, like a mould or receptacle, ready-fashioned for the flow of molten metal which was my hatred. And just as molten metal hardens in the mould into a cold instrument, so my hatred hardened and defined itself into a definite purpose – murder.

At this point Declan seemed to feel it safe to break off for a moment. His voice had dried up to a hoarse croak, and we had both finished our drinks long ago.

'Another drink?' he invited me. I nodded, all thoughts of escaping forgotten, so securely had he wound me up in the thread of his tale. Declan waved to the waiter and pointed at our empty glasses. We sat in silence until he had brought us replacements, and then, when we had slaked our thirst, he went on.

As a devout Catholic, I recognised that I was contemplating a mortal sin, and the eternal perdition of my immortal soul. But I had no power to escape the cold grip in which my hatred held me. I decided from the outset that I would spare my father until after my mother's death. I decided also that should the event occur which I prayed for fervently – the miraculous full recovery of my mother – then I would spare my father's life in turn.

But my mother continued to fade quietly into a thinner and thinner wraith, white against her white linen in the cool blue room. My father continued as before. He never brought his mistress home again, but often returned im- probably late from his supposed visits to the hospital. The infrequency of our meetings helped me to disguise my enmity. He was used to sullenness from me already, and perhaps put down my silences to the additional strain that my mother's illness was causing. He knew the strength of my feelings towards her. No doubt my passion shamed his own indifference. He perhaps avoided me in those last weeks as much as I avoided him. Meanwhile my hatred grew, like a cancer on my soul. And my prayers for my mother grew more fervent, for if I lost her I would lose my soul. I pleaded with God to strike a bargain with me – but God did not listen. One night my mother died, and I was abandoned to my sorrow and my vengeance.

The funeral service took place at a crematorium in the foothills of the Sierras. The sky was washed clean blue by a recent storm, and eagles wheeled high against the snow on the mountains. My mother wanted her ashes to be scattered on the waters of Dublin Bay and we drove away from the crematorium with her remains in a small cedar casket. It was a curious thing to hold in your hands, and to load into the boot of the car next to the spare wheel and the jack. Wedging it into place so it would not move, my father's hand and mine touched briefly. It was our only physical contact that day, and I knew it would be the last time I would touch his living flesh.

Nuala cried in the back seat all the way back to the city. I remember we stopped before going home at an ice-cream parlour, to comfort her a little. But she couldn't eat anything. Soon, I thought, she was going to be an orphan. I resolved that I would be the best father she could ever have as I looked at her tear-stained face.

You will be surprised perhaps by my callousness in intending to deprive my sister of her father. And indeed by my decision to avenge my mother's death upon him. I see the extremity of it all now. Frankly, I'll admit to you, it was a dreadful mistake. But in adolescence you walk along the edge of a precipice. All your fledgling emotions are poised for flight, and if the wrong things happen, then they take wing downwards, into the abyss. And what begins as a flight becomes a fall, a headlong terrible fall towards damnation.

My father's sin, in my eyes, was that he abandoned my mother in the time of her greatest need and suffering. Since I wished him to go to hell, I decided that he should most appropriately die by fire.

Outwardly our lives changed little in the weeks after my mother's death. The little casket of ashes was put into a cupboard, to await its journey to Dublin Bay. My father was still out until late most evenings, on a variety of pretexts to do with his work. Eventually he gave up explaining his absences, and came home almost every night after we had gone to bed. Maria, the maid, maintained a fragile domestic cohesion, collecting Nuala from school, preparing meals, washing clothes.

As for me, I was finishing my last weeks at school. I was preoccupied with an interrelated set of questions. Would I pass my exams well enough to go on to study for the priesthood? How was I going to murder my father by fire without any suspicion falling on me, and without hurting anyone else? And how was I going to provide for Nuala's future after my father's death?

Declan paused here in his tale and threw his tequila back with a quick motion of the head and a sinuous twist of his Adam's apple. The barman was drawing down the shutters at the window and I realised with surprise that the bar had emptied, and it was time to go. Declan paid for the drinks while I stood up and moved towards the door in a slightly disorientated way. Outside, Declan fell into step with me as I started off, uncertainly, in the direction of my hotel.

'You've a Dublin accent yourself,' he said, for the first time showing curiosity. 'Are you here on holiday or business?'

'I'm here on business.'

'And your business is in Dublin?'

'Yes, it is.'

Declan seemed satisfied with this, and did not enquire what business it could be that took me from Dublin to Mexico City. He must have been pursuing his own line of thought, for after a pause he said:

'I travel myself a good deal between Ireland and Mexico. And to other places . . .'

He seemed uncertain how to go on. Then, signalling me to wait, he took out a pencil and a small notebook and scribbled something in the light of a street lamp. He tore the page out and handed it to me.

'My addresses – here and in Ireland.'

I took the offered piece of paper and put it into my pocket without looking at it. I offered nothing in return. Now that the spell of his narrative had been broken and we were out in the cold streets, I wanted nothing more than to be rid of him and headed towards my bed. Something of my initial cynicism was returning – he was just an old soak, probably a little deranged, lonely no doubt. Certainly he seemed reluctant to leave me.

At that moment a taxi came along the street, with its 'Libre' sign illuminated, and I hailed it. In one smooth flow of movement I turned, shook Declan's hand, then climbed into the back of the taxi and, once the door was shut, gave the name of my hotel to the driver. It was done in an instant, and I felt a little guilty as I waved through the window at the suddenly isolated figure of my companion. He looked slightly stunned, his mouth forming an automatic smile which was belied by his sad uncertain eyes. Behind him, the street light cast his shadow high against the blank wall of a building, so that he seemed menaced by a huge black figure poised to strike him down. I thought that I would never see him again.

*　　*　　*

In fact, when I did see him again, about a year later, I didn't recognise him at first. It was in Dublin, in one of the bars off Dame Street. I'd stopped off for a guinness after work, as I sometimes do, and since I had no wife and children waiting for me, I had another one. There were only half a dozen other customers – three up at the bar and the others in little alcoves like myself. I was half way down my second guinness when an altercation at the bar caught everyone's attention.

'Hey! Do you want to set the place on fire? You are crazy!'

The speaker had his back to me, but the accent was familiar. He had jumped up from his bar stool, which had toppled over, and was standing beside two young men at the bar, obviously highly agitated. In an ashtray on the counter something seemed to be alight – perhaps a cigarette packet or a bit of paper.

'Keep your shirt on, old fellow! It's nothing!'

'It's irresponsible I tell you! Patrick, what do you say?'

He was appealing to the barman, who raised his hands in a gesture of neutrality. I was trying to remember where I'd heard that voice before. Then he turned to me.

'What do you say? Setting fire to things in ashtrays! We could all be reduced to ashes!'

He stopped, and peered at me more closely. The light was dim in there. Our mutual recognition was simultaneous. He had not had the advantage of hearing my voice, but I have a burn mark on my forehead which is quite distinctive. You might almost say it amounted to a disfigurement, of a minor kind. A dark lumpy raised scar of skin, in the shape of a cross. The result of an accident with a steam iron when I was a toddler.

A smile came to Declan Martinez's agitated features. He seemed to forget the business of the ashtray immediately and collected his glass from the bar to come and sit beside me.

'I thought we would meet again,' he said as he took his seat. His voice still rustled like leaves. Brittle dried-out autumn leaves. 'We were interrupted, weren't we, a year or so ago?'

I nodded. 'In Mexico. Yes.'

He sipped his drink. 'Would you care to hear the rest of my story?'

The question was rhetorical. He was going to tell me anyway. But the fact was that I had never forgotten what he had already imparted, and sometimes, without ever thinking I would know the answer, I had puzzled over his hatred for his father, and wondered if he had indeed murdered him one day. So I sat tight, and Declan resumed the quiet, inexorable flow of words whose elegant phraseology was curiously at odds with the horror of their substance.

You will remember my three objectives following the death of my mother: first to destroy my father by fire in such a way as to make it appear an accident; second to make provision for my little sister Nuala, who was seven; and third to gain a place in a seminary to study for the priesthood.

I decided to do nothing until I had taken my school-leaving exam, which was only a few weeks away. As I told you, Nuala and I saw very little of my father at that time. One morning a letter from Dublin arrived. The sender's address was on the back of the envelope, and I saw that it was from my Aunt Maud, my mother's sister, who had belatedly been informed of my mother's death by my father. She and my father hated each other, I now know, although an elaborate civility whenever they met had disguised their true feelings from my childish eyes. Maud was married herself, to a Dublin barrister. They had no children.

My father had already left for work, and I decided I would read the letter. As I did so, I felt a sense of being in the hands of a fate bigger than myself, for one of my three problems was proving to have a possible solution. Like a 'deus ex machina' my Aunt Maud was proposing that Nuala should go to live with her in Dublin. She suggested, in any event, that Nuala should pay an extended visit of a month or so, to help her put her mother's death behind her and to get a sense of whether a change of home would suit her. Aunt Maud pointed out that I would soon be leaving our home, and with my father's busy life that would leave my sister to be brought up by the maid. She did not dwell on her own desire for a child to look after, as she knew that would carry no weight with my father.

Nuala was duly packed off to Dublin. In her trunk went the casket with our mother's ashes for scattering on the waters of Dublin Bay. I observed her parting with my father like an assassin behind a veil, alert for any display of passion on either side which might stir doubt or remorse for what I proposed to do. But the leave-taking was calm on both sides.

Nuala's departure coincided with the end of my final school examinations. I felt I had acquitted myself well, in spite of the other claims on my thoughts. I could do no more than wait for the results to come out, and start writing to the seminaries where I hoped to gain admission. My parish priest, Padre José, on hearing of my sister's departure for Ireland, suggested the notion that I should endeavour to find a place in a seminary in that most blessed of countries. He had a special fondness for Saint Patrick, and promised to pray for his intercession in the matter of securing a place for me near Dublin. I wrote to the two addresses which he helped me to find. With all these concerns taken care of, my attention now turned fully to the question of my father's destruction.

We had, on an occasional table in the sitting room, a piece of kitsch worthy of the Mexican sense of the macabre, but which had actually come from Ireland with my mother. This was a small ashtray in the shape of a skull, with deep eye sockets where a cigarette stub could be gruesomely extinguished. On the forehead of this grinning skull was an epitaph: 'Poor old Fred/Smoked in bed'. This ashtray provided me with my inspiration.

My father was quite a heavy smoker. There was an ashtray on his bedside table, and by furtively visiting the room in the mornings, after he had left for work but before Maria had been in to clear up, I ascertained that he did indeed smoke in bed.

With Nuala gone, my instinct was to act quickly, and I made my preparations on the Sunday after her departure.

My father was out of the house, presumably with his mistress somewhere. He didn't trouble himself to discuss his movements with me. Maria was taking her weekly afternoon off, visiting her mother. I had the place to myself. In the garage I found the can of petrol we used for filling the lawnmower – we were wealthy enough to cultivate a lawn – and decanted a litre into an empty wine bottle. I secreted this in my bedroom, together with a quantity of old rags from a sack in the garage. I checked that a box of matches was in the usual place beside the fireplace, but did not remove it to my bedroom in case Maria noticed it was missing in the evening. Then I spent some time in my father's bedroom, rehearsing for the night's operations. I practised opening the door soundlessly. There was a slight unavoidable click when the handle was turned, but no creaking. I decided that I would need a torch to be certain of my movements and checked the kitchen drawer where we kept one. It was there, and the batteries were sound. I was shaking with a sort of fearful malevolence as I made these preparations, and was glad that no-one else would see me before I regained my composure.

One of my concerns was that the fire should not spread

from my father's bed to the rest of the room and then to the whole house. Our floors were made of wood, and I was anxious too about some of the wooden furniture in the bedroom, but could think of no plan other than to go straight to the fire extinguisher in the kitchen after I had set the bed alight. I didn't dare to move it anywhere closer in case Maria noticed.

My father came home for supper at about seven, which I had not really anticipated. He usually ate out now. We sat, as I alone knew, for the last time together at the big round dining table with the empty chairs of my mother and my sister mutely adding their absence to our company. He asked some perfunctory questions about my day, which I answered with little grace. He seemed thoughtful, and once or twice I thought he was going to begin a conversation. But I gave him no opening, kept my eyes fixed on my plate and hurried through the food. Only once did I steal a surreptitious glance at his face, as he fumbled for cigarettes and matches at the end of the meal. As if through a magnifying glass I saw the dark hairs of his eyebrows, the pores of the skin on his nose, the fragility of it all. For the first time I recognised the sadness in the lines around his eyes, and just for one moment my hatred was eclipsed by a sense of what might have existed between us, in a better world. Then he put a cigarette between his lips and struck a match, and the glow of the flame lit his features from below, like the flames of hell.

It was two in the morning when I deemed it was safe to act. The house had been silent and still since midnight, when my father had come up to bed. Maria's room was downstairs, so I had to be very quiet going down for the matches. As the thin beam of my torch illuminated the objects in the sitting room, each of them seemed isolated as if on a stage, each with its story to tell. There was my mother's photograph, with me beside her and Nuala a tiny baby in her arms. I heard my mother's voice saying 'Forgive and forget, Declan! Forgive and forget!' The torch beam moved on, to the little skull with its ghastly grin. 'Send him up in smoke!' it cackled, 'Send him up in smoke!' The torch beam wandered, picking out now this, now that. It seemed to move of its own volition, and as I stood in the centre of the room, the darkness filled with murmurings where the light had touched inanimate objects into life. Even the chairs and the tables seemed to hold their opinions.

'Have pity, Declan!'

'He deserves it, he hates you, he hated her!'

'Does your courage fail you, Declan?'

In spite of my attempts at calm and lucid preparation, now that my plan was in action I was sweating with terror. For I felt myself the focus of a struggle of forces greater than my own will, the oldest struggle of all, that between good and evil. I stood immobile, surrounded by contradictory urgings. I was paralysed, unable to act. My will was in suspension, a prize for the victor in the battle of voices.

I don't know for how long I stood in the eye of that storm, but eventually the voices fell silent and I found myself pointing the torch at the fireside, and moving forward to pick up the matches. And I swear to you the hand that reached forwards was not mine. Deep inside me, the small clear voice of good was pleading, exhorting, demanding, reasoning. But it was too late. The voice was powerless within a body possessed by evil.

Noiselessly I glided to my father's bedside and packed the petrol-soaked rags gently, ever so gently, around his sleeping body. In sleep he looked so innocent, and younger, and somewhere inside me the voice reminded me of my childish love for that younger man, long ago, before I knew anything of judgement. Silently it screamed out for pity, for mercy, for love, as hands, not mine, struck a match and applied it.

Then it was all too late. A sudden sheet of flames swept up the bed like a wave hitting the shore.

For some moments my father lay unmoving in his bed of flames, and I prayed he might die in his sleep. But then he woke, all wrapped in fire, and . . . I cannot describe . . . the horror of it. In his eyes the terror, the pain, the *recognition* as I fended him back on to the bed with the legs of a chair while he tried to rise. It was not a swift or an easy death. And amidst the fighting, the heat, the smell, one word only escaped his lips – one word: 'Why?'

Declan Martinez paused, and I seemed to awaken from a dark dream to become aware again of the dimly lit lounge, with its sprinkling of early evening drinkers sitting or leaning at the bar like grey ghosts. Cigarette smoke curled in the air, and I had a brief illusory sense that the whole place was quietly, greyly smouldering, like an ante-room to hell.

Declan finished his drink and went to the bar to buy us another. He was, in his way, a generous man. I watched his back with a sense both of horror and pity. As before, in Mexico, I thought of the Ancient Mariner, and felt tethered by some hidden bond to my story-teller. Why did he have to tell *me* his tale? When he returned with our drinks, Declan seemed to have divined my thoughts, for he addressed me in these words:

'You will be wondering why I tell you all this. The reason is that I think you may be able to perform a service for me. Don't worry – it will cost you nothing. Quite the reverse.'

'How can I help you? You know nothing about me. I could be a policeman and have you arrested for murder.'

Declan laughed. 'You are no policeman! Tell me – I'm sorry – what is your name again?'

'Tom.'

'Tom – are you a Doubting Thomas? We shall see. No, I

know nothing about you, but I know everything about you that is of relevance to me . . . may I?'

Declan reached out his hand and put a finger to my scar, my crucifix scar on the forehead. He touched it gently. 'How did you come by this, Tom?'

'It's a burn. It happened when my mother was ironing. When I was about three. I pulled the iron off the ironing board on to my head.'

'A curious shape for a burn. Do you believe that dreams can tell us things, real things, that otherwise we could never know?'

'Yes, I do.'

'Good. Because I was told about you in a dream. When I was at the seminary. I was told many things there in dreams: that I would be pursued; that my pursuer would never allow me to rest in a single place, and that I would only finally be released from my long flight by a man with a cross on his face. That's you, Tom. I saw you in my dream.'

'Who is pursuing you?'

Declan sank his whisky in two gulps. He looked at me as if assessing whether to trust me, sucking in his hollow cheeks. I sensed, for the first time, a hesitation.

'I think I must prepare you for that gradually, Tom,' he said at last. 'It is the hardest part of my story to believe. I would not want you to think I am mad. I must first tell you – *show* you – the evidence of what I know to be true.'

'Why should I be willing to help you? Just because you've bought me a drink . . .'

'Ah Tom! There's no way back now that we have come so far. You know that in your heart. There's an affinity between us – I know nothing about you, true, but there is something – something in your past which links you to me. We'll find out what that is – perhaps you don't know, perhaps you know already.' Declan looked at his watch. 'Have you eaten tonight?'

'No, I haven't.'

'May I invite you to my flat for a cold supper? I keep a flat here, in Lahinch Street. Just a few minutes away. Will you come? I have things there which will explain a little more about my plight.'

I felt enmeshed in a web spun from pity, curiosity, and something else, something deeper and nameless which made Declan's words ring true. There was an affinity between us, and he did not know, he could not know what it was. For *my* crimes had gone as undetected as his own.

We set off together in the gathering darkness of the Dublin streets. Lahinch Street was close by, and we were soon ascending four long flights of stone stairs up to the door of Declan's flat, which was painted in a rather old-fashioned dark green. Beyond the door was one of these gracious apartments with high ceilings you find in Georgian terraced conversions. The sitting-room curtains were open, and I walked to the big window which looked west and south over roof tops and across the glittering lights of the city to the dark hills beyond, whose shapes were still just visible against the fading sky.

Declan switched on the table lamps and smiled:

'It's a splendid view, isn't it? I always feel more at ease when I can see a long way. I will only sleep in a place with an extensive view – in Ireland, to the west; in Mexico, to the east. There's something else too, that I consider essential – come and look.'

He took me to the kitchen, which was at the back of the flat. There was an unexpected door there. Declan opened it, and we stepped out on to a cast-iron landing which hung over an enclosed courtyard, a sort of deep black pit whose sides were formed by the high stone buildings all around. A precipitous fire-escape snaked its way down from the landing into this pit, past dozens of little windows like eye-holes, the kitchens and bathrooms presumably of the dwellings all around.

'Wherever I sleep there must be two ways to get out, otherwise I would feel like a rat in a trap. I must never let myself be cornered.'

We sat in the kitchen to eat cheese and pickles and cold ham, and we started on a bottle of whisky.

I may as well admit that I've a little weakness for the drink myself, and between the two of us the bottle of whisky was soon half done. I was telling some story about my companions at work when Declan suddenly silenced me with a finger to his lips.

'Hssh! Did you hear anything?'

We listened. There was nothing – just the wind rising a little outside. But then there was a 'Tap! Tap!' on the windows. It came faster and faster, rain driven on the wind, and Declan relaxed again.

'I'm a little edgy,' he explained, 'because it is soon time for me to leave Dublin again. I am looking for the first signs that my – *pursuer* – is near. Come with me into my study Tom, and I will show you the things I told you about in the bar.'

Declan led the way, after filling our glasses, to a room I hadn't noticed earlier, opening off the small entrance hall and having the same view across the darkened city as the sitting room. The rain was beating into the window now with a splattering anger, turning the lights of the streets and houses into smears and blurs.

Declan turned on a lamp on top of a bureau, and the yellowish glow revealed a small room in which books, maps, papers and curious instruments of measurement and magnification were crammed on to every surface. Declan stood by the bureau and invited me with a gesture to look around me. The room was filled with clues to Declan's preoccupations, but they were clues I could not begin to interpret.

One wall was entirely taken up by a huge bookcase, with

titles covering mythology, mysticism, astronomy, astrology, oceanography, cartography and meteorology – and a great many other things beside. On a table in the middle of the room was a chart of the Atlantic Ocean. Scattered over it were a globe, a telescope, a magnifying glass, measuring tools such as dividers and set squares, a compass, and a mess of pens and papers and notebooks. On the wall opposite the bookcase was a great plan pinned to the wall, covered with dates and tiny handwriting, and divided up into boxes of varying sizes, coloured green, amber and red. On the bureau itself were tables of mathematical formulae and a calculator.

Declan was watching me as I took all this in, and when I turned to him with a quizzically raised eyebrow he motioned me to take the only armchair in the room, beside the window, while he sat on the wooden chair at the bureau.

From a little drawer he took out a leather-bound notebook. He balanced it on its spine on the palm of one hand, and it fell open neatly at a place somewhere in the middle. I could see that both pages were closely written on in black ink. Declan cleared his throat and read to me from the book:

'There are demons of the earth, who smother and strangle the benighted traveller, the walker of dark lanes in the country darkness. There are demons of air, who rip with their talons at the soft underbellies of aircraft, who break the bridges of fragile ice that carry the over-reaching mountaineer. There are demons of water, who drag down the drowning, who guide sharks to their prey and icebergs to their fatal meetings with the hulls of ships. But beware the demons of fire, for they are vigilant in pursuit of the transgressor. They are the torch-bearers, the wrath-carriers of divine retribution. They do not cease to follow their quarry, but are the hounds of the spirit kingdom. They consume those who have called them up.'

Declan shut the book and looked at me.

'I wrote that when I was at the seminary. It was the middle of the night, a stormy night, and I had woken from a troubling dream. The words had come to me in the dream – I had read them in the pages of a bible, but of course they are not there in the real Bible. The Bible in my dream was on an altar in a small chapel. It was night time, and the chapel was in the middle of a wood. The trees were bending and groaning in a wind, and the flames of the candles in the chapel fluttered like living creatures struggling for life. A sudden fierce gust blew open the heavy door of the chapel with a crash, and knocked over one of the candlesticks on to the altar cloth. The cloth caught fire at once. I looked around me for something to stifle or douse the flames, but there was nothing. Then the other candlesticks began to topple, and the flames spread along the wooden pews and even across the stone floor. I realised that the flames would soon reach the door, and I would be trapped. With a desperate dash I just beat the leaping fires to the door. I ran through the woods, and the chapel behind me was a howling crackling thing, a mass of flames. For a moment I thought I was safe, but then I saw the trees nearest to the chapel catching sparks in their upper branches, and the wind fanning the sparks into a frenzy. Then the trees were alight, burning like torches, and the fire was passed from tree to tree by the wind, until, run as I might, there was fire all around me – behind, in front, racing through the branches overhead! I felt the heat begin to sear my skin, and I heard the whispering triumph of the fire demon – I will never forget its words – "As you sowed, so shall you reap, Declan! As you sowed, so shall you reap!"'

Declan paused, and perspiration was standing on his brow at the horror of his recollection. He took a slug of his whisky and continued.

'That dream, Tom, was only confirmation of what I had

dimly suspected ever since my father's death: that I was accursed, that my sin was so great that hell would not wait for me, but had sent out into the land of the living a demon, a fire demon, to pursue and destroy me. My fate is to be dragged down by earthly flames into the everlasting flames of hell. I have spent over thirty years outwitting my nemesis.'

Declan was clearly anxious to be credible. He started to explain the things in the room. He began with a black and white photograph of a burnt-out building.

'This was my home the day after my father's death. I got it later from a press photographer who turned up. It all got out of hand, you see. While I prevented my father from escaping the flames, the fire spread to the rest of the bedroom. By the time he was dead it was too late to tackle it alone. I ran to the telephone and dialled the fire brigade, but – Mexico, you know – it was nearly an hour before they came. I was standing out in the street, with Maria the maid. The neighbours had come out from all around too. The house was like a bonfire in the darkness. I was mesmerised by the flames. To my eyes they formed a monstrous creature, crouched over the house and tearing at the walls and roof with teeth and claws. Every now and again it would raise its hideous head and look at me, as if to say: "You have brought me here. You have brought me into the world. Now you will be mine one day!" I turned and ran from the sight, and only dared return when the fire brigade had done their work, and the house was a grey smouldering ruin in the early morning light.

'It turned out that not only was the house well insured, but so too was my father's life. My sister and I even became the recipients of a special pension paid by the diplomatic service, since we were now orphans. My father's executors helped me to invest in such a way that my whole life has been unmarked by financial worries.

'Everything else fell into place over the next few weeks. Nuala did not come back to Mexico for the funeral – she was already settled into her new life with her aunt and uncle, and the news was broken to her gently in Dublin by myself a few weeks later. Yes, I was quickly in Ireland, for my exam results were good, and I was accepted for a probationary novitiate at a seminary here.

'Having satisfied my compulsion for revenge upon my father, I prepared myself, in the quiet prayer-filled life of the seminary, to set a first foot on the long stony path of remorse. For years, as I studied and eventually completed my training as a priest, I thought I was travelling along that path. I began to consider myself cleansed, purified – in spite of never confessing my mortal sin. How foolish I was, to think I could pretend it had left me unmarked. I prepared myself for the pastorship of a community, for the role of a parish priest. But then the dreams began, and the fire demon came more and more frequently in the night to tell me of how I was accursed. The night that I fled in secret from the seminary was the night that it burned down to the ground.'

Declan paused, and looked beyond me at the rain-lashed window. 'Other dreams have revealed to me the nature of the demon who has marked me for his prey, and what I must do to evade him.'

He turned to his enormous wall chart. 'This is the plan which governs my life. I keep a similar plan in Mexico City, and in other places around the world which my dreams have told me to keep secret. I need only visit these other places once or twice a year, to break the cycle and send the demon off on the wrong track.

'The basis for my movements is quite simple. Wherever I am, at any time of the day or night, the demon is moving towards me. I am like a magnet which draws it. But it can only move at the speed of a fire moving through a forest, subject to the variations of the wind. Let us say, in round figures, that it is 5,000 miles from Mexico to Ireland. And let us say, on average, that the demon can travel five miles in an hour with a steady breeze behind it. Then it would reach me in six weeks. But fortunately I can use the winds to prolong our separation. I have made a close study of the weather and the seasons, and have devised a course of travelling the world which I follow annually and which never permits the demon to be nearer than two days' journey behind me. On average I can remain in Mexico, or Dublin, or wherever it might be, for eight to ten weeks, before having to flee once more. Thus I have attained a sort of fragile stability for my existence, although several times in the early years I made miscalculations and nearly paid for them with my life.

'You may wonder why, if my soul is already lost, I should be so concerned to save my skin for a few more years of a harried and lonely existence. I do so because there is still a way to save my soul. It was explained to me by a "bruja" – a village witch or wise-woman – in the state of Morelos in Mexico. Her fame in curing possessions by evil spirits had reached my ears.

She told me that my spirit would be safe if I died by water. Water would wash and purify the sin in my soul and put out the flames of evil that had been lit there. But – and here was the difficulty – I must not die by my own hand, but by the hand of another. Who could that person be? Her next words struck a chord of truth deep within me, for they confirmed what I had already seen in a dream: "It must be a man who bears a cross – a cross on his forehead."

'So you can see, Tom, that my search has been a long one and at times, it seemed, a hopeless one. But when I met you last year in Mexico and heard your Dublin accent, I knew at once that we would meet again. Fate would determine when – I had only to be patient.'

Declan drained his whisky and looked at me. I considered his words. 'You want me to drown you?' I said at last.

'In a nutshell, yes,' Declan replied.

I started shaking my head.

'Listen to me, Tom!' Declan said urgently, leaning forward on his chair. His haunted eyes transfixed me.

'First, there are sums of money concealed in cash, in Ireland and Mexico, which will make you a wealthy man, able like me to live without working. I have been saving for many years. I could tell you where to find that money. Second, there is no danger to you in this. There is no connection between us that the police could ever find. No-one ever comes to this apartment – it would be many days, even weeks before I was found dead. You could be far away by then – or just carrying on your everyday existence, going to work, going home. As unsuspected and unconnected with the obscure death of an obscure man as you could possibly be. And it would be so easy to make it look like an accidental death. An empty bottle of whisky beside the bath. A lonely man, doubtless an alcoholic, drowned in his drunken stupor. You would hold me under, Tom. I'd take sleeping pills, be sound asleep. No struggling. It would be easier than drowning a kitten, or a baby.'

Declan's eyes were hypnotic, desperate: 'Save my soul, Tom! Save me!'

I stood up, unsteadily. I had to get away.

'I'm sorry, Declan, truly sorry. But I can't consider this at all. It's . . . impossible, that's all. Impossible!'

I staggered up and out of the room. Declan made no physical attempt to stop me. He followed me to the door of the apartment, repeating the same phrase over and over:

'Think about it again, Tom! Think about it again!'

My footsteps echoed strangely as I descended the flights of stone stairs to the street door, as if I were being followed.

Declan didn't give up. In the next few days he hung about

the streets near my workplace. Increasingly he looked shabby and ill-shaven, and he plucked at my sleeve with feverish desperation whenever he could get near me. He reeked of whisky. I felt myself trapped, horribly trapped, since his predicament and his desires coincided so closely with old desires of my own, desires about which he could know nothing. He spoke, when he could detain me long enough for speech, of how we were linked inextricably by fate, of how I was born to be his salvation, and branded on the forehead with the sign of the cross in token of my ineluctable role.

One day he approached me in even greater excitement than usual. His eyes shone with an unnatural brightness.

'I went to the registry of births and deaths, Tom. Your birthday – it was the day that I killed my father!'

I hurried away without replying. As the days had passed, my irritation, my sense of being trapped in an obligation, and my burgeoning desire to sin again as I had sinned in the past had focused to a fury which had Declan at its centre. Like Declan I had been having dreams – nightmares – and the conclusion of this business was growing clearer and harder in my mind. There was only one possible conclusion. *I was going to kill him.*

The next night, instead of avoiding him, I said that I was ready to talk. We went into a bar.

He was in a pitiable state, and I hurried him into a dark corner so that he wouldn't attract attention. He could have been taken for a derelict, so wild-looking had he become. As he gulped his whisky he revealed the reason for his desperation: in pursuing me he had neglected his calculations. His timetabling was awry, and he was afraid the fire demon could even now be moving across the west of Ireland. I must kill him that night, or it would be too late.

'It's the fires of hell, Tom, that I can smell and hear. As the demon gets closer I can feel my skin beginning to scorch and char. My soul is in your hands, Tom – deliver me tonight, or I'll be lost!'

We made our arrangements. He would go back to his flat. He would leave his kitchen light on and the strange little door on to the fire-escape would be open. I could gain access to the back courtyard through a passageway at the corner of the terrace, and climb the dark cast-iron staircase until I reached his landing. Declan would be in the bath at midnight. He would have taken sleeping pills an hour before, and probably would be asleep in the water, with an empty whisky bottle beside him. Once I had performed my task, I could make my way out the way I had come. My instructions for finding the money would be in a sealed envelope in the bread tin in the kitchen. We parted at nine, leaving the bar separately. I went home to make my preparations.

At five to twelve I walked down the passageway to the courtyard. I was dressed in dark clothes, wore soft-soled shoes, and carried a duffle bag containing such items as I needed for the task ahead. My pulse was racing with an excitement I had not felt for years. I had drunk enough to embolden me, but not enough to impair my thinking. If I were to be successful, and get away undetected and forever unsuspected, then I could afford no slips. I had always been meticulous in the past. Declan had chosen his executioner well, in that respect.

I climbed the iron staircase as a spider climbs its thread towards a fly. I felt evil coursing through me like fire, making my skin hot in the cool night air. Apart from Declan's kitchen window, almost all the other windows looking into the pit were dark.

I slipped into Declan's flat, shutting the kitchen door quickly behind me lest my silhouette be glimpsed by some unlikely watcher at one of the darkened windows. I called out softly: 'Declan? Declan?' There was no reply.

The first thing I did was to open the bread tin. There was a small sealed brown envelope. I ripped it open. There were two photocopied maps, tightly folded, one of an area in Ireland and the other of an area in Mexico. A handwritten letter described in detail where two metal boxes were buried. I tucked the papers into my trouser pocket and went on into the bathroom. Declan was there sure enough, a naked helpless creature snoring softly in the bath. So fragile and defenceless. The water was tepid. I spoke loudly: 'Declan! Declan! Are you asleep, Declan?' and pulled at one arm which trailed over the side of the bath. There was not even a break in his breathing.

Midnight tolled on a distant church clock. There was no wind, just a breathless, waiting stillness into which the chimes fell like pebbles into a silent pool. As the last bell struck I felt the weight of the moment like a fusion of gathering forces beyond all human control. There was Declan, lying in the bath, the curse of patricide stamped upon his wasted, driven existence. There was his fire demon, arrived on the stroke of midnight. And there was me, accepting the power of the demon, letting it possess me as it had possessed me in the past, letting the fire flow into my heart and soul. All the buildings I had burned to the ground in my youth were merely the preliminaries, the necessary apprenticeship for this culminating act.

I heaved Declan's dripping body out of the water and carried him like a baby to his bedroom. My body possessed a superhuman strength. I got him into his bed and opened my duffle bag. I took an ashtray with its stubs and ash out of its plastic bag and placed it beside the bed. I put matches and an empty cigarette packet next to it. One stub I dropped on the pillow beside his face. I sprinkled petrol from a gallon can on to the sheets and fetched books and papers from the study and scattered them over the bed. Then I stood back.

I struck my match, and watched the tiny flame dancing its desperate little fight for oxygen. Declan's soul had fought hard and long, but like mine its destination was sealed. I put the match to the petrol-soaked bed and watched the fire take hold of Declan's inert body. Then I fled swiftly down the fire-escape into the black pit whence I had come.